In My Time Of Need

Brandon Pomeroy

Elpida Press
Kansas City

Thanks to Sofia Pomeroy for help with editing and formatting.
Any mistakes that remain are mine.

-B.P.

Published by Elpida Press.
elpidapresskc@gmail.com

Cover design by Alison Janssen

ISBN: 978-0692633021
ISBN-10: 0692633022

For Jamie, who always knew I would.

1

Gulu, Uganda

Sweat had begun to roll down his forearms. It beaded precariously at the tip of John's right elbow as he attempted to get better exposure. The operating room was stiflingly hot, the vents only wheezing out recirculated air. His headlight shined brightly into the girl's abdomen. The large duplicated ureter identified, he was able to get a loop around it, and began mobilizing it away from its attachments.

"Stephen, can you hold here while I set up this Balfour?"

Stephen grabbed the hand-held retractor, toeing in to expose the right side of the pelvis as John adjusted, then readjusted the arms of the self-retaining one. The mismatched and worn components eventually allowed him to see where the ureter dove towards the bladder.

"Pickups."

"Pickups to me, too."

Alice handed Debakeys to both men as they worked on getting the two ureters freed down to the bladder where, luckily, they joined into one. It was tied and cut, then brought up, while continuing to free it further. Rose, the circulating nurse, filled the bladder with saline through a urethral catheter. This caused the bladder to bulge larger in the pelvis. John began incising its outer layers. The thin mucosa presented itself and John placed two retaining sutures on it, keeping it from retracting back. The mucosa was opened allowing the saline to stream into the wound. Once it was sucked out, John and Stephen began carefully tying the spatulated ureter to the bladder mucosa, using tiny fragile sutures.

"Careful with this stuff, we don't have very much of it," John reminded Stephen as he cinched down a knot.

"I will be."

In truth he didn't need to be told. Stephen was from a village very near Gulu in the area of Uganda north of the Nile River. He was used to getting by with very little. Nothing went to waste. Most of the surgical supplies at Lacor had been donated. They were either left behind by medical mission groups from Italy and the United States or purchased with donated funds. From the 5-0 chromic suture packets that the surgeons were currently using, to the operating room tables and anesthesia machines, nearly everything was a gift. The people in northern Uganda were very poor. Even though Lacor was a private hospital, the fees charged covered less than thirty percent of the budget.

Stephen had grown up during the war, when Joseph Kony and his Lord's Resistance Army terrorized the area, forcing many people to leave their villages, huddling together for safety. They crowded into refugee camps and sent their children by the thousands inside the walls of Lacor hospital every night. He was luckier than most. He was able to go to school, eventually to University, and now was an intern at Lacor Hospital. Friendly, outgoing, with impeccable English, John had taken him under his wing. On most surgeries in which an assistant was needed, Stephen was called. They had worked well together from the beginning, anticipating each other's moves.

John tunneled the ureter a little into the bladder wall, making sure to give it a wide attachment to prevent future problems with stricture. Once that was complete they began closing the abdomen. Two layers of deep tissue and then a subcuticular closure of the skin. Ninety minutes after the initial incision they were finished, satisfied with their work.

"I'll go talk to her mom," John said peeling off his wet

gloves.

"Sounds good. I'll make sure she gets to recovery and then I'm taking off. I have too much studying to do tonight. See you tomorrow."

Leaving the theater, as it was called in Uganda and other English influenced countries, John slipped out of his green clogs. He stepped over the four-inch barrier and put on his worn, frayed green Chacos. This little step was the divider between the theater and the rest of the hospital. Meant to be a physical reminder to change shoes and put on or remove a lab coat, it had been an effective addition to infection control during the Ebola outbreak in this part of Uganda at the turn of the century. The oversized rubber clogs were community shoes. Washed every night, they were shared by everyone in the surgery department. Rather than using disposable paper shoe covers, which cost money and generated waste, the shoe system worked well.

John found the girl's mother sitting on a mat on the floor in the hallway of the surgical ward. Nurse Mary helped with translation. Most of the poor rural people spoke Acholi and knew only a small amount of English. John had learned a few words of Acholi but not enough to communicate ideas or hold any kind of conversation. People that had been to school usually knew English, plus whatever languages were spoken at home. Acholi, Luganda, Swahili, and several others were common here. If one translator didn't know a language, usually someone else could be found who did. It was the old telephone game that kids play, passing information from person to person. While it worked adequately, details were surely lost. John felt like he really needed to learn Acholi but it just didn't seem to stay with him.

"We're all finished. Everything went well."

"Thank you doctor."

"It was her right ureter. Instead of inserting into her bladder it ended in her urethra. That's why she was wet all the time."

"So Fatima will be whole now? Normal?"

"God willing she will be. We'll remove her catheter in two or three days. Following that, she should be dry."

The woman made a quick, slight upward nod of her head,

raising her eyebrows a little as she made a "hmm" sound, a sign of great joy for this humble woman.

"You can't know how much this means to our family. You have given my child back to me. She hasn't been able to go to school for years. With her wet clothes she has been forced to stay at my side, not able to participate in village life. *Apwoyo matek*! Thank you so much. You know that we are very poor. We are a village of farmers, barely able to survive on what is grown and what little we can sell at market. I can never hope to repay you, but don't worry, God will pay you!"

"You're welcome. And God has already paid me many times over. But that's part of the deal right? We talked about this already. The way you can repay me for doing this surgery is to enroll your daughter in school. There is nothing more important than education for the girls of this country. You can't imagine the joy it would bring me to find that she had gone on to University, perhaps even become a nurse or a doctor. She seems very bright. You should be extremely proud."

"*Apwoyo*."

"*Apwoyo*. I'll be back to check on Fatima in the morning." John and Mary moved away from the woman. He glanced inside one of the patient rooms.

"Mary, since we're here, let's check on the inpatients. How's everyone doing?"

"Everyone is okay, Mr. John."

In Uganda as in England, surgeons were referred to as mister rather than doctor. It was true that their first name was not often used, but the mister was a compromise in John's case. He had always felt uncomfortable being called Dr. Reynolds in his previous life in the US. He preferred the familiarity of given names. He felt that titles and initials only separate people, causing alienation. Stratifying people according to titles loses something important.

He and Mary visited the five patient rooms. All were filled with several patients, each in a simple bed. They were lying either on the vinyl cover or on their own blanket. Nearly everyone had one or several family members sitting on mats on the floor. They

4

took up most of the floor space, even extending underneath the beds in some cases. They talked and ate their simple meals: cassava, boiled millet, a flat tortilla-like bread called chapatti, perhaps a bean soup with a few bites of fish. The patients were fed by their families who also acted as their caregivers, helping with dressing changes, emptying urine bottles, assisting with walking and getting in and out of bed. The few nurses were spread too thin to do all of the care themselves.

The rooms smelled of food, sweat, stale urine, feces and dirty clothes. They had none of the chemical odors of hospitals in more developed countries. John would argue that Lacor Hospital smelled better than the ones back home. He preferred the organic smells of abundant life rather than what he considered sterile, asthma-inducing cleaning solutions and air fresheners. The sound of families conversing with each other as they ate, filling each other in on village gossip or arguing about political candidates, filled the rooms. They moved smoothly from talking to helping. If someone didn't have family, if he had come to the hospital alone, maybe on a bicycle or on the back of a motorcycle taxi (a *boda boda*), members of a family in the bed next to him would help. He would spend his days talking with them, joining in their meals, becoming a temporary uncle.

"This is Ruth. She had a large hernia repaired today."

"Oh I remember. Hi Ruth. How are you this evening? Are you in pain? Do you need anything?"

"No Mr. John. I am fine. Thank you for what you have done for me. Will I be able to return to my village tomorrow?"

"Sure, but don't lift anything heavy for two weeks. Otherwise you'll tear the stitches and you'll be right back here again."

He said this knowing full well that Ruth would be back to her usual activities immediately upon returning home. She would be fetching water, pounding millet, making meals, washing clothes, and hoeing a small garden, all of the things that women did for their families. He did his best to repair the hernia securely, placing extra sutures to keep it from recurring, hoping that some amount of pain would also limit her activity, slowing her down for a week or two. But without Ruth present at home, doing all of her usual chores, her family was likely suffering, her daughters picking up the slack where they could.

Mary guided John around the rest of the patients. He looked at urine bags, palpated abdomens, changed dressings, joked and comforted. Once he was satisfied that everyone was doing well, that there were no major problems that would require an urgent return, he said good night.

He checked on his young postoperative patient in the recovery area. He found Fatima calm and stoic. She didn't move or smile, but neither did she complain. Lying on the bed with its rusty rails and cracked vinyl mattress, alternately nodding off and staring straight ahead, she looked very small and fragile. His own daughter's image flashed through his mind for a moment. He remembered the way she had slept so silently and peacefully at this age.

John left the surgery department and headed down the quiet, covered hallway. The radiology department was on the left. In the daytime it overflowed with people. Many with limbs wrapped in dirty rags, some sitting on the ground, some in homemade wheelchairs, or on crutches made of sticks and duct tape, others in the few chairs against the wall, everyone waiting hours for their turn.

The first area on the right, or west, side of the hallway was open to several long clotheslines where laundry was hung during the day. It became a photogenic, ever-changing, multi-colored collection of scrubs, bed linens and towels. It was like a pop-up, temporary display of art and it always managed to catch the eye of passersby. Tonight it was simply a collection of wires hung between poles. Next came several private patient rooms. One patient and their family per room with an en suite bathroom was a luxury that few could afford. But for those that could, these suites awaited.

Next he passed a large open area, a courtyard dominated by two very large thick-trunked Bougainvillea trees, their purple flowers and large leaves another source of beauty on the hospital grounds. The vegetation below the trees was virtually nonexistent as families gathered on their mats. Some were patients waiting for tests or recovering from surgery before heading home. Some were families of patients. Many traveled for days to bring their loved ones to Lacor. It wasn't feasible for them to return home, so they waited in the courtyard, setting up temporary camps. Eating, talking, resting, the place was filled with life, yet was still very quiet. No modern sounds of television, or even radio could be heard, only the community that had sprung up in its place.

He turned left, passing between two outpatient buildings for about fifty feet, then right again towards the gate leading outside the hospital grounds. The guard nodded as he passed through the metal door, crossing the newly paved road. This road didn't appear impressive by Western standards. It was freshly built by Chinese contractors and was wide enough for two container trucks to just barely squeak past each other. There were curbs at the edges and wide sidewalks for foot and bicycle traffic. Despite its shortcomings, it was a major transportation route leading from a major seaport in Kenya, through Uganda, and up into South Sudan.

On the south side of the road a small retail community had sprung up to provide services for staff and visitors to the sprawling hospital complex. *Boda bodas* were lined up facing the highway, their drivers sitting or laying on their cycles, some talking with each other, some were quiet, yet all were watchful for potential customers. John walked by them towards the small simple family businesses that lined the street. Everything was available there from a barbershop to clothing to phone cards to several general stores. There were restaurants and bars. There were small kiosks selling ready-to-eat meals like barbecued meat, roasted corn, chapatti and what John had come over for: samosas.

The samosas sold there were similar to ones available in any Indian restaurant. A mixture of meat and vegetables, which usually included peas and potatoes, were seasoned with spices, wrapped in dough and fried. John purchased two of the vegetarian variety. The woman wrapped them in paper, handing them to him as he gave her a few coins. With his warm meal in hand he headed back across the street.

The weak fluorescent lights on both sides of the highway barely cut into the darkness of the Ugandan night. The waning crescent moon was directly overhead, a reminder of the fact that he was very near the equator. Even with the moonlight it was very murky. He came back through the metal gate, this time staying to the outskirts of the hospital, walking down a shadowy service road. Past the empty chapel, past the nun's quarters, he turned east at the next footpath. Not able to see clearly by this point, as any light from the front of the hospital had long since been left behind, he found his way by habit. He had become used to finding his way around, although he did occasionally pull out his phone to use as a light.

The path eventually led to several modest apartments. They were fairly new brick buildings with green metal roofs that housed some of the doctors, nurses, and staff from the hospital. There was a small well-tended lawn that ran down the middle of the development. John greeted the few people that were outside as he made his way to his own apartment.

Once inside, he turned on a lamp. Electricity was not a given here. It came and went and wasn't something that could be counted on. Tonight it was working, allowing him to see his dinner.

The lamp illuminated the furniture in the apartment, which consisted of a kitchen table that was four feet on each side, and two wooden chairs with pale green paint that had worn away from the seat and the top of the front rungs. The chairs were pushed up on two sides of the table. There were two additional chairs against the wall of the same room. A single bed was in a separate bedroom, along with a standing chest of drawers, and a bedside table. In the bathroom there was a flushable toilet, a shower and a sink. The white kitchen contained an electric stove, a microwave oven, and an electric kettle.

John sat down to eat his samosas, pouring some water into a glass and quietly praying before taking his first bite. His prayer usually consisted of seven words. "Lord Jesus Christ, have mercy on me." A simple prayer that he had learned years ago, it comforted and centered him, calmed his heart and nourished his soul.

The Jesus Prayer, as it has been known for centuries, dates back to at least the third century. *The Philokalia*, a multivolume collection of ancient writings by the desert fathers and later writers, books that John had read in their entirety three times, contained many references to it. These holy men of Syria and Egypt, people like John Cassian, Mark the Ascetic, and Evagrios the Solitary, lived a life of simplicity, often spending years in a lonely cave. Later, communities sprung up in these areas but many of the practices remained. The men and women spent their existence in constant prayer, eating a simple diet, and leading a life of quiet contemplation. Orthodox Christians carried on the tradition of the Jesus Prayer, something that had always appealed to John, even before he had a name for it. This wasn't the first time that day that John had whispered those seven words. And it wouldn't be the last.

After finishing the meal he folded the paper and placed it in the trash container. He washed the glass in the sink, dried it, opened the cabinet on the far left and placed it right side up next to three other eight ounce glasses.

John picked up a spiral notebook that was lying on a stack of papers on the kitchen table, sat down, opened it to the page in which he had written "September 22" and began to write underneath that morning's entry.

"30 clinic patients
4 surgeries: 2 inguinal hernias, TURP, R reimplant for ectopic ureter
Noticed the moon tonight.
An old man who was missing his front teeth, but had the most angelic smile was in the clinic today. Nice conversation."

He read what he had written, tracing over some of the letters to make them more legible, looked back over the morning's entry as well as the two previous ones, then closed the notebook and placed it back on the pile in the corner of the table. He put the pen on top of the notebook as he rose to his feet to get ready for bed.

After brushing his teeth and washing his face, John removed all of his clothing except his boxers, plugged the cell phone into its wall charger, noted that it was nearly eleven, got under the sheet and laid on his back, his head on a thin pillow. The room was still warm, but a fan provided just enough air movement and white noise to make the room comfortable. The screened windows in the bedroom, bathroom, and living room were open to the cool night air.

"Lord Jesus Christ, have mercy on me," he repeated to himself over and over. His breathing began to slow. "Lord Jesus Christ," as he inhaled, and then "Have mercy on me," as he exhaled. In less than twenty repetitions he was asleep.

2

The cell phone alarm went off at five seventeen, the time John had awakened for as long as he could remember. For some reason five fifteen felt too early and five twenty felt too late, so five seventeen it was. He showered, brushed his teeth and examined himself briefly in the mirror. The rapidly thinning dark hair had grey infiltrating the sides. That and a short, incomplete white beard gave a scruffy, yet distinguished appearance. He was quite thin with somewhat sunken cheeks, prominent ribs and a flat stomach. His face, neck and forearms were tanned while the rest of his skin was pale.

He brushed his hair, boiled water for tea in the electric kettle, and sat down at the table in his underwear. There was no milk, but there was sugar. Two teaspoons of the brown crystals were stirred into the cup as the Ugandan tea bag steeped. After taking a first, cautious sip, he opened his *One Year Bible* and read the entry for September 23rd. The Bible had readings from the Old and New Testaments, Psalms and Proverbs. After reading the passages from Isaiah 42, Ephesians 2, Psalm 67, and part of Proverbs 23 he went back and reread the verses from Isaiah that had struck him that morning.

"I will lead the blind by ways they have not known, along unfamiliar paths I will guide them; I will turn the darkness into light before them and make the rough edges smooth. These are the things I will do; I will not

forsake them."

Taking the spiral notebook, he opened it to the first blank page. At the top he wrote "September 23," and then copied the verses on the first few lines. He closed his eyes and thought about the passage for a moment, the interesting arrangement of the words, then read it again.

"We are all blind," thought John. "What faith it takes to try new things, to leap into the unknown, to face the future- but it's necessary if we are to do good- if we're to create change."

He thought of the times he had been blind, when he had no idea where he was headed. Times when he couldn't feel God near at all, when he felt so alone.

"What comfort to know that God is right here, shining a light, creating meaning and smoothing the rough edges. Life has enough uncertainty and darkness even in the very best of circumstances. It's easy at times to allow that darkness to overwhelm us. But to know that we have a guide, an internal voice to lead us... Well, that's an amazing thought."

He made a few notes under the verses, closed the notebook and got up to place a saucepan partially filled with water on the stove. He added some red millet and brought the mixture to a boil, then covered the pan. With the millet gently boiling, he moved to the bedroom to get dressed.

In the freestanding bureau he pulled out a pair of khakis and a blue button up collared shirt. There were three similar shirts hanging in the dresser as well as two short-sleeved polos. In a drawer were five t-shirts in assorted colors, five pairs of underwear, also in assorted colors, and two pairs of black socks. He owned two pairs of shoes- the sandals and a pair of brown dress shoes that he rarely wore. He didn't have a tie or a sport coat, but did have a sweatshirt and a pullover sweater for the nights that he was out late. All of these things fit neatly in the chest of drawers.

Once a week he left a bag of dirty laundry on the front step of the apartment when he left for the day. That evening the clothes were returned, clean and folded. This was one of the nice perks of living at Lacor. John felt like he would rather wash his own clothes, but they came back smelling so nice that he continued with the small luxury.

Once the millet had boiled for twenty minutes, absorbing most of the water, he took it off the burner. He poured it into a bowl and added two teaspoons of sugar, mixing it in.

He ate while looking at his phone, checking his email and Facebook. He allowed himself only fifteen minutes a day for this, partly due to the expense of cellular data, but mostly because of an intentional effort to stay in the moment. Technology, the Internet, all of the ways to stay connected with people, in fact made him feel less connected. He did the bare minimum to have some idea of what was going on with his family and his US friends, but by this point he didn't return many notes, didn't post anything, didn't comment or share or like anything. He had unfollowed most of his Facebook friends, so he didn't see nearly as many posts as he once had.

That morning he saw pictures of kids going to homecoming games, cute dog and cat pictures, some humorous sayings, and where his friends had eaten or visited the night before. With the eight-hour time difference many people were likely still up. He only had seven emails over the past twenty-four hours. They consisted of a reminder to change the oil on a car he no longer owned, an appeal for money from MoveOn, newsletters from Grinnell College and from a band named Work Drugs, a daily meditation from Richard Rohr, a short note from Jessica, and a three line note from his sister:

> "Hey John,
> Give me a call when you can. It's about mom.
> Deb"

He read the note again, looking for clues. He had an idea of course but it would have to wait for confirmation. Clinic started soon and he didn't have time for a long conversation with Deborah. Anyway, it was after eleven there and she was likely asleep. If it were a true emergency she surely would have called.

Trying to put the email and its implications out of his mind he rinsed the dirty bowl, put it in the sink and headed out. There was probably a key to the door somewhere in the junk drawer but he had never used it. John preferred to live a life that didn't involve keys or locks. He held a very light grip on his few possessions.

The walk out of the small apartment complex took him past the huge mango tree that served as the picturesque backdrop to the Ebola martyrs memorial. John always slowed down a little here, glancing at the tree and taking in the peaceful scene. Today he stopped for a moment to read the names on the plaque, offering a brief prayer of gratitude for their sacrifice.

He left the memorial and turned towards the hospital. He had begun visiting Lacor on short medical mission trips several years earlier but his memories didn't involve the AIDS or Ebola epidemics, or the Joseph Kony years. However, there remained many people on staff who did remember and their lives were certainly affected by those events. It was truly a special place.

John arrived in the clinic area to find the hallway completely filled with people sitting patiently on long benches. Many would be waiting hours to be seen. John smiled and nodded at his nurse Agnes, who smiled and nodded back.

"Good morning Agnes, how are you?"

"I am fine, Mr. John. Did you sleep well?"

"I did. Like a baby. And speaking of babies, how about you? Did your little one allow you to rest?"

She laughed, saying, "Oh little Mary is very demanding but it is okay. She is worth it."

"That's the truth. She sure is cute. So, it looks like we have a full day ahead of us. We'd better get started. Have you seen David yet?"

"He is around. I'll go and find him. Here is your first patient," she said as an ancient man with a gnarled stick for a cane in his right hand hoisted his thin body off the bench and toward the exam room. His dirty papers were clutched tightly in the other hand.

John guided the man into the room as he watched Agnes glide down the hallway looking for David. Her long neck, straight spine, and square shoulders gave her the appearance of a ballerina as she walked. But even more muscular. He knew she was an amazing dancer. Like many Acholi she had learned the traditional dances at school. These were a source of pride and still played an important part of their cultural identity. The exhausting and hypnotic movements of hips and shoulders to drum beats, whistles, and shouts were a treat to watch. It was impossible to know whether the Acholi are graceful due to the dancing or if an innate gracefulness leads to their dancing ability. Probably a little of both. Whatever the origin Agnes definitely had that gift and it was visible in her every move.

Just as John was saying good morning to the first patient, in an attempt to assess the man's English to see if he could get started on his own, David came around the corner. He immediately greeted the old man in Acholi. They exchanged formal comments back and forth as David guided the man into the metal chair next to the examination table. John took his papers and began looking them over. Recurrent urinary tract infections, slow stream, and painful urination. He had already had a prostate ultrasound, an ultrasound for residual urine, even a biopsy. It was enlarged with no evidence of cancer.

"Tell me why you have come here to see me today."

David translated John's questions to Acholi for the man. Nineteen-year-old David was truly a godsend. He had been a patient himself around the time of John's arrival. He had a minor problem that was easily remedied and he had stayed around to be a fulltime translator. Not only was he able to speak and understand multiple languages, which was not that uncommon in this area and in much of the world, but he also had an amazing ability to take on the correct accent. Pacing, pitch, word emphasis and understanding of slang and idiom all combined to make him indispensible to John. He was dependable, enthusiastic and eager to learn more.

"I am having so much trouble passing my urine. It comes out very slowly. It is painful at times."

"Do you get up at night to pee?"

"Oh yes, all night. It is very disruptive to my sleep."

"Have you tried any medication for this problem?"

"An antibiotic. I don't know if it was helpful. Also I have used traditional medicines."

These few questions took some time and involved a lot of back and forth between David and the old man. David knew what John was asking, the medical nuances and what information he needed to make a decision, and he was an expert at getting to those answers and translating them back to a simple conversation. It was usually a given that the man would have tried many herbal remedies. Most villages had traditional medicine experts that offered treatments that might include herbs, parts of animals, incantations, and physical acts. These were treatments that had been passed down for many generations. They were much less expensive, more convenient, and for many people, generally more accepted than traveling for hours or days to a large medical complex. Many of the people that arrived at Lacor had been suffering for months prior to making the journey.

In the US, John would have prescribed a medication for the man. Inexpensive and fairly effective, the majority would rather take a pill than have surgery. Here however it was different. Most people were poor and couldn't afford a daily medication. They weren't used to taking a pill every day indefinitely. Follow up was usually not very good. Even if the man decided to get a prescription, they would not likely see each other again and he would run out of medicine.

"Okay, I need to examine you if I could please," John said as he took out a blue nonsterile glove and a tube of lubricant.

With David's explanation and help, the man stood up next to the bed and began unbuckling, untying and loosening several layers of pants. The layer closest to the body was rarely actual underwear, but more often something like basketball shorts.

Once everything had been pulled down to his knees he bent forward over the table. John placed his lubed, gloved finger into his rectum. Five seconds later he said, "Okay, that's fine, you can get dressed now."

The man resituated himself, using his cane and John's arm for balance. As he slowly lowered himself towards the chair, dropping the last inch as his arms gave way, John began his well-rehearsed speech.

"David, will you please explain to him that his prostate gland is enlarged. It's blocking the flow of urine from his bladder. Tell him that I can perform an operation called a transurethral resection of the prostate, or TURP, that will remove the obstruction. This will allow for his urine to flow freely, with better control. No cutting of the skin is necessary. He will have a catheter in the bladder for two days. There are no guarantees of course, but there is a good chance that this procedure will help him."

David had heard this explanation many times before. He had his own manner of describing the disease process and the surgery in a way that the man would understand perfectly. This was something that took practice and instinct. A precise word for word explanation would leave the man confused and anxious. In the same way that John changed his discussion based on the patient's background, using different words and descriptions for different ages, education level, professional background and socioeconomic status, David knew how to speak to each of the people that came before him. They talked back and forth for a few minutes, laughing at times, other times looking serious, while John filled out the medical record and the pre-operative forms.

"So, what did he say?"

"He said okay."

John knew better than to ask for details. They would involve inside jokes and anecdotes that he wouldn't understand. The important thing was that the man comprehended what was planned and agreed to it.

"Tell him I can do it tomorrow if he would like."

"Oh, he would like that Mr. John. He wants to have the surgery very badly. His concern is with the cost. He doesn't have the required amount."

The services at Lacor were heavily subsidized by donations and were ridiculously inexpensive by Western standards. A hernia repair could be obtained for a little over fifty US dollars, a major abdominal surgery for one hundred twenty-five. One of the problems was that people in Uganda weren't paid in US currency, or British pounds for that matter, they were paid in Ugandan shillings. One dollar could buy nearly four thousand Ugandan shillings. So the devalued currency, farm economy, ongoing government corruption, and widespread poverty meant that even the simplest surgeries and treatments were financially out of reach for most people.

"Tell him not to worry. He should talk to billing and just pay what he can."

The expression of gratitude and relief on his face and body was immense. He smiled, stood up straighter than he had in months and blessed John. He thanked him for coming to help the people of Uganda. For leaving his own country, which he knew was much more comfortable, to live and work there.

"You're welcome. Let's see how you do before getting too carried away though."

"Oh, I am sure I will do well in your hands. I am so happy. You know, I am just a poor farmer. We barely grow enough on our plot of land to keep from starving. There is no money for anything else. This is a great gift."

"You're very kind," said John as he handed him his papers. "Now take these up to Mary and she'll get you registered. Remember not to eat or drink anything after midnight." He had David walk him up to the charge nurse's desk to get him on the surgery schedule.

Before John had finished giving instructions to the man, another patient stood up from the end of the bench in the hallway, came into the exam room and sat down. He held his papers out to David who took them and started to make some notes in the chart. John walked back in, squeezed hand sanitizer onto his hands, rubbed them together until they were dry, took a swallow of water and sat back in his spot.

"So, tell me why you have come here to see me today."

3

This pattern continued throughout the morning. There was a parade of men and women, boys and girls, all needing attention for some kind of ailment. Thankfully not all required surgery. Some needed reassurance, others medicine, and some needed a referral to a different department or specialist. As always, the work was tiring, interesting, frustrating, and gratifying.

In the early afternoon, Mary appeared and whispered to John that it was time for tea. He didn't always take time to eat, but today he felt hungry enough to do so. Warm chapatti with just the right amount of oiliness, ripe flavorful bananas, and Ugandan tea with warm milk and sugar were the usual comforting fare.

In the lounge, John took a chapatti, sprinkled sugar on it, and peeled a small banana, placing it on the tortilla. He rolled the whole thing up and ate it with his tea, mainly listening as other nurses and surgeons came and went. He always enjoyed the company, but never quite felt a part of it. Everyone was more comfortable speaking Acholi, so most of the more colorful, descriptive conversation was lost in translation. But a break was a break, and community was community and he was glad for both.

Following tea there were two short surgeries. John let Stephen do most of the procedures as he assisted. He exposed tissue, blotted blood with gauze, directed, guided and encouraged the intern. Stephen had improved greatly over the past few months and needed much less in the way of specific instruction at this point.

They listened to music as they worked. John had thousands of songs on his phone. Music had always been important to John. His musical selection always seemed to match his mood. Today it was the band Made in Heights and Seattle songwriter Damien Jurado, as he was feeling a little pensive and mellow, although he couldn't quite pinpoint why. Stephen and Alice, for the most part, humored him and let him play what he liked. He tried not to push them too much though, staying away from the free jazz and abrasive punk rock side of his collection. All in all, it seemed to work, breaking up the silence, acting as a conversation starter or just providing simple entertainment as they worked. He missed having someone really appreciate his music. To understand it, banter back and forth with him about it. But that was another time and another place. Following the surgeries, John met David back at the clinic to continue seeing patients.

Although John worked seven days a week, had performed hundreds of surgeries and seen thousands of patients, he knew that he met only the tiniest fraction of the need. There simply weren't enough doctors, supplies, government support or foreign aid, and not enough hours in the day or weeks in a year to see everyone that needed help. Many people that came to be seen were turned away or became tired of waiting. Appointments were made weeks in advance. Despite that, a multitude came without reservations, hoping for a miracle. The odds were stacked against them. But this was nothing new, their odds were long from birth. And yet here they were.

The schedule seemed to fill up in a relatively random fashion. The staff knew what John could treat for the most part, but really the luckiest, most persistent, and best connected were the ones that received the attention. And not all of the patients that were evaluated could be helped. Lack of expertise, equipment, time or pre-operative diagnostic studies would lead to rejection. Looking for particular afflictions over others and trying to help those with greater need first also led to selecting one particular surgical patient over another.

Most of the Ugandan patients appeared very stoic. They betrayed little emotion with their eyes or their facial expressions, or at least little that could be easily read by John. A tiny flash of a smile, a raised eyebrow, and a quick upward nod was about all for "yes, we are on the same page." Disapproval was a "tsk" sound and a slight frown. And as patient as everyone was with the long wait, it was still difficult. A quick walk outside the operating rooms to the patient wards and veranda on a Friday afternoon was greeted with disapproving stares and a chorus of "tsk." After months of hearing and seeing this, it was still unnerving and disheartening at times.

Brought in by a family member, the next patient was about thirty and had a problem that John was not skilled in treating. John knew how important it was to stretch himself, to push the boundaries of confidence, energy, and expertise. If he couldn't help someone he knew that there might not be anyone else that could. But he still knew his limitations. In this neglected, poverty-stricken area of the world many people had problems that were beyond what could be treated for various reasons, and this was one of those patients.

When David told him that the doctor would not be able to help him, his face had one of disbelief. He seemed paralyzed with sadness. He had to be told again. It was like he couldn't comprehend what was being said. His eyes widened, he began to silently weep. Next he started shaking, staring straight ahead at a spot on the floor. John explained the situation through David in every way that he knew, trying to soften the blow. He said, "You will be fine." That maybe he can pay for an operation in Kampala (knowing full well that he was very poor). That he could still have a normal life. But all the man heard was "no." After an eternity of staring, trembling and then trying to compose himself, he was able to stand up. With a final, feeble sounding, "Sorry," from John he was led out by his friend. The door closed behind him, but not before one last "tsk."

Barely two seconds later the door opened again and the next patient came in, a cane in one hand and a black plastic bag in the other, the bag holding his catheter tubing. Like all of the others he was filled with an urgent expectant hope.

John tried to shake off that encounter and move on, finish up the day. He closed his eyes for just a moment before beginning to talk to the next patient. He pictured the look of anguish as the man wept for himself and for all others like him in the hallway and in Uganda. The memories would linger. They would return in flashes that night and in days to come. Failure has a cruel way of overshadowing success. For every surgery he performed in Uganda there were probably three patients that returned home disappointed. There were thousands all over the country with the same affliction who never even made the journey to Lacor, who perhaps mercifully never even tried.

John knew that life wasn't always filled with success or simple solutions, that even the most advantaged felt pain, could be overlooked, or be told no. He knew that there were times when everyone felt lost, forgotten, rejected and push aside. By tapping into that emotion instead of letting it damage him further, he developed empathy. He became a wounded healer. Certainly by experiencing loss, pain, and disappointment first hand he could more deeply understand his patients and those around him.

John offered a silent prayer that God would have mercy on him, on the man that he couldn't help, and on all those that long for healing, that they might find peace.

And then he forced himself to move on. To be present with the patient who was now in front of him in the exam room.

"So, tell me why you have come here to see me today."

When the last patient was seen, John put away his gloves, lube, and papers. He pushed the chairs back to the edges of the room, and went to find Mary. She was rounding with one of the three staff general surgeons, Mr. James. He was performing teaching rounds with some medical students and an intern named Carol. One of the Comboni priests was there as well. Everyone was standing just outside one of the larger patient rooms.

John had seen the priest before but had never had a long discussion with him. He guessed Father Paolo was nearing seventy. He had been at Lacor continuously for at least three decades except for brief infrequent returns to the main house in Verona. Perpetually smiling and friendly, he was one of the more visible clergy, often socializing with patients and staff.

St. Mary's Hospital Lacor, more commonly simply called Lacor, was founded by Combonis in 1959 and missionaries from that order have been involved with the hospital ever since.

Daniel Comboni was an Italian missionary to Central Africa in the 1850's. He began in Sudan and worked in other places in the area including Egypt. He understood the importance of involving Africans in their own destiny. His motto was "Save Africa with Africa," and he was a vocal opponent of the slave trade. He died in Khartoum, Sudan in 1881, but his work carried on. Missionaries arrived in Uganda in 1910 and began establishing Catholic churches throughout the country. Pope John Paul II canonized Daniel Comboni in 2003. Including Father Paolo there were over twelve hundred Comboni priests, with more than a hundred missionaries in Uganda alone.

Tonight Paolo was talking with the students, Carol, and Mr. James as they rounded. James was kidding with the students, asking when they had last been to mass. Most Ugandans attended either the Church of Uganda, which is part of the Anglican Communion (Church of England) or the Roman Catholic Church. A growing number were practicing Muslims and about four percent were Pentecostal Christian. Carol laughed at the question and said it had been about a month.

"When you were home then?" James said, smiling.

"Yes, I always go to church when I am home."

"Why not when you are here? It's easy, you can walk about forty steps and you are there. You wouldn't even be winded from the journey."

"Yes, I know. I guess I just get busy."

James asked the medical students when they had last been to church and got similar answers. None of them went regularly. All the while James and Paolo were exchanging bemused glances with each other. Medical students are used to being put on the spot on rounds, the addition of the spiritual questions in front of

Father Paolo was a new twist though and they didn't know what to make of it.

John spoke up at this point. "Do you attend mass regularly Mr. James?"

"Every day, Doctor."

"Really? I didn't know that about you. That's great. I'm really impressed. Do you feel it helps you? Offers peace? Keeps your life in balance?"

"I do. I find it necessary in my life to attend church daily. I don't think I could do what I do without prayer. It's a common thing. This is what I was demonstrating to Father Paolo. Most of us grow up with a faith. We go to church, we pray, we believe in something greater than ourselves. But then we go to school. We become people of science. In medical school most of us stop going to church. Maybe we think we don't need God. Maybe we're too busy. We think we are too smart. Maybe we discover girls. Or boys.

"But then comes a time when things get difficult. A patient dies. We miss our family. We have children who start asking too many questions. We have a low spot in our lives. Then we remember. Then we return to church. And then we pray. We seek God at church and in our hearts and in each other."

"You're right. That's exactly what happened to me," said John, impressed with James' insight.

"Of course it is. Children pray. Young people stop praying. But when we grow up, have a family, responsibility or a painful loss we begin to pray again. Right, Father?"

"Yes, I've seen it many times."

"Okay, we need to keep moving or we'll be here all night. Plus, these patients are tired of listening to my lay theology. Carol, who's next?"

Carol gave John a winsome smile, rolling her expressive brown eyes as she turned to the next patient saying, "This is Oswego Michael, he had a partial colectomy two days ago. His vitals are stable. Urine output has been good. He's been up walking. His bowels haven't moved yet but his belly is soft and he has good bowel sounds…"

24

As Carol gave her report Paolo caught John's eye. "May I talk to you a moment?"

John said, "sure" as he backed out of the doorway. Paolo followed into the hall.

"It's probably nothing but I was hoping to run into you sometime. I have been passing blood in my urine."

"Really? Any pain with it?"

"No, none."

"Red urine? All the way through? Or is it more like blood dripping after you pass urine, or just something you noticed on your underwear?"

"It is red urine."

"Any clots? Something solid? Or simply thin red urine?"

"A few small clots I think. It looked like I was passing dark red meat. Almost like tissue."

"When did this start and how often has it happened?"

"It's hard to know. Maybe six months. At first it happened infrequently. Last week though it was red for much of the day."

John signaled to Carol, who was now at the back of the group gathered around a different surgery patient. She came out into the hallway with the two men.

"Father, you know Dr. Carol. She's going to get you signed up for a cystoscopy tomorrow. I just want to take a look in your bladder. Make sure everything is okay. You'll be asleep for the procedure. If I find anything abnormal I'll go ahead and remove or biopsy it. Carol, could you also make sure Father has some blood work and an ultrasound of the abdomen?"

"Sure Mr. John. I'll take care of it."

"Thank you. I think he'll be the third case but please check on that and give him some idea what time to arrive in pre-op."

"I'll do it."

With that John shook Paolo's hand and smiled at Carol. He looked at the time on his phone and said, "Let me know if you need anything tonight, otherwise I'll see you both tomorrow."

He left the hospital, jogged across the highway and found his favorite kiosk. The cook spoke very little English, but John had been there enough times it wasn't a problem. This time he bought a bowl of rice served with a groundnut sauce that was gently simmering in a big pot on a charcoal fire. Simple, fairly bland but filling and vegetarian, she gave it to him in a bowl that he had retrieved from his locker for the occasion. He carefully carried the bowl and a ripe mango back across the road, through the gate, and down the path to his apartment.

Flipping on the light he kicked off his shoes at the door, stepping into the kitchen to pour some water. He did pretty well with the tap water at Lacor. It was supposedly filtered, but when possible he did try to boil it first before drinking. The water that had cooled down to room temperature in his electric kettle was perfect for the occasion.

He sat down with his meal, closed his eyes and quietly prayed, "Lord Jesus Christ, have mercy on me." He said it several times. Praying until he felt his mind slow and his heart open wider, until he felt present and mindful. Only then did he take the first bite of his dinner.

Once the bowl was empty and the mango was finished, he washed his dishes, put them away and took out his spiral notebook. Under the September 23 entry from that morning he wrote:

"35 clinic patients
2 surgeries: inguinal hernia, large hydrocele
Priest has blood in his urine.
Interesting discussion about prayer and attending church with James and Paolo.
Upset man that I couldn't help. His face..."

After rereading the words from the morning and from the two previous days, thinking about them for a few moments as he traced over some of the letters, he placed the notebook and the pen back on a corner of the desk.

He looked at the time on his phone. It was a quarter till ten, which meant it would be one forty-five in Kansas. His sister would be at work now and could hopefully talk. He took a breath and pushed her number.

"Hi Deborah. Sorry it took so long to call. The day got away from me a little."

"No problem John. I didn't want to do this by email. Are you okay? I haven't talked to you in a long time."

"I'm fine. It's mom, isn't it?"

"It is… she had a stroke…"

"When?"

"Yesterday."

"Is she…?"

"Yeah, she's gone John. The doctor wanted to talk to you, tell you himself. I told him I would do it. It's for the best though, you know? She wasn't herself. That person has been gone a long time now."

"You're right. Of course you are. We all knew this would happen. Thanks for letting me know…" He paused a minute then said, "Deborah?"

"Yeah?"

"I'm sorry I'm not there. I'll get home as soon as I can. Tell Fred I'm thinking about him, that he can call or email if he needs anything from me."

"Sure John."

"Great. Bye Deborah."

As he hung up, the Isaiah passage from the morning, the one that he had been thinking about throughout the day took on a more specific meaning. Once again he was blind, and once again he was dependent on God to lead him forward. He knew that the way wouldn't be easy but with his path illuminated and the edges smoothed by faith, he would be all right.

However, there were still some decisions to be made. Some difficult ones. He decided that the day had been full enough, that he would sleep on it, confident that things would be clearer tomorrow.

4

Placencia, Belize

Two Years Earlier

It was the best decision he had made in weeks. When John had seen the dark green Club Car XRT 850 with a For Sale sign on it during the long trek back from his second trip to the store that day, he immediately tracked down the owner. It was only two years old and well cared for. He didn't even bargain much. He drove it home, parked it under his house, and admired it for a long time.

It really hadn't taken long to get to this point. Six weeks ago he had arrived with a plan for a simple life. Walking everywhere. Enjoying the slow pace. Only buying what he could carry. But moving in, getting a few things for the furnished home, stocking up on groceries and simply going to the market every day, sometimes more than once a day, had involved a lot of time and a lot of walking. Also, he was kind of trapped in the area. He wanted to be able to explore further up the peninsula sometimes. He knew upon moving to Placencia that there was a chance he would need a vehicle of some sort and was glad he had at least tried it for a while. But having this cart would help so much.

John took the key with him and climbed the stairs to his home. It was a duplex on eight-foot stilts. There was an open sink and shower down below to rinse off sand. He had a spacious yellow veranda that ran the length of the front of the house. Two plastic chairs on the porch faced east. Sitting in one of the chairs with his morning tea, he could watch the sunrise. If he had his glasses on he could just make out the beach through a small gap in the buildings.

The inside was a clean and simple one-bedroom apartment. Two inexpensive wicker chairs, a small wicker couch, and a coffee table with a glass top made up the living room furniture. There was also a television that John didn't watch.

On shelves above the kitchen sink, there was rice, beans, peanut butter, local honey, canola oil, a large bottle of Marie Sharp's hot sauce, a few dry herbs and spices, a pineapple, two tomatoes, an onion and a small paper bag of chocolate chip cookies. A half-sized refrigerator, microwave, and an electric stove completed the kitchen area.

The bedroom furniture consisted of a full-sized bed, dresser, and bedside table. The walls of the entire apartment were medium brown, horizontally placed two by fours, with a walnut stain. The dark wood provided a comfortable feeling for John. It felt good to get out of the hot bright sun at times. Of course, it was often warm inside. There were two fans but no air conditioning.

He had found the place online before he arrived, and had signed a three-month lease for what he felt was a very reasonable thirteen hundred Belizean dollars per month. This was six hundred and fifty US dollars and included utilities and wireless Internet.

It was basically in the center of the village, only about two hundred yards to the nearest fruit and vegetable stand, and just a little farther in the opposite direction to the beach. He rarely heard any neighbors, including the fisherman that lived on the other side of the duplex. It looked perfect in the pictures and it was really almost as good in person.

John filled a glass with water from the kitchen faucet, took his Kindle and went outside to sit on the porch. He had been trying to read these past six weeks. He had only carried the Bible with him when he moved, but did have several books on the Kindle. The local library in the village mainly had travel books and popular mass-produced paperbacks, most of which were well read and several years old.

He was currently reading Dostoyevsky's *The Brothers Karamazov*, partly because it had been one of Dorothy Day's favorite. One of his goals for his time in Placencia was to take on some of the longer classics that he had never had time to read. So far the book was amazing. The three, well really four, brothers and their different personalities were fascinating to John.

Alternately sitting in one of the plastic chairs, standing at the railing, and pacing barefoot up and down the veranda, he read off and on for two hours. In the shade of the porch it was comfortable, not too warm. There were periods in which he would stop and just watch the darkening sky, or a person walking by on the sandy trail between the houses, or put on his glasses and watch the waves wash in on that little bit of beach that he could see from the corner of the porch. He had noticed over the past few weeks that he had begun to relax a little. There was less going on in his mind, which he took as a good thing. He had never been one to sit for long and that hadn't changed, but he did feel a little different inside than when he had arrived, and that was the point wasn't it?

It was dark now and he was getting hungry, so he went inside and pulled last night's leftover rice and beans from the refrigerator. He scooped a good portion into a smaller bowl and warmed it in the microwave. The kitchen table could be round or square depending on whether the leaves were up or down. John had one leaf down so it would fit tighter against the wall.

He sat in one of the two chairs with his meal, and after shaking on a liberal amount of hot sauce, he bowed his head and prayed. He gave thanks for the food, the lovely day, and asked God to bless the people whose faces bubbled up into his mind.

After eating he washed out the bowl, took down the pineapple, cut it into bite-sized pieces and put half of them into the fridge in the dinner bowl. The rest he left on the cutting board and ate while standing. Since arriving he had eaten pineapple nearly every day. They were so sweet, inexpensive and filling. In season, they were grown only thirty miles away on the mainland.

Taking out one of the two remaining chocolate chip cookies, he sat at the table and opened a spiral bound notebook. Turning to the page in which he had written "November 30" at the top, he read the Bible verse written below the date.

"Seven times a day I praise you for your righteous laws.
Great peace have those who love your law,
and nothing can make them stumble."- Psalm 119:164-5

John had read through his *NIV One Year Bible* eight times now, but it was only upon moving to Belize that he had taken the time to really pore over it carefully. Slowly going through each of the four passages every morning, he focused on whichever of the verses seemed to be speaking to him that day. He read the words out loud, and then silently to himself as he tried to discern the deeper meaning. Maybe it was just an emotion, maybe some new word or phrase that he hadn't noticed before, but he always seemed to find something new, some direction or theme that would carry him through the day, making it richer.

This morning it had been the two verses from Psalms. John liked the "seven times a day I praise you" passage and had intentionally stopped that many times to be present throughout the day. He wrote in his notebook under the Psalm:

"I look around and I praise God for the laws of creation. For the way everything is interconnected, whether we admit it or not. For the genius of giving us free will and individuality and yet making us dependent on each other. Meaning that for the world to work correctly we have to work together. The great peace that comes to those who love God's law, who love Creation, working for the common good, for sustainability. Nothing can make us stumble when we are living in the spirit of equality and the long-term health of our common home.

Whether watching the red, then orange, then yellow sun silently rise as it dispels the darkness, or swimming in the warm salty, buoyant waters of the

Caribbean Sea, or picking up trash on the beach, or finding a mutually agreeable price for a golf cart with another child of God, the laws of the Creator are perfect."

He wrote a few more lines about what he did that day, who he had talked to, what he spent money on, and then he put the notebook away. This was something he had dreamed of doing for years but just never had the time. He would lie in bed and remember his day, pray for patients and people he had met, take stock of the successes and failures, but that was it. He now had the luxury of time. He could prayerfully reflect on the day, how it all tied together from the initial *lectio divina* in the morning to the theme that was carried forward. How the people and thoughts that came before him seemed interwoven. He felt more in touch with his true self and believed it was one of the most important aspects of his new life in Belize.

He looked at his phone next, catching up on news, email, and Facebook. He replied to a few of the fifty emails, liked a few posts, and skimmed three articles from the New Yorker and NPR. He allowed himself no more than thirty minutes a day of social and entertainment Internet and phone time. It was a major change at first, difficult and stressful to himself and to others. But now thirty minutes seemed to be plenty. When the time was up he turned on the alarm that was already set for five seventeen and got ready for bed.

———————

The next morning, when it was still dark, he awoke in anticipation of the new day. This feeling had become more acute since arriving in Placencia. The time of awakening hadn't changed but the initial sensation had. Instead of an eyes-closed, begrudging walk to make tea, followed by stalling and leaving a few minutes late for work, he was so much more at ease. He loved this holy time, when it was dark and quiet, with the promise of daylight still unfulfilled. Even though he literally had nothing important to do, he felt more excited about each day.

After showering and eating warm oatmeal with two teaspoons of honey, he sat down with his Bible and read the passages for December first. They were from Daniel, 1 John, Psalm 120, and Proverbs 28. After reading all of them slowly and thoughtfully, he wrote this down from 1 John 2:9-10:

"Anyone who claims to be in the light but hates his brother is still in the darkness. Whoever loves his brother lives in the light, and there is nothing in him to make him stumble."

He prayed about this, meditated on it and incorporated it into his being so that this day he would remember to love others, to stay in the light.

By the time John had finished breakfast he was undisputedly in the light. It came streaming in through the windows, illuminating the floor and brightening the room. Per his new routine he put on his dirty white KC Royals baseball cap, swimsuit, and Chacos, stuffed his goggles, towel, Kindle, and a fifty Belizean dollar bill into a small backpack and headed to the beach.

The sand was soft and already retaining heat as he turned left upon coming out from between two souvenir shops. He walked up the little sidewalk, billed as the world's narrowest main street, until the restaurants and small hotels thinned. He put his bag under a palm tree next to his shirt, shoes, and hat and waded into the water. The sea was calm and clear. He swam out a ways, looked around to find the palm tree, and then began swimming parallel with the shore. He went perhaps seventy-five yards then swam back, doing this five times at a leisurely pace. He rested for a few minutes, and then did it five more times. He rested again, this time a little longer, and then did it a third time. Back and forth, fifteen times in all. He was pretty sure it was over two thousand yards. He had built up from six hundred yards six weeks ago and could already feel his lung capacity growing, his shoulder muscles healing and strengthening.

He took off his goggles and floated on his back. Just floated, looking up at the sky, listening to the sounds of the sea in his ears as they bobbed in and out of the water. This was one of the reasons he had moved here. To drift effortlessly and endlessly in the ocean. It was something he had dreamed about for years. Each time he had been to a beach, the thing that he enjoyed the most, what he remembered when he closed his eyes and tried to relax back home, was this. Floating on his back, looking at the sun and clouds, or on his stomach watching the coral or fish, or the sea grass moving back and forth with the action of the waves.

He lost track of time and it was later than usual when he got out of the water and dried off. From there he walked up to the nearby coffee shop. John had stopped drinking coffee and switched to tea several years ago on moral grounds that would be difficult for him to clearly explain. Something about shipping costs, the amount of waste generated, labor exploitation and problems with land usage. Plus, he was trying to cut back on caffeine.

There were two coffee shops in town and, being a creature of habit, he had never tried the other one. Holy Grounds had four things going for it in John's opinion: a great name, it was closer to his apartment by about seventy-five seconds, and he had figured out what was on the menu and how to order. He was certain that he would eventually visit the other one, but not today.

That was due to reason number four: Jessica.

5

Jessica was tan, with honey brown eyes, interesting cartoonlike tattoos on her arms and back, and black-framed glasses that gave her a studious hipster look. She had shoulder-length, straight sun-bleached brown hair that she usually wore in a loose bun. John liked it better when it was down and he was a little embarrassed that he cared that much.

"Good morning John," Jessica said as he came through the door, still a little damp from his swim.

"Good morning Jessica. How's it going?"

Her hair was down today. The way she flipped it, fussed with it, something about her hair made her face somehow even brighter, her eyes more warm and alive.

"Excellent. Hey, we have peppermint scones today. I know it sounds weird but they're actually pretty good."

"Okay, I'll try one. And a rooibos tea."

"You got it. So, how far did you swim today?"

"About two thousand yards I think. That's what I'm telling people anyway."

"Nice morning for it. The current didn't look too strong and there weren't any cruise ship people today."

A few years prior, a cruise ship company bought Harvest Caye, an island only three miles from the mainland and about five from Placencia. It had been completely reconfigured at a cost of millions of dollars and untold ecological damage, and had recently become a stop for twenty-five hundred passengers at a time, two or three days a week.

Luckily, most of them stayed on the boat or on the manufactured beaches, bars, and wave machines on the island. But some passengers made it up to Placencia. Even a hundred and fifty people arriving at once tended to overwhelm the village. The town was in a pleasant steady state of restaurants, tourist shops and public toilets. As it slowly grew, or maybe contracted after a hurricane or dip in the economic fortunes of the US or Europe, the subtle changes were taken in stride. But the periodic influx of a bolus of cruise ship passengers had thrown the town off balance. Few townspeople could see the value of it, even those who made a little more money on those days. There were rumors of more ships stopping at Harvest Caye as well. All of this had added some anxiety to the residents.

"You're really coming along though, huh?" Jessica continued, "Swimming farther each week it sounds like."

"Yeah, it feels good to get stronger. It's been a long time since I've been in any kind of shape. Like decades."

She handed him the scone and the tea, each on their own small white plates. He paid her with the Belizean bill and left some change in the tip jar.

John sat by the window at a table for two. Facing the front of the store, he was positioned in a way that he could look to his right to see the beach and people walking by, and to his left to watch Jessica as she busied herself behind the counter.

He took out the Kindle and tried to read a little Dostoyevsky. He wasn't the only customer in the store. At another table, two older men were alternately looking at computers and talking. One of them had a voice that resonated deeply in his chest, a voice that was made for radio. The other's was higher and softer which meant that John could only clearly hear half of their conversation. He had a difficult time concentrating when there were distractions and this pair was definitely a distraction. Over the next thirty minutes he read only two pages but had an intimate understanding of the deep voice guy's extended family. He knew how his grandkids were doing in sports, what the weather was like in Boston… he knew everything.

The scone was actually really delicious. When he had finished it and had given up on trying to read, he took his mug and the two plates to the dirty dishes bin. He looked at the corkboard behind it, filled mainly with papers announcing apartments for rent, bicycles for sale, or advertisements for deep sea fishing trips. All of it had been up there since John had been coming into Holy Grounds, the number of torn tabs at the bottom unchanged. However, there was one new announcement. It was from the Friends of the Reef, advertising a volunteer event scheduled for the next day. They were going to work on replanting mangroves in the water near the airstrip.

"Have you done anything with Friends of the Reef yet?" Jessica asked from behind him.

Startled a little, John said, "What, this? No, have you?"

"Yeah, they're kind of cool. You should go. There's usually a good crowd, so you're bound to meet some new people. The last one was a beach clean up. There were like thirty people there and we really got so much done. It's amazing how much trash accumulates in some of the areas around here, places that tourists don't see."

"Are you going then?"

"I am. I get off at eleven tomorrow. We can carpool if you want. You can take me in your new golf cart."

"Sure, that would be great… Hey! How do you know about the golf cart? You aren't stalking me are you?"

Jessica laughed, "News travels fast here. Don't do anything that you don't want to become public knowledge."

"Seriously! That's funny though. All right, we'll go around eleven then. Why don't you just walk over to my place when you're finished here? The yellow duplex. It's south about three buildings, then over a little ways. You know Maria's fruit stand? I'm parallel with her. Of course you probably knew all of that already," he said with a grin. "I'll be watching for you. Well, I may see you here in the morning huh? Anyway, we'll figure it out."

"Sounds good. They'll have the plants and any tools we need there. Just bring clothes that can get wet."

"They're the only kind I have I think…. Planting mangrove. How cool is that? People coming together, volunteering and helping their community. I love it."

A young couple wandered in, scanned the room and headed to the counter, looking up at the menu board. The woman looked a little annoyed, like there was some sort of ongoing disagreement.

"Hey, how's it going?" asked Jessica. "I'll be there in a second."

"Okay, no problem," the man answered as they continued to study the menu.

She turned back to John. "Well, I'd better get to work. See you tomorrow."

"Yeah, great, I'll see you. Have a good day."

John gathered his things and headed home. He had planned to read a little more and take a nap, but once he got there he couldn't relax. His mind continued to relive the conversation with Jessica. He hadn't expected to find a volunteer activity, much less a date, with his morning scone. Well, kind of a date anyway. He really didn't expect much though. Jessica was just hitching a ride and being friendly. She understood what it was like to be new in town.

What did he really know about Jessica anyway? Not much. He thought she was fairly new to Placencia herself. It seems like she was medical in some way. Well, he could learn more details the next day.

He was excited about the mangrove planting also. He knew that they were so important to the ecosystem. Mangroves help prevent erosion and protect the shorelines from storms and waves. They filter pollutants from the water and act as an important habitat for all kinds of fish, mollusks and crustaceans. To establish, or even reestablish mangroves would be very helpful indeed.

Probably just as importantly, it was something to do. He had been filling his day with small, simple activities. Reading,

40

swimming, eating, walking… He was trying to be patient. To not immediately fill his life with too many activities. This is what he wanted when he had dreamed of this place. Less stress. More time to think. More pure interactions with people. Time for in depth conversations and meaningful relationships.

He knew that people were the same everywhere. Everyone had the same needs. The same desire for belonging, friendship, stability, and safety. So he was confident that he would find friends in Placencia. It was a small community, by definition insular, but everyone had been so friendly on his past visits here. He knew that he would fit in somewhere and find his people.

Maybe Friends of the Reef were his people. He was sure that he would at least recognize a few of them. This was what he needed, an organized activity. Something to help the greater good. These were the kind of life giving actions that led to lasting, healthy relationships.

The rest of the day went by quickly. A long walk, a drive in his golf cart up the road to buy salad ingredients at a stand he hadn't been to before, and then listening to Mexican music on the radio as he made dinner. It was another good, laid back day. He'd had no arguments with anyone, no stressful encounters. Even the loud-talker at the coffee shop had been more amusing that irritating. And why not? This wasn't rush hour traffic on I-435. Or shareholder meetings with his old group. The low level of anxiety was still there, but it was far back in his subconscious, covered over nicely by the pleasant day.

After dinner he took time to write in his journal, adding words below the passage from 1 John. He felt like he had lived in the light this day. He had loved his brother, regardless of the timbre of his voice. He knew the passage was more about nonviolence. It was about loving your enemies, turning the other cheek, about not resisting an evil person. Those things hadn't really come up this day in paradise, but he felt like the peace in his heart right at that moment could smother out any hostile thought.

The next morning the daily Bible reading that spoke to him was:

"The Lord will keep you from all harm- he will watch over your life;
The Lord will watch over your coming and going both now and forevermore."- Psalms 121:7-8

John knew that God didn't keep people from all harm. People died. They had emotional and physical pain. They lost jobs, spouses, and children. They fought in wars and had domestic disputes. There was road rage and there were drunk drivers and there were misunderstandings that led to hard feelings that could carry on for years.

"Maybe that line looks at the long term," he thought. "The big picture. In the end everything will be okay. Our spirits will leave us intact, free from permanent harm. Through all of it God is watching over our lives, our coming and goings. Watching us, gently guiding us. Maybe God keeps the deepest part of us safe. In our quietest moments God is there. In the beginning, at the very end, and yes, in that long middle we are kept from harm if we live eternally rather than temporally."

Still thinking about all of this, he put on his sandals and baseball cap, went down the stairs and headed north up the beach. It hadn't begun to heat up yet as he walked past his swimming spot, past where the stores and houses thinned out, then turned back west towards the road. With all of the planting still ahead of him, he had decided to take a day off from swimming. He walked back to the end of the main road, waving occasionally at people walking or driving or bicycling by. He found a guy he knew, Tom, standing near the main pier.

Tom was also in his mid-fifties. He and his wife had lived in Placencia part time for five years. He always seemed to be either fishing, preparing to fish, cleaning fish, or telling fish stories. John knew him from church and he was pleasant in small doses. He'd been attending the interdenominational Living Water church. It was a small community so there weren't very many choices. Catholic, Jehovah Witness, evangelical and this one.

John felt fortunate that it existed. Composed mainly of Methodists and Presbyterians, he felt comfortable there. Services were at an old restaurant that had been out of business for a couple years. The volunteer minister was from Cleveland but spent about nine months a year in Belize. He was an extremely nice guy. His theology was compatible with John's, which basically meant that John didn't spend the entire sermon silently contradicting and arguing with him. There were about twenty people at each service and John had talked to most of them, including Tom.

"Hey Tom, how's it going?"

"Oh, hey John. Good! Out walking?"

"Yep. I'm about finished- heading back now- what are you up to?"

"I'm meeting some people. Taking them out fishing. Tourists. Looks like a good day for it. I need to get you out there sometime. You'd love it. I'll do everything for you. You just have to sit back, relax, and reel in the big one. I'll even give you a discount. The Living Water discount," he winked.

"Yeah, I don't think so. Fishing's not my thing. Thanks though."

"Well, you won't know until you try right?"

"You're probably right. Maybe sometime. Well, good luck. Will I see you Sunday?"

"You bet. Have a good one."

John knew he wasn't ever going to go fishing. He did like going out on the water. Speeding along or sailing quietly. It was so pleasant. Being from Kansas it wasn't something he was able to do often. He certainly wasn't going to fish though. Or be around when people were hauling fish out of the water by a hook. He was a vegetarian and just the thought of it made him squirm a little. Pulling the hooks out of their mouths, the sharp fins, the smell, the dying fish flopping around on the deck. He wondered how they were killed. Did you whack them on the head? Just cut right into them? No thanks.

He waved at Tom and walked back up the narrow sidewalk. There was a group from a cruise ship in town. They were recognizable. They dressed differently and seemed a significantly more rushed. They were a little larger in general and selfie sticks were in use everywhere he looked. Of course, there were more people in the shops and walking around, but there were only a few staking out spots on the beach. He assumed the ones that wanted a beach would have stayed on Harvest Caye and not paid extra to come to Placencia. There really wasn't room for people to pass each other on the sidewalk so he had to step off a few times to get around tourists. But besides that, it wasn't a big deal to him. He tended to like people in general. It didn't matter whether they were cruise ship passengers or beach bums, natives or winter Belizeans. People were people really.

John peeked in Holy Grounds and saw that three of the five tables were taken. He opened the door and waved at Jessica, who looked past two women ordering at the counter and waved back. She gave him a "sorry I'm so busy right now" look and he smiled and shrugged.

"I'll see you later," she mouthed.

John gave her a thumbs-up as he backed out the door. He slipped between the buildings towards the main road, stopping at Maria's fruit stand. This was not only the closest one to his house, it was also the best as far as he was concerned. It had friendly people and nice produce, much of it local. There was usually a guy selling cinnamon rolls at a picnic table. It felt vaguely subversive buying from him, like he was a dealer or something. They were sweet, sticky, and wonderful.

The guy at Maria's put green peppers, mangos, and a big ripe pineapple into the cloth bag John always brought along. John looked at his phone and saw that it was nine thirty. He dropped his produce off at home and walked down to the office supply store near the dock. They rented computers with Internet access. His phone was fine for most things, but he liked to pay bills and do financial things on a real computer. He rarely had to compete for access here and this morning was no exception.

Belize's retirement program was one of the best in the world and was one of the main reasons John had chosen this location. Belize had a stable government, many people spoke English, and it had beautiful beaches. John was unsure how permanent this move would be, he only knew that he loved it here and wanted to give it a try. If he lived carefully, bought mainly local food and didn't travel too often, the cost of living would be much less.

Certainly his apartment was a great deal, about half what he would pay in Kansas City. Transportation was a fraction of the cost as well. He just had to be very careful with his phone. That was one thing that was more expensive in Belize. As a result, he didn't make many calls and only texted over Wi-Fi.

For now he was simply being mindful of his spending. He checked his credit card balance, paid a phone bill, and looked at his kids' student accounts at Grinnell and Texas Christian. He replenished their meal cards and transferred some money to pay a bill at Grinnell. He looked over his financial accounts, made sure the money was still there, something he liked to do weekly. Reassured, he logged out of the accounts, caught up on Facebook for a few minutes and returned some emails.

Michelle, a friend who had been his secretary, had written a little office gossip. She was mainly just checking in on him. He sent a picture of a Placencia sunrise and a brief note letting her know that he was fine. To be honest, he missed work, especially if he thought about it too much. That was one reason he limited his computer time. He was trying to live in the present, and really felt that it was necessary to make a clean break. It was so tempting sometimes to call and say it was all a mistake, that he'd be back on Monday.

Like most people, his identity was defined by his work. He didn't want it to be that way. He wanted to see what else there was inside of him, to discover what other self there was, once he slowed down and stripped away the vocation. It was definitely risky, but it felt necessary. He knew that at his age it was now or never. So his replies were thoughtful but short to the people back home. He tried hard not to burn bridges as the future remained very unclear.

Logging out he paid the guy at the counter with a few coins and hurried back to his place. It was now almost eleven and he didn't want to keep Jessica waiting.

6

He arrived just as she was walking up. She was wearing a Bully baseball cap; her hair pulled though the gap in the back.

"Cool cap. You know Bully?"

"Yes! Love them. I saw them play in Chicago. Totally rocked. I'm impressed that you've heard them."

"I love anything that resembles punk. 'I Remember', 'Six', those are such great songs. Loud guitars, just singing her heart out. How can she scream like that? She says that her voice is fine, that the screaming doesn't bother her, but you have to wonder… I don't make it to many shows anymore but I definitely still listen. Well, are you ready to go?"

"I am. Let's see what this baby can do," she said, patting the golf cart.

He got it started and they headed north, talking about everything and nothing at all on the way. It took about ten minutes to reach the airstrip. John parked south of it a little ways, in the dirt where the other volunteers were.

As they arrived, a small plane was taking off. A Cessna ten-seater, it drove slowly to the end of the runway, and then turned around to face the other way. It sat for a few seconds, the propellers gaining speed. Then the plane accelerated down the runway, lifting up just as it appeared to be too late. They watched as it soared out over the sea, and then banked around until it was headed northwest, back over the land, headed towards Belize City.

Some of the volunteers were already calf deep in the water of the little bay, planting and talking.

"Hi Bev," said Jessica to a fifty-ish year old woman with naturally styled, short gray hair, thin rimmed glasses, and a No War t-shirt.

"Hi Jessica. Welcome. I'm glad you could make it. There's plenty left to do," she said excitedly, including John in her smiling expression.

"Bev, this is John. He's kind of new in Placencia. He's a doctor from Kansas City."

"Was a doctor," he corrected with a grin. "It's nice to meet you Bev. This is great. I'll bet this took a lot of work to organize, but what an important project. Thank you so much for doing it."

"Thanks. It did take a lot of work. But it certainly wasn't all me. I basically just organize the volunteers. Get the people here. It was the mangrove restoration specialists that designed and implemented the project. All the hard work has already been done, so we just have to stick them in the ground. Here, I'll help you two get started."

She took a bundle of plants, waded out into the water a few yards. It was about ankle deep. With John's help she dug a six-inch hole and lowered the plant into it, being careful not to bend the roots too acutely. She gently patted the mud back into place around the plant.

"That's all there is to it. Simple enough. Keep them about two feet apart. They don't have to be perfect. In fact don't put them in straight rows. Offset and more random rows work better for mangrove. Got it? Well, grab some plants and get started. Anywhere in this general area is fine. Have fun!"

Jessica grabbed a bundle of mangrove propagules and John took a shovel. They found a good spot away from the other volunteers to begin planting. They got wet, muddy, tired and had a wonderful time, enjoying the work and the company.

"So, tell me about your daughter. She's five right?"

"Yes, she's in kindergarten at the International School. She loves school. It is very hands on and interactive. There are all kinds of children there. Kids from England, Mexico, Germany, and from right here on the peninsula. I was worried a little at first but feel like it's okay. We would never have stayed if I didn't think that Stella was going to get a good education."

"How long have you lived here?"

"Almost two years. We had visited with my ex-husband. When he left there wasn't much holding me in Chicago. Stella and I needed a change. A big change. So we just up and moved here. I had no job and not much savings. I get a little child support, but it was still a big leap of faith."

"Brave."

"Yeah, or stupid. But it's worked out great so far. I was able to get a self-employment work visa. I kind of stumbled into the woman that owns the coffee shop. She needed help, her previous business partner had recently moved back to the States, sold out her share. I just stepped in as her new partner. It was amazing timing for both of us. It seems to work. I basically run the place, all of the day-to-day operations. She puts up the money, takes the financial risk. Her name is Sandy by the way. She lives here about half time. Winter and spring. In fact, she'll be here next month sometime. I'm sure you'll meet her. She's so nice."

"So you like the coffee shop then? It's a good fit for you?"

"I love it! I had never worked retail before. I was an x-ray tech back in Illinois for quite a few years. Had absolutely no idea how to work an espresso machine, how to manage employees or inventory. But I guess I'm a fast learner because we're doing okay."

"Well, you're a natural and you're obviously doing a great job. The place seems busy and popular."

"Thanks. It's fun really. I mean work is work. Most of us have to do it." She winked at John. "But this is good work. Making coffee and pastries, gossiping with locals and meeting new people. The hours are good and my three employees are wonderful. They can pretty much run the place. Like today. I don't worry a bit about skipping out for a few hours to plant mangrove."

"Speaking of which, let's start over there now," John said, pointing to an open area with his elbow.

"Okay, I need to get some more plants first."

"I'll go with you. We could both use some water."

Filling their water bottles from one of the big coolers, they talked with a few of the other volunteers. There was a family of four that was only in Belize for the week. The kids needed service hours so this worked out perfectly for them. They caught up with a local retired couple as well. It was a good group. Happy laughter, bonding and sharing, everyone with the feeling that they were doing useful work, of making a small difference in the ecological balance of the beautiful yet fragile place.

"So what about your kids? Twins right? They're in college?" Jessica asked as they resumed their conversation and the planting.

"Yes, right on both counts. They're both sophomores. Kate's at Grinnell. Do you know Grinnell? It's a small college in Iowa. Kate had said there was no way she was going to school in a state that started with a vowel. You know... Iowa, Ohio, Oregon, Idaho. Well, I don't remember talking about Arizona or Alabama, but the I's and O's anyway. She just didn't like the sound of them. But Grinnell was a good fit. She loves it. It's a very small town. Small classes. She's made good friends already."

"What does she want to do when she graduates?"

"Kate has always said she's going to be a doctor. Maybe ER. She also talks about surgery. We'll see. But that's the way she's been headed for a long time.

"And Sam's at Texas Christian. A horned frog. He plays baseball for them. Just having a great time. Taking a lot of different types of classes. He's a biology major, but we'll see how it all shakes out. He would like to do something in medicine as well. He's a good kid. So laid back and kind. Caring for others comes extremely naturally for some reason. Problems and stress just seem to roll off of him. Kate and I could use a little of his type B personality. They were always yin and yang growing up. They really balanced each other out. They still do.

"I know they text and stay in touch by Snapchat and whatever. I think it's been difficult for them to be apart from each other. And with me away now… well, that's hard and is something we'll have to keep working on."

"Do you talk with them much since moving here?"

"Yeah some. You know, they don't need me as much as they did. Not to be physically around. They have their friends and their own lives. We talk some by FaceTime, and we email. It seems to be working so far. We're all meeting up for Christmas in Kansas City. It'll be weird since we don't have a place to stay really. We're going to stay with my sister. It'll be cramped but she was kind enough to invite us to try it. Squeezing in with family feels better than staying in a hotel. This time anyway. We'll see how it works out."

"It'll be fine. Just another adventure, right? How long will you be gone?"

"Only a week. Like I said, the kids have their own lives. They'll want to get back to their friends. Baseball practice for Sam starts right after New Year's. What about you? Have you been back to Illinois?"

"Not yet. My mom visited once. My sister's been here. I haven't been up to see them though. It's too expensive. Believe it or not, I'm not getting rich at the coffee shop. We get by but don't make enough to fly to the States on a whim. I've taken some time off, traveled around Belize a little, even drove up to Mexico once, but for the most part I just work and hang out with Stella. It's a good life. I don't feel like I'm missing anything."

"Speaking of that, what do you miss the most about life in the States? There must be something."

"Hmm… today the answer is fall. The cool dry air and the beautiful colors. We kind of fake it down here with the pumpkin bread and lattes. So maybe that's why it popped into my head first. But cold weather would feel nice. Sounds weird, huh? I never really liked cold weather before, but now…. To get up on a frigid morning, slip into warm slippers, a heavy robe, put my hands around a hot mug of coffee… I guess it's always what we don't have. The grass-is-always-greener kind of thing. What about you? What do you miss?"

John thought for a moment.

"That's a tough one. I don't miss cold weather yet. Cold and I have never been friends… I guess my job. I so looked forward to retiring. I thought about it every day. But even when I was off for only a week, if I weren't on a busy vacation, I would start to worry. I would be anxious, depressed, look for little things to do, anything to take my mind off the blankness ahead of me. I really hoped that having a long, indefinite length of time ahead of me would help with that feeling. Give me time to work through it. Being that busy was killing me, like it kills most of us. And for what?

"So, yeah, I miss my job. But I think more specifically I miss the feeling of being needed. No one really needs me now. I mean yes, the kids do to some extent. They need my money of course, but they also occasionally need to talk to me, to try out ideas, ask for advice, even to have me put limitations on them. But that's intermittent at this point and it really doesn't fill that hole like it used to when they were younger.

"At work I would see a patient, answer questions, make a diagnosis, comfort him or her, and maybe challenge a long-standing thought pattern about something. I would walk out and then go right back into the room next door to see another patient. Throughout the day I would answer questions from my nurse about prescriptions or lab work, from the office manager about call schedules or personnel issues, and from my secretary about patients that needed to get in to see me right away. There would be emergency room and primary care doctors calling me. The operating room might call, asking for help placing a stent or a catheter. The hospital called about new consults. After the day was finished I reviewed the lab and X-ray reports in the electronic record. I would call patients about their new cancer diagnosis or about a large stone seen on a CT scan, or about a wound that didn't seem to be healing right.

"All day long people needed me. Honestly, it was too much sometimes. I was needed at home of course too. Helping with homework, driving kids to lessons, making dinner occasionally, fixing whatever was broken, or buying something.

"It tends to create our identity doesn't it?" John continued. "How much we're needed, who all needs us. Our feeling of self-worth is bound up in this. It's our culture for sure, but really I think it's in most cultures. The difference may be that traditionally, for thousands of years and still today in many developing countries, a lot of the relationships were static. Nuclear families, extended families, others in the village or tribe, all had clearly defined roles. Everyone truly needed each other. Old and young and everyone in between interacted with each other and were important. Once people could no longer work they were still useful and respected for their wisdom.

"Today in cities and suburbs in developed countries we no longer have that. Even our nuclear families are transient in many, if not most, cases. Even for the families with two parents, the children grow up and move away.

"So we have our jobs. And when that's gone, well, I guess we have to figure out who we are apart from who needs us. I know it's possible. Children do it. Countless elderly or disabled or ill people do it. They come to terms with life at its most elemental. They need others and yet they have only themselves to offer. Nothing more."

"Wow John, that's amazing," said Jessica. She had continued to work beside John as they talked, carefully placing plant after plant in the shallow water. "I can tell that you've given it a lot of thought. I know what you mean. I feel better about myself and about the world when I'm working. But the times when I haven't been working I've been out looking for a job, so that changes things I imagine."

"Right. When work ends, intentionally or not, with no possibility of resuming work, again intentionally or not, a void develops. Maybe it's retirement or a disability, either way there is an emptiness that has to be filled in some way. That's the challenge. Am I able to piece together a life that is much smaller?

Will it still be meaningful? Might it be more meaningful? With more time to focus, more time to have long lazy discussions like this very one with an actual person, will I grow as a spiritual being? Even more importantly, will I be more effective at helping others grow?

"Do I really believe that God doesn't keep a running tally of my good works? That I'm loved no matter what? That quality is as important as quantity? Maybe I do. I'm starting to anyway."

"Good! I do think you're on to something. Who knows what will come next? This is a time of transition for you, John. You know that. It's necessary but temporary."

"I'm trying not to look at it that way. I feel like I'm all in. But ultimately you may be right. We can't grow without really making a radical change. Sometimes the change is made for us. But either way, when things are in flux, that's when true growth can occur. No one said it would be easy."

They had run out of mangrove and places to put them so they returned to get more water and to recover a little. Once again they met other volunteers. They talked about the day. The way that the bay appeared more alive already. They dreamed of how it would look in the future, healthy and sustainable, the mangrove twisted and thick, holding the soil and sand in place. Everyone was hot and tired, but had enjoyed their time together.

John and Jessica wanted to continue their conversation, but she needed to be home before Stella got out of school. He drove her back to the village, dropping her off in front of her small stilted home. They hadn't talked much on the way back, but it was a comfortable silence. Lost in thought, they sat quietly, letting the wind cool their sticky skin.

Jessica leaned over and kissed him on the cheek. "Thanks for a great day. I'll see you tomorrow morning, right?"

John couldn't hide his grin or compose a sentence more original than "Yep, I'll be there. See you later."

She laughed as she went up the stairs.

He smiled all the way home, not thinking of anything except Jessica. By the time he arrived he remembered that there were no leftovers, nor did he have enough energy to cook. So he parked the cart outside his apartment, and walked down to a small place that served local cuisine. He ordered sides of callaloo and fried plantain to go.

Callaloo is a relative of collard greens. A leaf vegetable, it is cooked and simmered with salt, onion, garlic and other seasonings. He tasted coconut in the local version. It was a fresh, inexpensive and filling meal. He listened to fragments of conversations as he waited on a barstool, not joining in and yet feeling comfortable. He heard bits of Spanish, Creole and English. People talking about fishing, about their day, or about what was planned for later that night. The voices lulled him to the point that he didn't notice when the waitress handed him the paper bag with his meal.

"That will be eighteen dollars Belize."

"Oh sorry. Great, thank you so much. Here you go. Keep the change. Have a good night."

Back home, he cut up one of the mangoes and half of the pineapple and ate the fruit with the callaloo. It was a great dinner. One that he had already enjoyed several times here. He didn't think about the number of calories the meal contained. That kind of thing hadn't been on his mind lately.

After cleaning up the kitchen he looked in his journal, slowly reread the Psalm from that morning and began to write about the day. He wrote about the walk, about talking with Tom, and mostly about the deeply satisfying conversation and afternoon with Jessica.

"God created day and night, death and rebirth, changing seasons. All of it is an integral part of nature. And so it is with us. We change and grow. But no matter how temporary things feel, however out of sorts we are, God never leaves us. God is with us here, now, and forevermore."

John put away the journal, and went outside to look at the sky. The lights of the surrounding buildings were dim enough that he could make out a few stars with his glasses on. He could hear the waves, the wind, and people softly talking. He heard Spanish voices on a radio in the distance, and occasionally a woman's joyful laugh. He felt more at peace than he had in weeks, just standing, listening, and watching. As he retreated into reverie he could still hear Jessica's voice. He could remember her smile and that unexpected kiss. He knew that it was getting late and that he should go to bed, but he didn't ever want to lose the feeling that he had right at that moment. The feeling that all was well. It was a feeling of contentment and endless possibility. An expansive feeling of being truly alive. And so he remained right there for a little while longer.

7

Kansas City

Nearly thirty-five years earlier

Somehow Larry found out that she was in town. Decades before social media, he had an uncanny way of hearing about these things. He was very unclear on the details but knew the address, that it wasn't a real party, and that she would be there.

John was leaving the next morning to return to Rice. It was winter break of his freshman year and he was flying back a few days early, mainly to spend time with his girlfriend. She was the perfect girl for him at the time. She was gorgeous, laughed at his craziness, brought him food, and had her own car. He had been excited to return to Texas until he learned about Kristin.

They had driven around in Larry's Tercel for an hour, drinking Old Style, listening to a Clash cassette and telling stories as John was working up the nerve to go see her. Larry's intimate knowledge of the city's streets and social happenings, his willingness to drive, and access to his dad's booze made him a good friend in times like these. John had no money, no car, no fake ID, and his parents didn't drink alcohol. He was dependent on the kindness of others when he needed to get out of the house, and Larry was happy to help.

The year before, Kristin and John had watched each other during passing periods in the high school halls for weeks.

Watched and then smiled and then eventually talked. Even though two years younger, she was everything that John was not. Self confident, articulate, graceful and so beautiful, her oversized hazel eyes always looked slightly amused, especially when she was talking to John. He was distracted, shy, immature and busy with a lot of other things his senior year in high school.

She came to watch him swim once. Indoor swim meets were loud, hot, and excruciatingly long for spectators. From where the swimmers were gathered he could see that she sat very straight and yet appeared comfortable in the way that dancers do. Her dark hair had become wavier in the humidity. She seemed out of place sitting on the hard metal bleachers. A ruby among a pile of stones. John was proud to have her there and yet they spoke perhaps twenty words to each other at the meet.

There was one other event. She invited him to the Lionel Ritchie concert at Kemper Arena. Her aunt and uncle would drive and chaperone. Not a fan of top forty pop, he still jumped at the chance. As the day neared, his social anxiety grew but he still went through with it. It was an uncomfortable night. Kristin standing by her seat, clapping and dancing to 'All Night Long' and 'Running With the Night', swaying to 'Hello' and 'Endless Love', while John remained seated, too self-conscious and embarrassed to stand with her. She couldn't comprehend his reluctance to get up and he couldn't understand it either, he simply knew he could not.

It was a quiet drive home. They both realized that even though they saw something in each other, something that the other was lacking, it just didn't seem like it was going to work. They were too young to realize that life is truly a matter of timing. A little more maturity and insight, a few more days spent together, things might have turned out differently.

That summer he heard that Kristin was leaving high school. She had moved to New York to try to make it on Broadway. John had faith that she would succeed and was proud of her. But the thought of her moving across the country, the fear that he may never see her again, created a sick feeling that stuck with him off and on until that day in January.

58

By now John and Larry were feeling sufficiently fortified, brave enough to ring the doorbell of a stranger's house. To their relief, it was the right one. A girl that they both vaguely knew from high school opened the door.

"Hey, you found us! Come on in. We're all just hanging out in the family room."

John and Larry followed her to the back of the house where Kristin was sitting with another girl, looking casual but unmistakably New York stylish and even more beautiful than John remembered.

"Hi! Oh my gosh, you look great," she said, rushing over to give John a hug.

"You do too. You remember Larry, right?"

"Sure! So, how have you been? How's college? Do you like Texas?"

"Everything is excellent. It's going really well there. I made it through one semester anyway. It seemed to take forever but then went really fast too, you know? I'm on the swim team there. What about you? What have you been up to? Still in New York?"

"Kind of. I'm touring with Cats right now. We're on a break for a week and then it starts back up again. It's very difficult but exciting. It's been a great experience. There are so many talented people there. I'm learning so much more than I could have imagined."

"That is so awesome. I'm really not surprised though. I always knew you would be a star."

"I'm not a star yet," she said, laughing. "But it's a start."

He sat down on a chair near the couch where she had been sitting. The girl that opened the door was on the other end and a younger girl was in the middle. Larry sat in the remaining chair. There was an uncomfortable silence for a moment. They looked at the carpet, the decorations on the wall, and each other.

Kristin and John quickly discovered that they weren't relaxed enough with each other to continue their conversation as everyone else looked on. So, the girls talked to one another while Larry and John tried to look cool, occasionally talking privately, laughing at inside jokes. Both groups attempted to draw the other in, but it really was no use. John and Kristin sneaked sideways glances and half smiles but were never able to resume their conversation.

It had been barely forty-five minutes when someone said they needed to get up early the next day, and then someone else remembered they were supposed to be home by eleven. Larry and John stood to go, and Kristin walked them to the door. Her heart shaped mouth was still smiling and those eyes still looked amused and light hearted. John wouldn't have noticed the pain behind them.

"It was so great to see you," she said warmly and genuinely.

"You too, Kristin. We need to stay in touch better. I'll write this time okay?"

"Do! We barely even got to talk. It's a shame that we're both leaving tomorrow."

"At least we were able to see each other tonight."

"Yeah, this was nice. See you John." She hugged him tightly.

"See you Kristin…"

They wrote each other only once and then faded out of each other's lives completely. He would always remember the way she looked that night. It would take decades for John to figure out what happened, why what seemed so perfect on the surface didn't work in reality. Why his immense nameless emotions couldn't translate into anything useful. In another place or time he might have had the words. He might have seen more deeply into her eyes, perceived that Kristin had emotions also. She had taken all of the risk in the relationship, yet in the end she needed him far less than he needed her. He didn't realize it yet, but that mature, calm, kind spirit that Kristin so effortlessly exuded was something he would spend many years trying to find again.

————————

Twenty years later

It was the perfect storm. One of those very few times in John's life when God was so near that the separation between the

60

present and eternity seemed to blur. To start, his grandfather had died of pain the winter before. Chronic, unrelenting back pain that turned a formally healthy, active, grouchy but never whiny man into a whimpering shell. No real cause or cure could be found and he simply withered away. John, Ellie, and the twins, who were four years old at the time, visited him in the hospital. The children took turns bouncing on their great grandfather's bed, pushing his walker up and down the hospital corridors, and asking everyone about the function of various tubes and catheters.

When he finally, mercifully passed away John struggled with the kids' questions about what came next. The word heaven sounded so foreign on his tongue at first, but repetition bred familiarity. As spring turned to summer he tired of the usual songs on the radio and his CDs, so began listening to talk radio. Sports at first, but then preachers. Evangelists like Lester Roloff, Ravi Zachariah, and Billy Graham. It felt like a lark in the beginning, but they started to sound more informative and thought provoking as he listened on his commute.

John went to church every Sunday as a child. Sunday school, youth group, choir, the whole thing. But as often happens, once left to his own devices he didn't regularly attend church. Maybe occasionally if a girlfriend wanted to, or when he was home on break from college or medical school, but for the most part it wasn't on his radar. However, his grandfather's death and his children's questions had started something. The AM radio preachers began to fan the tiny spark that still faintly glowed deep inside. The same spark that everyone has, the kingdom of God that is within us.

By August, he and Ellie were looking in the paper for a congregation that felt right. They found one. It was a traditional Disciples of Christ church in their neighborhood. It had a small choir, an organ, an abundance of octogenarians, a preacher that was very kind and welcoming and who gave safe, sleep-inducing sermons. It was perfect.

John read the Bible, attended the adult Sunday school class and eventually taught it. He began tithing, giving ten percent of gross income, with most of that going to his church. When a Wednesday night worship service began, he always attended that as well. He loved that church, the people in it, the way it smelled, the unused nooks and crannies, the big fellowship hall and the sanctuary with the stained glass. He began listening exclusively to Christian rock. His heart enlarged and his mood felt so light.

And he began to quit things. To simplify. The first things to go were the voluntary hospital committees. If a meeting or dinner wasn't mandatory, directly related to his job, or church related he didn't go. He resigned from his position as vice president of the medical staff at the hospital. He dropped out halfway through an MBA program. He refused to read anything except the Bible and spiritual books. Ellie was used to John's changing hobbies, interests and fixations but she could tell that something was fundamentally different.

Four years later

A nearby church, larger than John's, held periodic presentations by local nonprofits that he attended when he could. On a Tuesday in August there was to be a talk about poverty in the historic Northeast. John had always been interested in poverty and planned to go, assuming that it would be about the Boston area, or some such place in New England. It turned out that the Northeast is a location in Kansas City. Just east of downtown, it is a poverty stricken area. Many people had lived there for decades, while others were just passing through. Racially if not economically diverse, there were homeless people, prostitutes, and new immigrants from all over the world. And there was a Catholic Worker house.

Or more correctly, catholic. With a small "c". Meaning ecumenical, all-inclusive. At the presentation John learned that Loaves and Fishes Catholic Worker was based on the ideas set forth by Dorothy Day and Peter Maurin. They began the first Catholic Worker in New York City in 1933. It was a newspaper and a movement that was still very much alive. Jacob from the house talked a lot about the kinds of problems they faced and how they used nonviolence and love to try to overcome them.

It was a lot of information to take in all at once. John had never heard of Dorothy Day or Loaves and Fishes, and didn't know the northeast part of the city at all. He stayed and talked with Jacob and asked if he could come visit sometime to find out what the place was all about.

Two weeks later Jacob and his wife Rachel served John and Ellie soup, green beans, salad, bread, and a slice of cake. Most of the produce came from the garden that took up both the front and back yards. Everything was homemade and delicious.

"So, I don't have Dorothy Day's book yet. It's on order still. Can you tell me a little more about her?" John asked Jacob once they were all situated at the table in the cool, dark kitchen.

"Sure. She was a journalist who was involved in the women's suffrage movement during the early part of last century. She had a conversion experience in the early thirties and had been on the lookout for kind of a mentor, somewhere to put her energy and passion for the poor and marginalized. In walked Peter Maurin, a French peasant with lots of ideas and a gift for pithy statements. They hit it off immediately. The first paper came out in 1933. It was filled with Peter's short poems and Dorothy's essays. Circulation increased rapidly. It's still being published for only a penny a copy.

"The Catholic Worker was founded on three principles really. They wanted to create houses of hospitality in which the poor were welcome. This could mean a soup kitchen, a place to sleep or maybe a place to have a hot shower and a change of clothes, like we offer here. The second idea was to have frequent clarification meetings. These were times side aside for people to get together and discuss important issues of social justice. Peter loved to talk and he knew how critical the free exchange of ideas was. We do this monthly. We invite speakers or hold roundtable discussions on a wide range of topics. The third principle stressed the importance of land. Peter pictured having farms where the poor could go to learn a trade, as well as to stay in touch with nature. Today's urban farm movement is an outgrowth of that idea. We've converted our lawns and some of our parking area into gardens. We plan to have chickens. Maybe even bees at some point.

"They were very involved with politics as well. Dorothy Day considered herself a Christian anarchist. She opposed all war and thought the central government wasn't necessary when there was love and mutual aid."

"A Christian anarchist. I've never heard that term before but I love it." It was like a new world was blossoming in front of John as he listened and learned about this alternate reality. Jacob referred to it as a Sermon on the Mount theology. Truly loving one's enemy, praying for those that persecute us.

Jacob gave them a tour of the old house where the small community of eight people lived. Those who had outside jobs worked no more than twenty hours a week so they could be more present and involved at the house. They shared all of their income, receiving a weekly allowance. They prayed together many mornings and had their evening meal together.

After lunch they went next door to visit an old brick building. The second floor held three apartments for either community members or as a short-term solution to get a person off the streets. The first floor's space held a dining room with a small kitchen, two bathrooms with showers, a living room where people waited their turn for a shower, and a room that had been converted into a walk-through closet. Guests that wanted a shower signed up that morning. When it was their turn they chose clean clothes from the closet, took a shower, then left their dirty clothes in the laundry basket. These would be washed and hung back up in the closet in a day or two.

All were welcome. There were no forms to fill out, no background checks, no income verification, and no drug testing. There was always a hot meal available to anyone who was hungry. A person would sit at the table and be served. No standing in line. Jacob explained that poor people spend entirely too much time standing in lines.

No cell phones were allowed. The idea was for people to be as present as possible. They were encouraged to interact with the volunteers, with the Loaves and Fishes community and with each other.

"It's not always peace and love," Jacob said, "but we do pretty well. Everyone is treated with respect and kindness. It's Matthew 25, you know, the sheep and goats."

Even though John had been attending and even teaching Sunday school for four years he didn't know what Jacob meant by that and said so.

"In Matthew 25:31-46 Jesus talked about judgment day. He indicates that there will be an accounting. It's a passage that doesn't get as much attention in Protestant churches as it does in Catholic. And it's a big one for Catholic Workers. Those that treat the down and out and the marginalized as their own sister or brother will be rewarded. And it doesn't necessarily mean in the hereafter but also in the here and now. We are to welcome the stranger into our home, to feed and clothe the hungry and naked. We are to visit the prisoner and comfort the sick. These are ways in which we care for Jesus. These are the corporal acts of mercy and they are taken very seriously here. It's how we continuously create the kingdom of God."

"I love that. It makes so much sense. Truly following Jesus rather than simply worshiping him."

"That's right, we try to model the way the beloved kingdom might look. Building up a new world in the shell of the old to paraphrase Dorothy Day, who I'm sure was paraphrasing someone else. She had a lot of those types of sayings."

"You've given us a lot to digest here. I feel like I need to learn even more. Do you think I could come and help out sometime? When's the best time to do that?"

"We always need volunteers. We do showers during the week. Arrive by eight. You'll be out of here by eleven thirty. Also there are community workdays once a month on Saturdays. That's a good time to bring a group. We do all kinds of work.

Gardening, repair work, sorting and organizing. It really helps us out a lot and ends up being kind of fun. We come together for lunch to wrap up and reflect."

"Okay, that all sounds great. I'll look at my calendar and see when I can come. This is all just amazing. I need to go home and process it a little, I think."

About the same time, John decided he needed some time off. He was allotted six weeks of vacation per year but had only been taking two or three. These were usually spent out of town visiting extended family, or on a beach somewhere in the Caribbean. He began taking off one more week per year to catch up. He did small projects around the house and in the yard. He wrote stories and wrote songs on his guitar. He had lunch with friends and began to volunteer. This became an important week, one that he would look forward to all year.

Most of the other doctors in the practice also took a half-day off per week. John had never done that, but over time he began to take off one Friday per month so that he could work at Loaves and Fishes. He would work there in the morning and at a free health clinic that he had discovered in the afternoon.

The clinic was in a suburb that had many low income families. Patients with preexisting conditions, recent immigrants, and people living in poverty all received care here. The goal was to keep them out of the emergency room and provide continuity of care. It was funded partly by local hospitals, as in the end it tended to save them money. Patients with cancer, infections, urinary problems and other conditions were seen there. It was interesting and satisfying to be able to help in that way, and somehow it didn't feel like work to John. No charge, no insurance to deal with, no push to see a certain number of patients, and simpler charting. By removing the stressful part of medicine, everyone benefited.

Spending time away from his paying job helping others was new but felt natural. True, people in health care help others. But this was different. It was spending spare time, or better yet, carving out blocks of time, to intentionally work with those that through circumstances often beyond their control such as skin color, place of birth, mental illness, sexual abuse and a multitude of other possibilities had been left behind. As Jacob had taught him, he was looking for Jesus in the guise of the poor.

Jesus also came as a man who gave a rousing impromptu sermon as he waited for his turn in the shower at Loaves and Fishes. The guest tied together a hard-to-follow story about painting houses, and having Jesus speak to him as he slept in a park, and trying to keep young people off drugs. It was really something beautiful. Following his message he gave John a blessing that he would always remember. He spoke expansively and honestly, so that John knew without a doubt that he had seen Jesus that day.

John and his family changed to a new church. Younger, more socially and environmentally aware, it was located downtown and was an anomaly in the way that it continued to grow and change as other churches stagnated. He met more people who challenged him in the way that they lived holistic lives in which their vocation and their avocations intertwined. God wasn't a God of rules, limitations and favoritism but one of love, inclusiveness and peace. Not one of scarcity but abundance. These months were exciting and new and he once again felt his faith deepening and his heart enlarging as his world continued to expand, uncovering previously unknown people and places.

8

Around five years after he found his way back to church, John had started thinking about meat for various reasons. Mad cow disease, mercury in fish, the terrible way farm animals were treated, the unsustainability of it all, the hormones, pesticides, carcinogens, the list seemed to go on and on. His family switched to a local butcher for beef. They were careful about which fish they bought. They only ate free-range chicken. All of these things were important, but as John thought and read more about meat and the fact that most of the world eats very little if any animal protein, he began thinking he should stop eating it altogether. He wouldn't need to change breakfast or lunch which had been vegetarian for years. He started with meatless weekends. About three months later he eliminated it from all meals.

"Why are you doing this, John?" asked Ellie, whose patience was being tested with all of the changes.

"Well, it's hard to explain. The short answer is that I've had plenty of meat in my life and I don't feel like I need any more. You know? I think I've had enough."

"Well, I've had about enough also, John. That's crazy. You need more protein. You work too hard to not eat properly. I'm pretty sure that you've already lost some weight."

"I just feel like it is something I need to break free from."

"You're not trying to tell me that you feel like hamburgers control your life, are you?"

"Well yeah, I suppose that livestock does control our lives in a way. Do you know how much water it takes to produce beef? How much methane is produced? How much manure? The fertilizers and pesticides that are used to grow the corn that feeds the cattle? All of the same holds true for pigs, chickens and fish. All of it is bad and it isn't necessary.

"You know how over the past few months the pork chops have been tasting strange to me? Like they're rotten or infused with chemicals or something? Now it's happening with beef too. The other day when we had those tenderloin tails, they didn't taste right. I think that it's a sign."

"Well, I think it means you're losing it. I'm not making separate meals for you. And the kids still have to eat meat."

"I totally agree. We don't need separate meals. I'll just eat more of the side dishes. Maybe eat an egg instead of meat sometimes. We don't make too many things in which it's mixed in. I guess I'll have to give up Hamburger Helper. But that's probably a good thing," John said, trying to lighten the mood a little.

The first few weeks were the hardest. John worked out grams of protein to be sure he was getting enough. It turned out that because he still ate eggs and dairy it wasn't an issue. He discovered that people in developed countries end up stressing protein too much, that we really needed much less than people think. He read labels carefully, which among other things meant he had to give up some of his favorite candy.

Even though it was never the goal, he did actually feel much better. He had more energy, slept harder, his bowels functioned better. But the biggest impact was on his mental well-being. Once again a weight that he never knew was there was lifted. He felt at peace that he wasn't directly participating in the livestock industry. That he didn't have to worry about hormones and carcinogens, on how much mercury he was putting in his body. That, like much of the developing world, he was getting by on less. The rest of the family wasn't vegetarian, but despite her initial reluctance, Ellie admitted that it hadn't been too difficult to separate out the meat.

———————

That same year John went to Africa for the first time. When he was first invited to go for a one-week medical mission trip it was as if a secret prayer had been answered. One that hadn't even been completely formulated. For years he had longed to go somewhere to help. He considered going with his church group to Central America but that never felt quite right. It involved building projects and he just wasn't much of a handyman. He investigated fistula hospitals in Africa but they didn't have a need for him, their volunteers were mainly support staff rather than surgeons. The surgeons were already experts in repairing complicated fistulas in developing countries.

So when a pediatric surgeon had to back out of a trip with a local medical mission group, leaving a spot that needed to be filled quickly, a wide net was cast. And the net caught John. It was a life-altering trip. Traveling in a large group with three other surgeons, there were experienced nurses that helped him pack. It was all extremely overwhelming: the preparation, gathering medications, packing clothing and supplies. Not knowing exactly what kind of surgeries he would be doing or what all he would need added to the stress, but also to the excitement. He studied about Uganda and the medical needs there. In truth, there was no way to fully prepare, no way to understand what it was like without seeing for himself.

It was an indescribable experience. Everything made him cry there: the blazing red sunsets, the smiles of the people, the bright yellow moon, and the warm dry air. Exhausted, homesick and completely overcome with emotion, he was surprised yet not surprised at all that the people he met were just like him. Culturally different in many ways, yet all had the same needs. They had the same worries, found joy in the same things. They were truly his sisters and brothers.

Every night they worked until well after dark. On the walk back to the compound there were no streetlights, no lights in the dwellings, only the occasional cooking fire. They only had their headlamps to light the way. The heavy dust in the air decreased visibility even more. Men glided by on bicycles, a woman would suddenly be next to them with a heavy, perfectly balanced bucket of water on her head. Children appeared out of the darkness, smiling, grasping for their hands, talking excitedly in Acholi. As they walked, John had several children around him, their warm dry hands in his. They would travel the rest of the way to the camp like that, faces beaming up with the joy of being recognized and noticed. They let go just as they reached the camp and then disappeared into the darkness. This also made him cry, knowing that Jesus had walked with him.

One night he stayed behind at the clinic. All of the surgical cases were finished, or so everyone thought. Somehow one young man with a hernia had been missed. It was a miracle that in the mass of patients more weren't missed. Mr. James, the amazingly energetic Lacor surgeon, said he would stay and repair it using his team. John asked for permission to stay behind and watch. It was an unforgettable experience to be back in the operating room, this time as an observer. Mr. James' experienced team performed the hernia repair using local anesthesia. The young patient was so calm, appearing to meditate throughout the procedure. The male nurse patted his cheek and spoke softly to him. The open windows let a little of the evening breeze into the hot room. The dim lighting was like a dream. Less than an hour later the procedure was finished. The patient was asked to stand up and walk to the recovery area where he would rest for an hour or two. He winced but did as he was told. Patient, surgeon, and observer, all came together as if God had willed it that way.

When they finished that night it was well past ten. The mission team had long ago returned to the camp. By now, John knew the way back and was not nervous about walking. But as he came out of the clinic with his headlight on, he could barely see an open van door about ten feet ahead. The ambulance driver was waiting to take him back. Mystery was everywhere. How did he know? Who told him? John was glad the driver couldn't see his face as tears rolled down in gratitude and exhaustion. They drove back in silence. The driver's English and John's tired mind weren't up to the challenge this late. But the comfort and the grace were enough.

When he arrived, more grace. The team clapped as the car rolled up. Questions about how it went. His vegetarian meal prepared by the wonderful and beautiful cook. But he couldn't eat. He sat and listened to stories and thought and prayed. He thought about how the light shines in the darkness throughout the world, lighting every corner and bringing comfort and grace to places like that, as well as to a free clinic in the suburbs, and a shower house in Kansas City.

He had read a passage from Isaiah 50 that day that seemed appropriate.

"Let the one who walks in the dark, who has no light, trust in the name of the Lord and rely on their God. But now, all you who light fires and provide yourselves with flaming torches, go, walk in the light of your fires and of the torches you have set ablaze."

The vision of light, of trusting in God as we walk in darkness. It all seemed so perfect.

Following that trip, it was difficult to adjust to life at home again. It took several weeks before the streets that were empty of people, the calm traffic that stayed within the dotted lines, the huge grocery stores with a hundred different types of cereal all began to seem normal again. He didn't want it to seem normal and hung on to the feelings that he had experienced in Uganda. He missed the warmth of the people, the smell of cooking fires, the bright red sunsets and even the grueling long days in the operating rooms.

It was after that first Africa mission that he really began to simplify. He traded his Mercedes for a Ford. He sold his watch collection and cleaned out his closets. Contracting his carbon footprint, simplifying his life, decreasing waste, increasing his tithe and his volunteer time. All of these felt intertwined to John.

He felt like he needed to be an example to his family, coworkers and friends. He was voting with his choices. By living smaller, he felt closer to the earth and closer to God. It's a cultural characteristic to live loudly, to consume, spend and display. To hoard and save. To spend money on expensive entertainment, on luxuries and novelties. It's countercultural to live humbly, and below one's means, to give rather than take, to share rather than strive for profits.

By living simply and denying himself worldly pleasures he kept his focus on the eternal. Deep down he knew that God didn't require these things from him. God loved every single bit of creation equally and he couldn't win favor by any act of mercy or self-denial. But the fact was that living smaller seemed to be working for him.

Writings from the *Philokalia* and other early spiritual books inspired him to try harder. He took these words to heart, sleeping and eating less while praying and reading more. There were so many examples of ancient holy women and men who would live on a crust of bread, who never slept, who stayed in their cell and prayed, only occasionally offering a word of encouragement to others. By meditating on these words John felt better equipped to face the world. It kept everything in perspective. Practicing what Ignatius of Loyola called spiritual indifference his mind became freer.

As busy as he was at work and with his family, John searched for time to write. In the morning before others arose or at night when everyone was fast asleep he wrote. He started a blog and wrote devotionals for church. He wrote poetry, song lyrics, and long emails to friends, anything that got what he was feeling outside of himself. The writing helped him make sense of his days. By pulling the events of the day, his interactions with others, his readings and even his mood together into a few sentences of contemplative writing, his life seemed more focused and relevant. He was able to see that our lives are a small part of a larger whole.

However, there never seemed to be enough time to write, something that John regretted as his life rushed by. On a quiet

Sunday morning in his home office in the basement, or late at night in Africa after a marathon day when he was finally able to begin to collect his thoughts, or in a house on a beach in the Caribbean as everyone was relaxing after a long day in the sun, these were the times that he was able to write. These were the times he felt most at peace, healthy and content. He was able to reflect and share what he was feeling with whoever was within range of his words.

On a day-to-day basis however, there was little writing. There was working, worrying, and the daily activities of a busy modern life. He tried to live intentionally and question his habits. He loosened himself from activities and habits that felt constraining. Thus the fasting, the letting go of meat, carbonated drinks, drinks in containers, food that had traveled too far, frozen food, food that came in boxes, food that had too many ingredients, or unknown ingredients. He truly did dream of living as a desert monk on a loaf of bread and a little tap water. Unfortunately, one of the problems was that John wasn't a desert monk. In fact he was a father and a husband. He had a demanding job that required a lot of energy. And he was starting to make people nervous.

———————

Immediately prior to his trip to Africa he had weighed himself and was shocked to find how light he was. That was the first time John had stepped on a scale in years but he had been feeling thin, and knew that he had lost weight. He assumed it was due to the stress involved in the lead up to his first mission trip. But when he returned it got worse. He worried that he really was sick, had possibly acquired some kind of gastrointestinal illness in Africa. He started counting calories, trying to add in more food. But mainly he was fooling himself. It seemed like the more attention he paid to his weight the lower he dropped. Late that spring he hit a new low. About the same time he fell trying to hurry out of bed to shut off the alarm. He felt light headed and just went down.

"Okay, that's it. You have to go see a doctor," Ellie said as she watched him get back up from his knees and stumble into the bathroom.

"I am a doctor. I just got up too fast."

"You always get up too fast, but you've never passed out before."

"I didn't pass out. I got light headed for a second. I think maybe I was sleeping too hard or something."

John really wished that she hadn't seen that. That he could have recovered more quickly. He was worried about what would happen now. He really did think he was fine, but he was a little concerned that he couldn't get his weight turned around. What if something physical was going on and he wasn't simply a desert-father-wannabe nutcase?

"Will you do it for me please?"

"Okay, I will. I'll see someone, get some blood work. I'll make sure that I'm healthy. I really just need to eat more. It's as simple as that. For some reason it's been tough to do these past few months but I will."

"Well, you aren't going back to Africa until you gain ten pounds."

"No problem. I will. You're right. At this weight I don't have much of a cushion if I were to really get sick. Like if I got the flu or something. I'll tell you what. I'll eat more desserts. Like apple pie. I've always loved any kind of fruit pie. And ice cream. And maple flavored fudge from that one place, remember? It's an excuse to pig out on all of the things I love. Good thing I'm not diabetic."

"If that's what it takes, it's fine with me. I'll go buy an apple pie today."

"Awesome. That actually sounds good. It'll be something to look forward to tonight. Okay, I really need to get ready for work now."

John did eat that apple pie. And there were more pies and desserts. His exam and blood work all turned out fine and by mid-summer his weight had climbed ten pounds. He was feeling stronger and mentally was doing much better. When things were going well and his stress level was low he ate normally, but when life got too busy or conflict arose he began to lose weight. He wasn't out of the woods yet.

9

"Do you have everything you need?"

"Yeah, I think so."

"Books? Clif bars? Phone charger?"

"Check. Check. Check."

"Pretty good packing. I can't believe everything fit into one suitcase."

"Well, to be fair, it's one suitcase and a very full backpack."

"Still. Pretty good."

"I think it's plenty. My guess is that I'll only use about half of what I'm bringing."

"You shouldn't need much in paradise. This is going to be good for you, John. And Placencia looks so beautiful! I wish I were going with you. But I guess that would sort of ruin the whole point of moving huh? No, you need to do this on your own. I understand and I support you completely."

Michelle was one of the handful of people who did seem to understand. She had been John's secretary for several years and of course knew him pretty well by default. But her insight went much deeper than that. They had clicked immediately. They felt an instant connection, seeing some of the same pain in each other's eyes. They shared an understanding of the beauty as well as the absurdity of the world. John was always amazed when he found someone like her. They appeared if he stayed awake and watchful. People who seem to be a part of the same whole. "Cut from the same cloth" always felt like an appropriate cliché.

Michelle had great bottomless empathy that was innate and natural. That is what John had seen the first time they met. Even though she left to take a job closer to her home, or maybe because of that, they had stayed close friends. They leaned on each other for support and he was understandably worried about not having her around in Placencia.

She hugged him as he started to tear up. "Hey, sorry, I'm not making this any easier. You'll be fine. Seriously. And I'll be here if you change your mind and decide to come back next week. Or next month. You'll have Internet there right? We can talk, FaceTime, whatever. I'm still here for you, John."

He often wondered why they had never taken the next step. Why they were just friends. Really close friends, but still. He was pretty sure it was his fault. She was a beautiful girl but he rarely thought of her in that way. Never thought of anyone that way anymore. Intimate relationships. It all seemed so complicated and unnecessary. Maybe he just wasn't ready yet. It would have certainly changed their relationship, and he needed to do this on his own. It was so much cleaner and easier to leave a close friend than to leave a girlfriend. Their friendship would continue. They hadn't really talked about it but he assumed she felt the same way. She seemed content anyway.

"Thank you Michelle. I know you are. Thank you for everything. I could seriously not do this without you. Knowing that you've got my back. It means everything."

"I've got it. Let me know when you get there okay?" She smiled, her eyes sparkling and damp.

"I will."

They hugged one last time. Both were reluctant to let go. When at last they did, she gave him a sad smile then turned and walked away.

———

Ten months earlier...

John was in the middle of clinic when his phone rang. He turned off the ringer without looking at it and resumed listening to the patient's list of complaints. A few seconds later it vibrated, letting him know there was a message. As he led the patient out of the room he took the phone out and saw that the call was from the Overland Park police department. His heart sped up as the possibilities flashed through his mind.

He leaned against the wall, steadying himself as he heard the words, "This is Chief Bob Hartley from the Overland Park police department. Please call back and ask for me. There's been an accident."

Time seemed to stand still as John went to his office and without a word, closed the door, sat at his desk and called the number, waiting while Chief Hartley came to the phone.

"Mr. Reynolds?"

"Yes?"

"It's your wife. Ellie… I'm sorry to tell you that she's been in an auto accident…. She didn't make it."

When John didn't say anything, Chief Hartley said again, "I'm sorry."

There was another long pause before John managed to speak. "Was anyone else hurt?"

"The other driver will be okay."

"What happened? Where?"

"At that big intersection at one hundred nineteenth and Metcalf. A driver ran a red light. I don't think she suffered, Mr. Reynolds. She was gone by the time the emergency crews arrived. We need you to come down to identify her body and collect her things. We can send someone out to get you if you would like. I can't tell you how sorry I am."

"No…it's okay…I'll be there in a little while."

He took down the information, hung up the phone, and just sat there. Too stunned to cry, or to tell his staff what had happened, or to think about what comes next. It was more than fifteen minutes before Michelle finally, tentatively knocked on his door and peeked in.

"Dr. Reynolds? You've got a whole waiting room full of patients. Everything okay?"

"Hey Michelle. Do you think you can help me out? I don't think I'm going to be able to see any more patients today. Will you please reschedule everyone? Tell them how sorry I am."

"Sure. No problem. I'll take care of it. Is there anything else I can do?"

"No. That'll help a lot. Thank you Michelle."

She closed the door behind her. He waited a few minutes, long enough for all of the patients to be led out of the exam rooms, then left quietly and quickly. He drove to the hospital to which Ellie had been taken. He identified her broken body, signed some forms and returned to his quiet home. He had no idea how he was going to tell his children.

———

By the time the funeral was over it was clear that Ellie had been a victim of an all too common occurrence. A seventeen-year-old kid named Jarius had rolled through a stop sign in front of a police officer. When the squad car started following him he panicked. He sped up. He worried that he would get in trouble with his mom. He had been in a wreck the previous month. It was only a minor fender bender but she had threatened to take his car away. She worried about him driving all the way into Johnson County for his job. Why couldn't he have a job closer to home? She knew there weren't any jobs where they lived, but she still worried.

So he ran. Of course it didn't make sense, but he was seventeen. Teenagers never made sense. John had just lived through those years with his twins. By the time Jarius got to the intersection he was going almost ninety, the police car right behind him. He swerved and slammed on his brakes. Ellie swerved too but not in time. He slammed his 1985 Accord's left front fender directly into her door. Somehow he survived with only a broken femur and a mild concussion. Ellie died. And the policeman was able to write a ticket for failing to fully stop.

Somehow John was never angry. Not at the policeman who engaged in a high-speed chase over a minor traffic violation, something that John discovered happens nearly every day. He certainly wasn't angry with Jarius. John knew that he was just a kid. That he had his whole life ahead of him. He desperately wanted Jarius to get this behind him and learn from it. To not let this be the defining moment in his life. To get a job, have a family, and help make the world a little better.

No, he was just incredibly sad. Sad and scared. He hadn't lived alone for over twenty years. And even back then he wasn't very good at it. He drank when he was lonely. He had girlfriends. He had ways to block out the pain. This was completely different. The house was so quiet.

He missed things that he had taken for granted. Talking and worrying about the twins with Ellie, for one. He would never have guessed that, but it was true. Most of their conversations had centered around Sam and Kate, how they were doing in school, what they had done that was funny, irritating, disrespectful, lazy, or insightful. He realized that those talks were unnecessary in most respects- the kids were fine without the constant worrying and fretting and reminding- yet he missed them. The way that he and Ellie had bounced parenting ideas off one another. The way they adjusted and amended as they went along. It had certainly worked. Both of them were amazing, intelligent, competent young adults. Or else they were faking it well enough like everyone else.

He missed going for walks with Ellie. They had always taken the same route around the neighborhood. She walked too slowly and he too quickly. They would talk about the events of the day and then plan for the next. They would dream and begin preparing for the next phase of their lives. He definitely missed having a meal ready when he arrived home, and the way that clean clothes magically arrived in the closet, or groceries in the refrigerator. Things weren't perfect between them by any means. But the sudden loss was overwhelming.

He talked to Kate and Sam most nights. It helped all three of them to stay connected. They would catch up on the activities of the day. He might help a little with some homework. Or they would at least pretend to let him. FaceTime was a wonderful thing but it was still a very poor substitute for physically seeing them. To be able to hug or pat them, to be able to look over and see them there. Maybe Sam was just lying on the couch, looking at his phone. Maybe Kate was sitting in her favorite chair, legs crossed, watching some show on the iPad. He always felt comfort in simply having them around. But now... well, he was grateful for what he did have.

They had come home as soon as they found out, stayed through the funeral but were now back at school. This was their freshman year and John wanted them to continue to do well. They were both off to a good start. They were making friends, enjoying the freedom and the experience and both knew that their mom would not have wanted them to drop out or to do poorly. In fact, Sam seemed to have a new motivation. He had done amazingly well on the last round of tests.

John continued to work. That surely helped more than anything. To take the focus off himself for those hours. And work certainly did just that. Even in the midst of the stress and the busyness, rushing from room to room, filling out electronic medical records, he still found comfort. Every day he saw things that made his heart swell and gave him such gratitude for what he had, rather than regret for what he lacked.

Patients were so kind. He received countless cards, cookies, homemade bread, and books. Many wanted to talk about Ellie more than themselves. Those minutes in the exam room with caring patients, healing each other with grace and loving kindness, were more precious than anything else John could have imagined.

Over the next month or two, his attitude about work changed dramatically. With nothing else to do, no one to come home and talk with at the end of the day, John didn't mind working long hours. When a call came in the night that someone was having catheter problems or increased pain, rather than simply giving suggestions or walking the nurse through it over the phone, he would go in and see for himself. Driving the quiet dark streets late at night was soothing, almost spiritual. He would put on Ryan Adams or Damien Jurado and feel like he was gliding through space and time.

The hospital at three in the morning is a completely different place. There were hushed voices, dimly lit hallways, and patients that were exhausted, scared and lonely, but very grateful for the care. He felt like he had more time to talk to the patients. To get to know them a little better. He began to appreciate the night shift workers at the hospital so much more. The people that are there when everyone else is asleep. Surely it was a strain on their bodies and their relationships. But there they were, up all night.

He found that he needed even less sleep than before. He went to bed late and got up early with the occasional middle of the night run to the hospital thrown in as well. He didn't necessarily feel like he had more energy, but had simply lost interest in sleeping. For one thing, time felt short. He always had worried about the finite amount of time he had on earth, trying to get as much done as possible, but that feeling had intensified. Sleeping felt like such a waste of time, unfaithful almost.

He went to work early and stayed until late. There wasn't anyone to pick up from a lesson, no meal waiting for him, and no appointments. When he did get home, he made dinner and ate while reading. He then cleaned up and read more, or maybe called Sam or Kate. He watched movies. Something he hadn't allowed himself to do previously. There was always too much going on in his life to focus on a film. But now he found them comforting. Nothing violent or frightening, nothing that felt too upsetting. A diversion is what he needed, and movies helped.

John did go back to Africa. He had already planned it and had requested the time off. The anesthesia provider and two nurses on his team needed him to go. They had also taken time off from work and made plans. He was just getting into some kind of routine at home but felt this was for the best. He loved his trips to Africa more than about anything. The warm air, the smell of cooking fires, and most of all the people. Stepping off the plane gave him chills. It felt like home.

The translators and drivers welcomed everyone back to Uganda. The big group got their luggage loaded onto the truck and the volunteers climbed into the vans, exhausted after the long journey but excited to be there. It turned out to be another magical week. It was extremely busy but not stressful. The fact that he had meals prepared and waiting at breakfast and dinner was a welcome change. Not having to plan, prepare, and clean up was a luxury. As was having people to talk to. On the vans, in the operating rooms, at night under the stars in the camp, the free and easy conversation was liberating. He stalled going back to his room and had trouble finally falling asleep.

As had become his habit in past trips he got up early to read the Bible and a little from another spiritual book. He then wrote down a passage that had caught his attention. As he thought about the verses, he began to feel more present, more in touch with where he was and what he was doing. Late at night when he came back to the room, when he was having trouble resting, when he knew that sleep wouldn't come for hours still, he would write again, tying together the morning meditation, the evening mood and the work in between into a nice package.

On Wednesday of that week he wrote in part:

"It's a common saying that at the end of one's life no one ever says they wish they had spent more days working. First of all, I think that statement is absolutely true. Second of all, it proves that what we do on these missions is not work. I may very well dream of Africa on my deathbed. I would deeply regret not coming on these trips and could write for days on what I have gained from Africa. The statement also makes me think about other things I would regret and helps me guide the way I use my time. This eventually leads to the same old problem of worry and hyperactivity and guilt about not doing more.

"But really in the end it isn't about the calendar is it? God exists completely outside of time right? So in my heart I know it isn't about how many days or weeks I did this or that. I don't think there is a scorecard. I really don't. Not when I stop and ponder the complexity and subtleties of us all. That life is really not a race – or a competition. And we don't have to start things or even finish them. We aren't coming in at the beginning or the end usually- but in the middle. Just jump right in and go."

When he returned to the States, he tried to fit back into his routine. But this time it was different. Immediately after Ellie's death he needed the act of going to work, seeing patients, staying busy, but now he wasn't so sure. Those meditations on time stuck with him. The fact that God lives outside of time and that in the end it is irrelevant. The tiny flash of existence... did it matter how many more patients he saw? Whether he outlived Ellie by one year or forty? He'll be there soon enough either way.

He knew that it did matter, but was having trouble staying motivated. Part of his heart had been left behind in Africa. Part of it had been incinerated with Ellie's body, her ashes now scattered in Kansas and Colorado. Part of it was in Grinnell, Iowa with Kate. Part of it was in Fort Worth, Texas with Sam. He simply wasn't sure there was much left.

He knew that one thing he needed was someone to talk to face to face. The little stories and anecdotes he shared with his nurses at work, or in the operating room, or with other people he had short, standing up, informal chats with didn't help very much. He needed formal chats. He needed sitting down, looking into someone's eyes, not checking a phone or a watch, long meandering meaningful conversations. He needed to feel valued and heard, not judged. He needed to say something the whole way, to get the whole thought out. Then to listen and to fully take in the other person's story. He needed to be able to remember what he wanted to say, and then have time and permission to say it. To not be forced to wait until next time. Not to find out the moment had passed and that it was too late to finish the thought. He needed to smile and laugh and cry and understand.

It is unbelievable how important these interactions are. And how rare. They are as important to one's soul as praying, as helping others, as sitting on a beach simply watching wave after wave, not a single one the same. There may not be a more important aspect of civilization, than the simple act of one-on-one conversation.

John tried to remember the last time he had sat and talked to someone like that in Kansas City. Being trapped together in a foreign country with no cell coverage for hours at a time tended to encourage deep conversations. That was one of the things he loved about the Africa trips. But what about in his real life? Very rarely. It was nearly always a scheduled event. Intentional. Not spontaneous.

So, he decided that he was past due for a relaxed heartfelt conversation or two. Perhaps that would help clear up some things in his head. Certainly what he was doing now wasn't working. He emailed three people that night to set up coffee dates: Jacob, Michelle, and his pastor, Ann. By late morning the next day they had all responded and he felt hopeful and peaceful as he worked through his day.

10

John still tried to take off at least one Friday a month. He no longer worked at the free clinic on these days. Nor did he clean showers at Loaves and Fishes. Life had become too busy even before the accident. This was partly due to the Africa trips. Preparing for them, being gone those days, then catching up and recovering from them. It all took a great deal of energy.

Besides, he needed the day to catch up. To run errands, to go to appointments at places that weren't open on Saturdays, and, if the stars were aligned just right, he would have coffee with a friend. Or tea, although lately he had loosened up that restriction on himself a little. He convinced himself that it wasn't a major moral failing if he had a decaf coffee now and then.

So, here he was, at a coffee shop in Westport on a cold, blustery day talking with his pastor, Ann. It wasn't lost on him that for many years this was the week that he and his family would be on a beach somewhere for spring break. He had talked to the twins about going somewhere, but unfortunately they had different weeks off. They did come home to hang out with their Kansas City friends, study, and relax at home for a few days. John was glad to have them around a little these past two weeks.

He and Ann tried to meet at least quarterly. She was a great comfort to him. One of the few people that he felt safe talking to. And one of the very few that he felt was smarter than him.

She was more insightful, better read, had a deeper understanding of the world. So, he looked forward to these days.

She always did at least comment on his weight. No one else mentioned it. It was a relief to be able to talk freely. She didn't push him too hard. Probably not hard enough, but at least she brought it up and he had a chance to talk a little about it.

"So, how much do you weigh now?" she asked bluntly.

"Um... wow okay... I was one thirty last week." He always fudged upwards a couple pounds.

"That's a little higher right?"

"Yeah, it's coming up."

"Well, you are still too thin. Did you call that guy? I gave you his number a while back. He was a pastor. He doesn't necessarily specialize in weight issues but I think you would understand each other. You kind of speak the same language."

"No, I've got it some place. I'm all right. Like I said, I've gained some. I think that's pretty good considering all I've been through."

"Listen John, I understand. I've had my own weight issues so I get it. And I know you've been through a lot these past few months. I can't even imagine. But I care about you. You would do better if you gained about ten pounds. You would feel better about yourself. I know you feel like you can't eat sometimes because of stress, or in solidarity with Africans or the homeless or whatever. But I want you to think about the message you are sending. If you're writing or talking to people about justice issues, or living simply, or being healthier, the message will come across a lot stronger if you look healthy. You'll be more apt to be taken seriously if you don't look like you are going to die. You know? I love you but it's the truth."

"That's really a good point. Thank you. It's one that might actually help. As you know, I'm not really interested in my body. Or my health for that matter. I've certainly lived a lot longer than I ever thought I would. But I do worry about the quantity of what I do. I want the quality to be better as well, but I like the idea of helping more and more people. Of changing the world for the better in some way. I know it's not ideal for me to be this thin. I promise I'll keep working on it okay? In fact why not right now? Do you want anything else? Their chocolate éclairs look really good."

"Sure, why not get two?" she said, looking pleased.

John was so thankful for Ann. Her sermons inspired him every week. Their progressive, inclusive congregation really felt like a shining light. It was relevant and alive.

When he returned with the pastries they resumed their conversation. They talked about their children, about the church, about Ellie and about what John saw as his next step.

"That's funny. I've been thinking the same thing in the same way- the next step. Like I need to make a change. But I'm not sure what that step is yet. Maybe Africa. Although I'm not sure how that would look. How I could make that work long-term. I'm also not sure I want to work that hard. I'm tired. I've also thought about simply retiring. I'm pretty sure I would be okay. Now that the kids are in college. Health insurance is always the big question. But I'm thinking about starting to investigate it."

"Well, no one here wants you to leave. But I know that you have many things you would like to do. And maybe this is the time to really take a look around and see what else is out there."

"Right? I know. And I feel like I need to do it soon or I won't do it at all. I get lonely- and I worry that I might act out of loneliness. I haven't dated anyone since Ellie died. I'm not sure I even want to. One of the things I worry about is jumping too soon into a relationship. We were together for over twenty years. The years went so fast and now they're gone. And I wouldn't change anything. But now I feel like I need to do something different. Something big. Daring."

"Well, I'm here for you. You know that. I love you and I support you. Let me know if you need anything. And let's do this again soon okay?"

"Yes. For sure."

They did one of those small, embarrassing half hugs, then went their separate ways.

A week later he met Jacob at the same coffee shop. He worried that he was turning into one of those mysterious guys who sit all day in coffee shops. What were they doing? What kind of job was it that required sitting for hours drinking coffee in public? John was jealous but also felt a little sad for people like that. It seemed a pretty isolated existence. He got his decaf and found a table away from the nearest solitary computer guy to sit and wait.

A few minutes later Jacob strolled through the door. He purchased hot tea and came over to join John. Since Loaves and Fishes had stopped offering showers and breakfast on Fridays they hadn't seen nearly as much of each other. An occasional Saturday workday or a clarification meeting, and these rare talks were about it. John was always inspired and encouraged by Jacob. He lived in the sort of authentic way that John dreamed of. Being eye level with the poor and marginalized on a daily basis, growing much of their own food, the chickens, the bees, the solar panels and the rain water usage, all of these were attractive to John. Not to mention the justice work, the protests, the street theatre and the gentle, organic way their message had spread over the years.

The two friends caught up with each other. They traded stories of their children, of their churches and of their jobs. Jacob was a minister and a teacher but chose to live in such a way that neither was a full time job. He and Rachel were the founders and spiritual leaders of their Catholic Worker house and he spent most of his energy there, with the day-to-day mundanities of being immersed in a large household. They had a long talk about Ellie. About what life without her had been like. Jacob was one of the few people that he could be honest with and it felt good to talk about everything.

"So, how's work going?" Jacob asked.

"It's okay. That's one thing that hasn't altered. My partners haven't really acknowledged the fact that my life has changed. In a way that is refreshing. I can always count on them to be insensitive and self-centered. Like a law of thermodynamics. Unchangeable."

"I guess that's good. If you look at it that way."

"On the other hand I guess they haven't made it more difficult either. Haven't complained to me about the extra days off I've taken. About how I've missed some meetings and have been a little disconnected as to the day-to-day operations of the business. I haven't had much interest in that kind of thing for quite a while but it has been more noticeable lately I'm sure. I can focus on seeing patients, doing surgery, keeping my charts up to date, patient care stuff. Anything else... just not interested."

"I can understand that. It seems only natural with all that has happened."

"Yeah, that's part of it. But you know me well enough to realize that I've been fading out of the business side of this for a long time. From holding medical staff positions at the hospital and being on the executive committee in my group and even starting an MBA program, to working towards becoming a hospital administrator, to where I am now. I haven't been to a hospital meeting in over seven years and I dropped off all of the committees with our company. So it's a continuum. Downward mobility. A movement away from business and hopefully more towards people. That is where my interests lie. In taking care of individual patients.

"But saying that, I do feel a little tired. Probably burned out is the best way to describe it. I do fine when I'm at work, seeing patients, doing surgery, but my attention and interest fall off quickly when I'm alone. I don't worry about patients like I used to. I would always pray for my upcoming surgeries. I would think about people at night before I went to bed. Say a quick prayer or at least give a positive thought to those that were on my mind that day. I've noticed that I haven't been doing that lately."

"I wonder if you could take less call. Work a little less. Do you think your partners would go for it?"

"Probably not. But I don't really think that would help. If I'm not busy I'm more stressed, not less. I enjoy being called in to help in the middle of the night. It gives me something to do and makes me feel needed. Same with busy days at work. If I saw fewer patients in a day, or went home early it would just make me sad and paranoid. No, I think my two choices are the same as they have ever been. Keep working hard or just quit."

"So, have you thought seriously about quitting? What would you do?"

"Do you have an extra room?" John said, laughing.

"We would make room for you anytime. We would love to have you. In any capacity. But is that what you want?"

"Sadly, I don't think so. I think I'm too selfish. I don't know if I can live in a community. I'm too private, grouchy, and whiny. I'm just not sure it would work. But believe me, I've thought about it. For years. And more so lately. I could find a way to work as a doctor part-time somewhere. Help with community life. It is a good dream but I'm just not sure."

"Well, like I said, you're welcome. We would figure out a way to make it work."

"I've actually been thinking a little about taking a sabbatical. I need to do some research, find out if it's possible to leave for a year, or maybe longer and still keep my license and board certification. I'm not brave enough to quit, burn my bridges and not be able to return if I find out it was a big mistake. "

"Assuming that's possible, what would you do? Where would you go?"

"I've thought about Africa of course. To go work at Lacor Hospital in Uganda or somewhere. But I worry that jumping from one busy, high stress practice to another may not be the right choice. It sounds like more of a lateral move."

"Yes, I can see that. I know how much you love Africa, but that might not be the best idea right now."

"I'm thinking about Mexico. Like a little village near Manzanillo on the Pacific coast. Or maybe Belize. Somewhere warm, Spanish speaking, inexpensive. Someplace that I can just exist for a while. Write, read, think, and try to figure some things out. Slow down my life. I never have time to do those things. I haven't properly mourned Ellie's death. My life feels like it is going way too fast. How did I get to be this age? I still feel twenty-five most of the time."

"Hmm…a beach bum…not what I expected you to say. But somehow it makes sense."

"Yeah, we'll see. I've had big ideas for years but I haven't done anything about most of them. I'm still here in the same town, doing the same job."

"It's an important job. You do good work. You help people in a way that most people can't."

"I know. And I am grateful for that. For that responsibility. But I can't do it forever. It's felt like a sprint. And I'm getting tired."

"I'm with you John. Everything you're saying makes sense. Thank you for sharing this with me. I want you to know that I support you one hundred percent in any decision you make. You're doing it the right way also. Intentionally. Prayerfully. Bouncing ideas off of people. In the end there won't be a precisely correct solution, but keep gathering information and thinking about it. And keep me in the loop okay?"

"I will. Thanks for meeting me and for listening to my crazed ramblings. You're a good friend Jacob."

"Anytime. But right now I need to get back. I'm going to show around a small group from Avila College. Try to explain what we do there."

"Sounds good, see you later."

"See you John."

They parted and John went home to his empty house.

Well, not empty. It was definitely full. He began looking around, making a mental list of what would need to be done to get it ready for market. Refinish the hardwoods. New windows upstairs. Fix some minor cracks in the walls and ceiling. Get rid of a lot of things. A tremendous amount of things. For someone who had tried to simplify his life, John was startled by how full the house was.

There wasn't much of monetary value left anymore, but there were boxes upon boxes of things of sentimental value. Items from college, high school, even elementary school. Ellie had not been a hoarder (or collector, as he preferred to think of it) like John, so most of it was his. He had old letters, cards, newspaper clippings, and stacks of magazines. Collections of Hot Wheels, the remnant of a massive comic book collection that he had gutted a few years back, and enough Christmas tree ornaments for at least three trees. Clothes, books, artwork, and papers that belonged to the children. Hundreds of CDs, records, cassettes, video tapes and DVDs. Games, televisions, stereo equipment, non functioning computers. And books. Shelf after shelf of books. Most of them John's but many of them were inherited from his grandmother. She had said it was like peeling off her own skin to give them to him. What was he to do with all of these books?

Then there was the furniture, the African statues and masks, the artwork, the extra beds, all of the things that he would eventually have to sell in order to move. That is what he was thinking. That he would move, downsize to an apartment. Someplace big enough that the twins would have their own bed, if not bedroom. It was the first step anyway. A noncommittal first step. He could sell the house and most of the contents. Move into an apartment. That would make it easy to leave when he wanted to go on mission trips or vacations, if nothing else. To not have to worry about the lawn or all of the many things that can happen to a house that is left unattended would be a small blessing.

He knew that Kate and Sam preferred that he stay. This was the only house that they had known. An apartment wouldn't feel like home. Not at first anyway. It would just be another reminder of how radically things had changed. But John couldn't help the fact that things had changed. The more he thought about it the more sense it made. He decided to call a realtor in the morning.

He met Michelle for tea the next weekend. It was a little place in Midtown that had interesting teas and juices. They also carried hard or chewy vegan desserts with not nearly enough frosting. Michelle was already there and had ordered a beet colored juice. She was thin, with short dark hair, startlingly green eyes and thick lashes. John felt a flash of pride that he was out in public with such a beautiful woman.

"Hey, thanks for coming. I know you're busy with Kayla and everything."

"Hi! No problem. It's good to see you," Michelle stood up and gave John a hug. "Do you want to get something to drink? I already have mine."

"Sure, I'll be right back."

John ordered a peppermint tea and a granola thing that was dipped in pretend chocolate. He wasn't clear why it wasn't real chocolate. It wasn't terrible though, and he reasoned that it was dense enough to count as a meal.

"So, how's it going? How's everyone at work? Is your new secretary as good as me?" She teased.

"You know that's not possible. But we get by. What about you? Everything going okay? Work? Your daughter?"

"Work is work. It's fine. My boss is pretty nice. We get along. I do like that it's close to home. And I have to be honest I don't miss the drama in your office."

"Seriously. I'm afraid it hasn't improved very much. My partners... Gross, let's not talk about that. So, Kayla? Still dancing?"

"She is. She loves it. She has a spring performance in May. They're working towards that now. She's doing really well. Likes fifth grade still. I'm enjoying this age. Well, I like them all but this is a particularly good one. I can talk to her like a human and yet she isn't a teenager. I worry about those years. I was awful to my mom."

"They aren't that bad. I loved having teenagers around. Yes, they keep you on your toes, but it was entertaining. But you're right, every age is fun really. You just have to kind of go with the flow. And keep adjusting your perception of them. We parents tend to lag behind a few years. When they are ten we treat them like eight and when they are fourteen we treat them like twelve. It's important to frequently look closely at them. To listen and to try to hear them. To try hard to stay up with them as they mature and grow. If we want our children to respect us then we need to respect them. That's the tricky part."

"That is great advise. That's why I keep you around, you know? Your Yoda-like wisdom."

"Funny."

"No, I'm serious! So, what's really up? Something was on your mind when you asked me to meet you."

"I just felt like I needed to see you. Catch up. We haven't really talked since my last Africa trip in January."

"Yeah, I know. So are you holding up okay? I know that coming back is always a tough transition. Probably even more than usual this time. Hey, did I read somewhere that your guy was sentenced?"

"Jarius? Yeah, he was. I worked hard from my end to get him a lenient sentence. He got the minimum for the charges he ended up with. Should be out in three years. He's a good kid. I've forgiven him and he's punished himself enough already, you know? I'll do what I can to help him get through these years. Prison can't help but damage him, but I'll try my best to limit the damage."

"You're more forgiving than I would be."

"Well, there's no sense in destroying another life. Ellie is gone and there is no amount of emotion that will bring her back. At least by loving Jarius I feel like I honor her life in some way. She wouldn't have wanted me to hate him…"

John paused, took a drink of tea.

"… I did want to run something by you though. An idea that I've had. It's not a new idea. It's something I've been thinking about for years, but now I feel like I've reached the point of no return… I'm thinking about quitting."

"Your job? Really? How rich ARE you?"

"Not rich enough," John said, laughing. "But I think I can do it financially. My needs and expenses really aren't much. I'll definitely have to watch my spending. I won't be able to buy a new car every two years, or take European vacations all the time. But if I'm careful I'm pretty sure it can be done. Or I should say of course it can be done, and if it can't it's my own fault. So from that standpoint it's a good challenge. It will force me to live even more simply."

"What will you do? Fish? Play golf?"

"Yeah, I think you know me a little better than that. I'm not sure, to be honest. I'm just ready for a break. I feel like it's now or never. I mean the kids are gone. There isn't really anything holding me here now. If I wait too long there may be grandkids and then I'll never want to leave!"

"I guess that makes sense. But you do like working. Being a doctor. Taking care of people. Operating. It's part of who you are."

"Right. Part of me. But not all of me. Obviously. I was someone before I was a doctor right? I was a student. A son. A boyfriend. A punk rocker. A swimmer. A writer, even then. A gardener. A child of God. And I'm still something other than a doctor. And you're something besides your job. We all are. We are complex and uncategorizable. We can assign names, but in the end we are unnameable. That's where I am starting with all of this. From the beginning. Letting go of one of my final attachments. Cutting a last string that's tethering me to a life that has become more confining than I would've ever guessed."

"So you're just going to float away?"

"I'm not burning bridges. Whoops, sorry, different metaphor. And I'm not going to float away. But I am ready to float freely. To not be tied to a job that takes ninety percent of my time and energy. Being on call several times a week. Answering questions all day long. The legal and regulatory crap. The stress of working in a group with partners. Feeling like I have to see thirty-five or forty patients in a day to keep my numbers up. Trying to keep office staff, partners, patients, hospital administrators, operating room people, coding people and God knows who else happy all the time. It's exhausting.

"I'm not a very good employee. Listening to authority has never been my strong suit. But being a boss or a leader, isn't easy for me either. It doesn't come naturally. So yeah, it's all difficult and I think I've had about enough. I've been here for what? Eighteen? Nineteen years? It's been a long time. I would venture to say that it's longer than most people work at one job."

"Okay, you're making a good case. But, I'll ask again. What

will you do?"

"Oh, I guess I have been dancing around that a little. I'm thinking about moving to Belize. Have you been there? It's so pretty."

"Seriously? I make fifteen dollars an hour. I haven't been anywhere. Well, Cancun once. Belize is right below there right?"

"Yep, directly south. Ellie and I and the kids visited different parts of the country. The most popular place is Ambergris Caye. It's nice there, but even ten years ago it seemed too busy. I'm sure it's worse now. And more expensive. We stayed in the jungle too, but I didn't like that as much. It's less expensive, but it would be a little too isolated for me. I want a place that has most of what I need within walking distance. Food, drink, beach, you know, the basics. There's a little village called Placencia that has all of that."

"That all sounds good to me. But what are you going to do there?"

"Nothing. I really need to do nothing for a while. Like I said, I just kind of want to live simply. Figure out some things. Get to know myself a little outside of the labels and titles that I've been encased in over the years."

"How long will you stay? Forever? Are you going to buy a place there and just disappear?"

"No. That's not the plan. I'm going to apply for the retired person's visa, or whatever it's called. Try to convince myself that it's a long-term move. But nothing is forever and we'll just see how it goes. I've been wanting to write. To read more. To pray more intentionally. To think and daydream and have extended conversations exactly like this one."

"Uh... you could do all of that here."

"True. I could. And believe me it will be hard to leave you, also Sam and Kate, my church... but I feel like I need the physical separation in order to make any kind of internal change. And that's what I'm striving for in the end."

"Okay, well, I don't completely understand it but I support you anyway. What can I do to help? What are you going to do with your house?"

"I've called a realtor and there are workers over there right now making some minor repairs. I would like to get it on the market in the next month or so. My goal is to have it sold by late summer so I can move to Belize in September. I'm pretty sure that's a reasonable time line. What do you think?"

"It all seems a little fast to me. I'm still trying to absorb all of this. But yeah, it seems like that's about right. Assuming your house sells. Do you need help cleaning? Getting rid of things? I've moved enough times, I'm pretty good at purging."

"I would love some help. What about tomorrow?"

"Sure, I can make that work. Have you even started?"

"Some. But there's a ton more to do."

Their tone had been matter of fact. There was a problem and Michelle was helping to solve it. But inside they began to feel a lonely sadness that wasn't there an hour ago. The thought of having to potentially end what had become an increasingly comfortable relationship didn't appeal to either one of them. They finished their drinks and parted ways.

Michelle did go over to help the next day. And many days after that. They sold furniture, electronics, the Hot Wheels, the ornaments and most of the comics, mostly on Craigslist at fire sale prices. They donated hundreds of books, records, and CDs to the local library. Within a month the house was fairly empty except for necessities, leaving enough furniture for staging.

Mercifully, the house sold quickly. John was unsure how long he would be gone. Whether he would be back at all. So, he rented a large storage unit, put enough furniture in it to furnish a one-bedroom apartment and sold the rest. He stored the remnant of his library, his great-grandmother's Bible, some pictures, his grandfather's pocket watch, a few keepsakes from his own childhood, as well as some of Ellie's and the twins' things. He sold or donated the remainder.

His sister and her husband had agreed to let him move into their basement for the next few weeks. This was a blessing as it provided him someone to talk to at a time when he would have been extremely anxious and lonely. Selling the house and contents had hit him a lot harder than he had expected it to. Ellie and the house were all mixed up together in his heart. He had to convince himself that this was normal, that it was okay to mourn. This chapter of his life was coming to a rapid completion and it would take everything he had to hold it together.

Work was busy enough to keep him occupied. The patients kept coming even with the news that his practice was closing. His office and surgical schedule was full right up until the last day. Most wanted to say goodbye, talk about his plans, give their good wishes or advise. With the end in sight, John's mood lightened and he started to second-guess his decision. He told himself that he could always come back.

And it was true. His manager had done his homework. His state licenses would remain active, the only requirements being a yearly fee, and fifty hours of continuing medical education.

He had known doctors who had left, moved to a different practice in a different town, figured out fairly quickly that they had made a huge mistake, and then moved right back. John's situation was different as he was moving out of the country and for all intents retiring, but those kinds of stories did bring him some comfort. He knew that he could return if needed.

He had found an inexpensive place in Placencia and was excited about the move. His main object was to have no set plans. This was something he had to pray about, being a natural researcher and planner. If he ended up finding a volunteer position, something to do in the community, then fine. But the first few weeks he simply wanted to tan, swim, eat fresh fruit, smell the salt air and go for long walks. He wanted to pray, write, read and think and to have a chance to learn to live with himself as he was. He wanted time to regroup, adjust, and perhaps work on being a little less worried about every little thing. And maybe even make some new friends.

11

Placencia, Belize

Plastic bottles had always bothered John. He had the opinion that there was literally nothing good about them. He could still remember when he was about thirteen years old and drank Coke from a two liter plastic bottle for the first time. It didn't taste right. It was kind of flat. Not as crisp or something. And then it started showing up in those twenty ounce bottles. It was the same thing. The taste was completely different. It wasn't long before glass bottles disappeared in the US. In recent years he had noticed that they were back in some places but these were small, expensive, no deposit glass bottles.

He fondly remembered the first time he had come to Belize. There were cases of glass Coke and Belikin beer bottles waiting in their room. They paid for the drinks and the deposit and received some money back when the empties were picked up. He didn't remember seeing plastic bottles on that trip, although he probably wasn't looking for them. Today of course they were everywhere. Glass still existed but more and more people drank soda and juice from single use plastic.

And water! One of the biggest scams in history. How did it happen that in the United States, with arguably the safest drinking water in the world, people started buying municipal water from other towns in plastic bottles at a ten thousand percent mark up? Not to mention the petroleum used to make the bottles, and the carcinogens involved in drinking from them. It continued to amaze him years after it became the norm. Privatizing water sources caused terrible access problems all over the world, and yet very few people spoke out.

Of course in countries where the local supply was a little iffy, it made sense to buy clean water. Usually available in reusable and refillable five-gallon containers, Belize had these deliverable to homes, restaurants and places of business. Placencia's municipal water was perfectly drinkable though, as it was throughout much of Belize.

So, in Placencia, most of Belize, and in much of the world including the States there was clean, drinkable tap water, there were big refillable containers, and there was glass that could be refilled at a bottling plant. From a hydration standpoint, and from a safety or taste standpoint, there was no reason to drink anything out of a plastic, one use bottle.

Why then did people in the US buy over fifty billion of them every year, consuming nearly nine billion gallons of mainly municipal water at grossly inflated prices? Why were there over two hundred brands of water in the States? Why were there empties everywhere in Placencia? They overflowed the public trashcans. They littered the beaches and the land around town. Following long sea journeys, they washed up by the thousands onto the shores of Long Caye near the Great Blue Hole miles and miles from the mainland. There were millions in Belizean landfills and billions in the US every year, with only a small percentage ever sent for recycling.

Laziness. That was the only answer. John didn't believe that people were innately evil. Selfish and thoughtless yes. And definitely lazy. If there were a way to drink water, juice, soda or other liquids that was as readily available, inexpensive and convenient as a plastic bottle, people would likely switch. If there were a way to easily and conveniently recycle plastic, people would probably do that as well. In the US about thirty percent of plastic bottles were recycled. In Switzerland that number was above eighty percent. In Belize only a tiny fraction were recycled.

All of the waste, all the trash, all the unnecessary expense bothered John immensely. He had seen the plastic problem worsen in the ten years that he had been coming to this part of the country, and he didn't feel like there was any opposition. Driven by profits and allowed by apathy there was little incentive to do anything about it.

Over the past few months John had found his cause.

It had begun at Holy Grounds. At the coffee shop most drinks were consumed in the store and were served in glass or ceramic ware. Plastic was used for cold drinks that were taken out. They also sold water and juice that came in plastic bottles.

John had talked to Jessica about alternatives but so far the conversation had been more theoretical in nature. He knew her well enough now that he felt it was time to bring it up.

"Hey Jessica, I think Holy Grounds can really be plastic free. You really don't need to sell any products that come in single serve plastic containers."

Jessica was wiping down the table next to where John was sitting. He had paper and pen out as usual. This time rather than writing letters or reflections, he was jotting down ideas about the plastic project. She gave him a "Seriously? We have to do this right now?" look.

He ignored the look and went on. "The solution here wouldn't impact the bottom line much. It might even help if we market it right."

"Okay. I'll bite," she said. She could tell he wasn't going to let it go this time, and really it was something she was interested in addressing as well. "What do you propose we do?"

"The first step is easy. Stop using plastic cups. Use the same paper to-go ones that you use for hot drinks."

"Yeah, I'm honestly not sure why we use plastic. Habit I guess. Have you tried it? Does the paper hold up as well for cold drinks?"

"Why wouldn't it? I don't see how temperature could impact the cup. If anything, I would think heat would be harder on a cup than cold. And how long does it have to hold up? Five minutes?

Thirty minutes? It isn't long. What do you think? Can we try it today?"

"Sure, I'm willing to try it."

"The other way that plastic goes out of here is when people buy bottled water or soft drinks or juice. I say you stop selling all of it."

"Okay, now you've lost it! We can't do that. We actually sell a fair number of those things here."

"Well, let's take it all one by one. Start with the soda. That's the easiest one. Glass bottles. That's it. We have a great bottling company in this country and there is no reason to have plastic or even canned soft drinks here. Even if tourists aren't able to bring a bottle back for deposit they won't likely throw it in the garbage. They'll leave it somewhere and it will eventually be reused."

"But not every drink is available that way. What if someone wants Pepsi and not Coke for instance?"

"Well, if so they may have to get it somewhere else. I think all of these initiatives will require education and explanation. Most people appreciate thoughtful decisions. There will still be a cola, a lemon lime soda, several Fanta flavors, even a diet soda. And we both know that it tastes better in glass than in plastic."

"That might work. But people also like juice and the flavored waters. What about them?"

"Get rid of the flavored water. That's an abomination. Do you really need to sell that? For juice, I have two solutions. Some juice comes in single serve boxes. Those still end up in the landfill but they have to be better right? They compress down and they surely don't last as long as plastic out there. The other solution is even better. Sell more fresh juice options. We have such amazing fruit here. Why would anyone want to drink imported juice out of a bottle? You already have the juicer. Let's just use it more."

"It's kind of labor intensive. And people tend to come here for coffee, and grab a juice as an afterthought. But yeah, you're right. We can brighten up that part of the menu a little. And I like that idea. We really don't need the bottled juices if we have fresh and boxed as options. All right, I'm on board with that. Now what about water?"

"I'm glad you asked. This is a little trickier, but again, it's just a matter of marketing. Standing up for the health of the village. We need to stress the common good over our individual comfort or immediate gratification. But why not set up a water cooler here? You could either charge a little or just offer it for free. Maybe charge a quarter and people could drink from a paper cup, or their own reusable water bottle. You could sell those little flavor packets for people that can't stand to drink plain water."

"So, the only people this would affect are those that grab a water to go with their sandwich or whatever. The ones that don't carry water bottles around with them."

"Yeah, well, it might not be a perfect solution, but those people can either bring their own water bottles or they could get a paper cup of water to go. It wouldn't be any different than if they were carrying a coffee, right? I seriously think people want to help. We're just making it easier for them, you know?"

"The eternal optimist. All right, I'm in. If you make a list of what we need to do to make this happen, an action plan, I'll run it by Sandy, but I think she'll be on board. I'll stop buying drinks that come in plastic bottles for the shop."

"Awesome. This was even easier than I thought it would be. Thank you so much. I can help with the Facebook page too. We can stress that we're becoming plastic-free for the good of the long term health of the village."

It all sounded simple enough and even self-evident once they had talked it out. Over the next week and with John's help, Jessica started to make the changes in the shop. She had a water cooler and several big refillable bottles of water delivered from the local supplier. She decided to offer water free of charge for the time being, until she had a better idea what the impact on the bottom line would be. They worked on some new juice recipes, and began advertising them on a sign outside the store. She ordered apple juice and milk that came in cardboard, and only soda that was available in returnable glass bottles from the local bottler.

By the end of the month, the change seemed to be a wash financially. There had been a little bit of local buzz about the changes made at Holy Grounds. The weekly paper did a short piece on the shop, quoting Jessica, saying that the changes really weren't much and that any inconvenience for the customer would be minor. She challenged other shop owners to follow her lead.

John was excited about the results but had already begun planning a much larger project.

12

"Do you think there is any way to choose a favorite Ryan Adams song? Like an absolute favorite?" Jessica asked as they sat on John's porch, feet up on the railing, watching the sky darken.

"I don't think so. There are way too many. I don't think you can choose one song from any prolific artist or band. Maybe if a person didn't know many of the songs, I guess. I mean there are one-hit wonders who keep churning out albums for years. So, I guess in that case it might work. But no, if you love a band, or a songwriter, and have a ton of their music I would think it would be impossible to pluck one song out and say, 'Yep, here's the perfect one.'"

"I'll bet I could. Sometimes there really is a perfect song. Like all of the artist's talent and creativity rolled up into one glorious four-minute masterpiece."

"I made a Drive By Truckers favorite songs playlist the other day. It's has fifty-six tracks on it."

"What? That's pretty lame. You can't seriously love fifty-six of their songs so much that you think they belong on that list."

"I do. And I had to hold myself back from adding more. It's pretty heavy on the first two albums and the Jason Isbell years... It would be the same thing with the Cure, the Replacements, Steve Earle, and the National... Even like U2 or the Clash. It would be more of a favorite song playlist. Not 'a' favorite song."

Since that day spent talking and planting mangrove they had become friends, but the last thing John wanted was to get serious with someone in Placencia. He wasn't sure how long he was going to be there. He didn't want to hurt Jessica and he didn't want to hurt himself. It was the same reason that he hadn't pursued a relationship with Michelle. At this point he needed friendship infinitely more than he needed anything else. They had come up with these back porch dates to just hang out, talk, philosophize and dream.

The Holy Grounds project had been good for John. It made him feel like he was contributing to the health of the peninsula. He had bigger plans as well, but was trying to keep the evolution natural. To not push too quickly. He kept to his routine of Bible reading, swimming, journal writing, keeping his life as simple as possible. He knew that if he let it, the plastic project would take over his life. He was unclear what the future held, but he wanted to hang on to the mindfulness that he had achieved in these last few months.

One way in which he was keeping things slow and intentional was by having these long relaxed conversations with Jessica. They had a standing balcony date twice a week that was different from their discussions at the coffee shop. John looked forward to them more than he wanted to admit.

"Okay, you did a pretty good job of changing the subject. But let's get back to it. If not the number one favorite Ryan Adams song, let's at least hear your top five." Jessica knew that John liked to change the subject to avoid answering questions. He was a master at it, and it worked more often than not.

"Hmmm… that's going to be hard as well. But let's see what we come up with. I may have to cheat. I don't want to miss an important one just because I don't have a list in front of me. Can I look at Spotify on my phone?"

"I guess so, but aren't there any that come to mind without cheating?"

"Well, yeah, of course. 'In My Time of Need' from *Heartbreaker* will always be one of my favorites. It's devastatingly beautiful. The lyrics and the way he delivers them still make me cry, even after all of these years. There is a lot of 'we' all through it, which adds to the beauty I think. Even introverts like me are social beings. We need someone to walk through life with, a person to share the pain as well as the joy."

"I like that one too. Those two old timers reminiscing over their long lives together, not regretting so much as just telling it like it is. There is fear and sorrow but also so much love in that song. What else?"

"'Factory Girl.' For sure."

"From the first Whiskeytown?"

"Right. It's kind of a bonus track at the end. Was it an EP or something originally? Anyway, I love that song. He just watches her. Wants to be close. She's the reason he gets up in the morning. He smiled at her one time but got yelled at by his boss. He's just so shy and so in love. Maybe not with the factory girl but with his idea of her. She's a place of beauty in his sad life."

"All right, that's two. What else?"

"This one is a little different. From the *29* album. 'Strawberry Wine.' I don't know for sure, but it feels like it's ten minutes long. It's a slowly developing story in which he gives himself time to tell the whole thing, just like we do on these nights. The characters are all somehow tied together by strawberry wine."

"I don't know that song."

"Don't feel bad. That album didn't do as well as a lot of others. It has 'Night Birds' on it also. That's another beautiful song. I can't remember what else is on it without peeking, but the whole thing is good."

"You're doing great. Only two more."

"My choices would probably be different if I could look at a list. But let's see, I guess 'Stop' would be on there. It's from *Cardinology*. I'm not even sure what it's about, but it's the last song on the album. It's slow and beautiful and feels really hopeless. I remember listening to it a few years ago at a really tough time in my life. I don't remember what was going on exactly, just that I felt crushed with stress and worry. I had pulled into the garage one night after work. The garage was shut and yet I continued to sit and was just listening and crying. Literally sobbing. And right at that moment I wanted everything to stop. And Ryan Adams felt it too, I thought. Life is so hard sometimes. You know?"

"I do. That's the amazing thing about music. How it speaks to us. How maybe at a different time in your life 'Stop' wouldn't have been important to you at all. So, I've noticed there's nothing upbeat or even remotely popular on your list. I mean Ryan Adams doesn't really write dance music but they aren't all slow, sad and depressing. What about 'Let it Ride' or 'New York, New York' or 'Drank like a River' or 'Come Pick Me Up'? Or even something from *1984*?"

"I'm telling you, I could easily come up with fifty favorites and some of those would be on that list. But you're asking me to do this from memory. And to only list five… Okay, here's one. The last one I guess. And it's definitely not a dirge. 'All You Had to Do Was Stay' from *1989*. We could take this conversation in a whole other direction and just talk about Ryan's cover songs but I think this is truly one of his best. The whole album is amazing, but Taylor's lyrics and Ryan's voice and the reimagined melody on that one gives me chills."

"It's not a dirge but it isn't exactly a happy song."

"No, you're right but isn't it amazing? And isn't it true? Relationships are so messed up. It's rare for two people to be in the same place at the same time. To have similar feelings. Everyone seems to be a little early or a little late. I've been both and either way it's tough… Anyway, it's a breathtaking song and it catches that emotion perfectly."

"I agree. It is. And that whole album is fantastic. I listen to it the most I think."

"I know. You sometimes play it in the shop, huh? So, what do you say, did I pass?"

"You did. You narrowed hundreds of songs down to five favorites. I do want that greatest Ryan Adams songs playlist though when you make it."

"You got it. I'm still not convinced that the top five thing is accurate so, yeah, I'll work on a good playlist with fifty songs and get it right."

"Because it is so very important, right?" Jessica said with a laugh.

"Yes! It is the most essential thing in the world right now. You know, I spent too many years putting my career and success first. Working ridiculously long hours, hurrying here and there..."

"You don't think work is important?

"Of course it is. But work means a lot of different things. And I don't think it is necessary to do something for sixty hours a week plus call time in order to obtain the rewards of work. A job is important. It was killing me though...and towards the end I decided that I would rather live."

"Do you miss it?"

"I do. Sometimes...I definitely miss the feeling of being needed. Of feeling like I have a purpose. But that's one of the reasons I'm here. To kind of build a life from scratch. To start over. Call it a mid-life crisis if you want, although my kids would tell you I'm way beyond mid-life. I wanted to see if there's anything behind the school, the degrees, and the titles. I wanted to be left alone with myself and see what remains."

"Is that a hint that I should go?"

"No. Definitely not. I'm just talking. Thinking out loud. I've nearly proven to myself that I can do this. I'm in a better place mentally that I've been in years. Plus, now we have the recycling project."

"Ugh. Let's not talk about that right now. Now you ARE talking about work."

"John laughed, "Okay. You're right. Your turn then. Favorite Goo Goo Dolls song. And you can't say 'Name,' 'Iris' or 'Slide.'"

"Easy. 'Better Days.'"

"And not 'Better Days.'"

"What? Listen I'm not as old as you. That's about as far back as I go."

"Nice. All right, you can use Spotify to refresh your memory. Maybe we should make it one that Robbie sings."

"Hey, now you're just being crazy."

They were both laughing. Sitting in the plastic chairs with their feet on the railing, they were turned so they could see each other's eyes. It was dark now and beginning to cool off that beautiful tropical evening. Their hearts matched the climate. And if they had been thinking of such things they would have realized that they were more at peace right at that moment than they had ever been.

But this wasn't a time for reflection; it was a time for living.

13

Once the changes had been made at the coffee shop, John started looking around for other ways to help. He had participated in beach cleanups and mangrove replanting. What he really wanted to do was to preserve the health and beauty of the peninsula, rather than just play catch up by picking up trash. He found that there was, in fact, a small recycling program already in the country. It was a private endeavor named El Mundo that collected and then sold plastic. John called them, wondering if he could set up something similar in Placencia. It turned out they were interested in expanding into the area and were thrilled to have a contact.

El Mundo agreed to deliver a large dumpster that would act as the central collection station. It would be hauled away, and a new one would be replaced every other week. Once it was full the plastic would be crushed, baled, and shipped to buyers in other countries.

The prospect was exciting for John and he was eager to get started. He talked to several local businesses and landowners and found one who was willing to keep the dumpster on his property. He promised that he would personally see that it was used only for plastic, and would keep the surrounding ground free of trash. He and Jessica talked to the local paper to generate some excitement about the new endeavor. Being new to the area, it was great to have a local business owner help as the project rolled out.

They went to a town council meeting, asking to set up separate recycling trashcans in public areas. They were told it would take time, that they couldn't just put them up overnight. The council would have a period of discussion, vote on it and then allot money from the budget. But they promised to help, and understood that it was a step in the right direction.

John, Jessica, and a writer from the local paper were present to meet the recycling dumpster when it arrived. The Placencia paper was more of a flyer, but it was widely read and the online version had followers from around the world. A small, curious crowd gathered as the dumpster was deposited. John smiled as he tossed in two plastic water bottles that he had found in a lot on the walk over. Pictures of that first act of recycling on the peninsula were everywhere that week.

John slept well that night, convinced that they were off to a good start. With the dumpster in place it was just a matter of education now. He needed to begin changing patterns that were ingrained in many people to simply toss plastic in the trash.

The next morning, over a breakfast of fresh mangos and a slice of toast, he read his *One Year Bible*. For April 7th the Gospel passage was Luke 12:8-34. It was a lot to take in all at once. In past years he had sped through all of the readings, as he had to hurry to move on to the next activity. In his new life, however, he was able to linger and really think. These verses were full of good and challenging advice. The parable of the rich fool, the verses about trusting in God, and then there was 32-34:

"Do not be afraid, little flock, for your Father has been pleased to give you the kingdom. Sell your possessions and give to the poor. Provide purses for yourselves that will not wear out, a treasure in heaven that will never fail, where no thief comes near and no moth destroys. For where your treasure is, there your heart will be also."

That is what struck him on that perfect, comfortable morning. Enjoying a simple breakfast, the windows open, with the warm tropical breeze blowing in. The salty air, the sound of sea birds, the waves, a truck backing up, people saying *buenos dias* to each other. *It has pleased God to give you the Kingdom.* It wasn't something that had to be earned or strived for. God is pleased. An extravagant welcome right here and right now. And so the line about selling all belongings and giving money to the poor wasn't a prerequisite to receive the joys of the Kingdom. Rather, it was a response to the grace that preexisted.

John wondered if he was doing enough. He certainly was receiving the fruits. He felt so at peace in beautiful Placencia. The weather, the food, the cost of living, the friendliness of the people, the pace of living. He had plenty of money, friends, and family. He had shelter, clothes, and even that cool new golf cart.

He had given so much to the poor, had sold or donated most of his belongings, but he couldn't fool himself into thinking he had done enough. Being a busy and thrifty surgeon for twenty years had resulted in a large amount of money. What kept him from selling everything, giving it all away like in the scripture? Fear mainly. He didn't know how long the money would need to last. He was still paying for college. There may be medical school in Kate's future, graduate school in Sam's. It all cost so much. At times he thought that he should have the twins take out loans like he did. But he had plenty, and didn't want them to start out their lives in debt.

He knew he couldn't use his children as an excuse. He could easily calculate how much they needed to finish school. But what about the rest? Wasn't he being unfaithful? He was scared to let go.

He remembered those years in college and in med school when he lived on next to nothing. He had no income. There were times that he felt hungry. Times when he couldn't go anywhere because he didn't have a car. He depended on others and lived in community. All shared what they had, or what their parents had given them. A girlfriend's gas card to buy food, or a free meal from a roommate's visiting parent, or frozen sauce from another friend's freezer, it all worked out. The birds of the air, the lilies of the field, and the college students all lived for the day and they didn't worry. They knew that life was more than food and the body more than clothes. And in their time of need they had each other.

And what about what he had seen in Africa? How little they had. Just barely enough for the day, at times. There were no leftovers, no extra freezer in the garage stocked full of food, no running out for dinner at a restaurant if someone didn't feel like cooking. Just enough. There was room for everyone to sleep even though they had no king sized beds, no down filled pillows, fans for ambient noise, or en suite bathrooms. In Africa people slept where there was room. There was a spot for everyone.

God provides enough. And God is pleased to do so.

As he thought this through he knew that although he wasn't where he needed to be, he was getting there. He was glad for time and for grace. The rule is not to make any big changes in the first year of retirement. Well, he had blown that one. By selling his house and moving to Belize he had done everything wrong. But he knew that this move might not be permanent. That he still needed to be cautious. His plan was to give away his money, but it would be little by little as his path became clearer. And in the meantime he would live as simply as he could. With self-reminders to continue to scale back.

John closed his Bible and notebook and picked up the phone. He glanced at the weather in Iowa and in Fort Worth. Snow at Grinnell and rain at Texas Christian. He texted Kate.

"How's it going? Looks like snow. Does it feel like spring will ever arrive?"

She answered about five minutes later.

"Seriously. I love cold weather but I think I'm actually looking forward to being warm again!"

"You should come visit. It's going to be hot and sunny here."

"Ugh, I didn't say I want to be hot. Or covered in sand. Just warm."

"Ha ha. I don't know where I went wrong. Why don't you love the beach? We visited enough of them when you were young."

"Too much exposure maybe. That's a thing, you know."

"Maybe. You still have to come visit sometime."

"We'll see. When are you coming to see me?"

"Touché. This summer."

"That's too far away!"

"I know. I miss you."

"I miss you too. I need to get ready for class."

"Okay. Have a good day! Love you!"

"Love you!"

He returned some emails quickly and sent a short one to Sam. He knew Sam wouldn't be up yet so he didn't bother texting. They talked several times a week, but it was easier to catch him in the evening.

The plan was to spend two weeks that summer in Kansas City. He would stay in a long-term stay hotel. One with two bedrooms and a little kitchen with room for the twins. He tried not to think about them too often, or at least tried not to linger on the thought. It had been a major change to move so far away, where communication was difficult. The year before, when he had lost Ellie and when the kids had gone away to college, was unimaginably hard. He felt like he was doing all right overall, but it wasn't easy and he missed them terribly.

Occasionally he still had flashes of memories of the four of them in Placencia. There was the long walk back to the condo from the village with Kate carrying a pineapple. Sam had the tomatoes and mangos. Ellie had the towels and beach things, and John had everything else. It was hot, and they went back and forth across the dirt road trying to stay in the shady spots as they traveled. John encouraged the others as they mildly complained about the walk, wishing that he had rented a golf cart. He couldn't justify spending that much money simply to avoid a nice walk twice a day. Plus, he explained, they saw more this way. Big lizards, that mango tree, the houses in various states of renovation and disrepair, the sounds of village life all around them. Even with all the whining he would give anything to have those days back.

But this would be a good day also. Things were simpler here. A full day in Placencia would have been a wasted day in Kansas City. He had missed a couple morning swims lately and was anxious to get back in the water. The cool buoyant saltwater, the gentle waves, the hot sun on his back, all of this combined to feel like heaven's riches. Something that no thief could steal or moth could destroy. He was rich in comfort and peace when he was in the water, when he was sitting on his balcony, when he was slowly reading the Bible or having long conversations with friends. He felt minor pangs of guilt when he thought this way. Who exactly was he helping these days besides himself? Life ultimately wasn't about comfort and peace was it? Giving away all of his belongings wasn't the end game right? It was only a start. Shedding everything, cutting strings, loosening attachments so that greater work could be done, that was the point of the scripture.

———————

John had finished his swim, was drying off and getting his things together, preparing to visit Holy Grounds when he saw Bev, the Friends of the Reef lady, down the beach. She had seen him and was headed his way.

"Hi John. I've been hoping I'd run into you."

"Hi Bev. How have you been? Any volunteer events coming up?"

"There's one in a little less than two weeks. A beach clean up. That's related to what I want to talk to you about. How's the recycling project going?"

"Well, it just started. The dumpster has been delivered. It'll get picked up two weeks from today. I don't know how full it will be. We'll see. On one hand I hope we can't fill it up. It would be great if I found out that we really don't throw away too much plastic here. Unfortunately I think there's more than enough to fill it. El Mundo is giving me a two-month trial period to see if we generate enough to make it worth their while."

"Do you need help? Selling the idea? Collecting trash?"

"Oh my goodness. You know I do. All the help that I can get."

"I was thinking we could market the beach cleanup as a plastic recycle project. We'll bring separate bags for plastic and for other trash. You know, we get pretty good crowds at these."

"That would be so great. And all of those people who come, they have their own friends and contacts, they go to restaurants, other businesses…it'll really increase awareness. This won't work if it's dependent on me digging through trashcans."

"That's exactly what I was thinking. So, the volunteer day is on that Wednesday."

"That's two days before the dumpster gets picked up. Perfect timing."

"Right! So, what else can I do for you? I really want this to take off."

"Well, I need to figure out a way to get trash containers for recyclables around town. You know, put them next to the regular trashcans. I talked to someone on the city council. They have to discuss it, vote on it, that kind of thing. It's on their agenda but it might take a while."

"Yeah, those things always do. I know someone on the council. I'll talk to her this weekend; see if there is a way to speed up the process. You're right though. It will be critical to have the trash separated at the source. We don't want to be digging through public trashcans if we can help it. Who knows what all's in there? What else?"

John thought for a moment. "Well, as important as the tourist on the beach with a Vitamin Water is, I feel that we need to really work on the residents and the guests that are staying on the island. Work on changing their habits. We need to make it easier to recycle. Make it as easy as tossing it in the trash. You know, people for the most part really don't care where the empty goes. I imagine that very few people lose sleep over plastic bottles and landfills and the Great Pacific Garbage Patch like I do."

"Oh I've lost plenty of sleep over all of that. But you're right, most people don't worry about it. They recycle if it's convenient and they don't if it's not."

"Exactly. So, let's make it easy. No one's going to carry all of their plastic to the dumpster. I say we start with the condos and small hotels."

"That makes sense. We can get several households and rooms with one conversation."

"Yeah, if we can talk to the property manager, get them on board, that would be great. We need to get a big garbage can and put it right next to their dumpster or other cans. Maybe we can have them advertise on their newsletters or websites. If nothing else we just park it there with a big sign," said John.

"I love that."

"Same thing with the hotels around here. I'm going to wait on the bigger resorts farther north. I don't really have an effective way to get their plastic back down to the dumpster. Just collecting from all of the cans around here will be difficult enough at first. I'll buy, or better yet borrow, a trailer attachment for my golf cart. Do you know anyone with a pickup?"

Bev replied, "Probably. I can ask around. What we should do is make a list of the inns and condos with more than, like, five units. With that information we can divide and conquer. I'm happy to visit and get them signed up. You can do some of them and I'll bet we can find others to help."

"Hey, I know you have other things going on, so don't feel like you have to take on too much of this."

"No, I want to help. We've needed to do this for a really long time. I'm elated that you've taken this first step. I'll do whatever I can to help."

"Okay. Well, thank you. How about if I get a list together and we can start working through it on Monday morning? How does that sound?"

"Sure. Anything."

"This weekend I'll walk and drive around and kind of map out what we need to do. I should've been better prepared and done this before the dumpster arrived. But, you know? Island time… and it just didn't seem real until it was here."

"Well, I think it's just great. It's a good start. And God bless you for trying."

"Thanks. Well, I'd better get going. Have a great day!"

"I will… and you too. Talk to you later."

After lunch John spent the afternoon driving his golf cart and walking around the peninsula trying to get a feel for how many garbage cans he would need. He quickly became overwhelmed. Just in the area of the peninsula that was south of the airstrip there were at least twenty hotels and inns. Condos and apartments were everywhere.

He checked at the hardware store and found that ninety-six gallon garbage cans were two hundred Belizean dollars. So, if there were as many big apartment and condo developments as there were inns it would cost eight thousand Belize to allot one trashcan per location.

He talked to a store manager. They had five of the big garbage cans in stock, and he could get as many as he wanted within a week. By explaining his plan, John worked the price down ten percent and said he would come back for all five of them later.

He had very little to do the rest of the day. Just the way he liked it, really. He decided to go and check his email at the office supply shop, maybe pay some bills. There was always a computer open for him it seemed. He tried to hold it to an hour at the most. With unstructured time it was a temptation to waste all afternoon on the Internet.

There was an email from his stepdad about his mom. She wasn't doing well. Her dementia had been rapidly progressive. She was now in a memory care center near their house. Fred did an amazing job with her. He was always by her side during the day. John knew that Fred felt guilty about having her there at all, but she just required too much care now. She didn't know anybody, didn't remember anything. She had been so smart, so independent; it was tough to think of her that way. But life was cruel at times. And it was a harsh reminder that we aren't really in control of our lives. We may think we are strong and don't need anyone. Individualism is one of the most prevalent false idols of the developed world. But infants, the elderly, the mentally and physically disabled, they all teach us otherwise. Hospice nurses, nursing home workers, and those that work in group homes are underpaid saints. Their worldly rewards are subtle at times, but they are surely storing treasures in heaven.

John's mom was slowing down. She was starting to lose weight, wasn't eating as much. She had stopped walking about six months prior, and now no longer initiated movement. She just sat in her wheelchair, even looked at the TV if her chair was pointed that way. That was the most striking example of her dementia to John. She would never have watched television for longer than about fifteen seconds at a time when she was younger.

John wrote Fred back, thanked him for the update. He got caught up on Facebook, checking the Holy Grounds page. An update about the dumpster was on both the Holy Grounds and Friends of the Reef pages. He shared both posts, and then wrote Sam a short note about his day.

By then it was about time for the shop to close, so he paid and went out into the late afternoon. He walked along the beach. The cruise ship passengers were long gone and the sand was nearly empty. He hurried over to Maria's to buy a pineapple, more mangoes, and a cucumber, and then went home to make rice and beans.

He ate the filling meal on the balcony, listening to Gordon Lightfoot on a small speaker that he had set on the table next to his chair. Gordon always seemed appropriate when John was in a contemplative mood. His smooth voice, amazing acoustic guitar work and libertine lyrics were just right for that evening.

A day old croissant mopped up the bean juice. Half of the pineapple completed his typical meal. John hadn't been able to weigh himself since arriving in Belize but he felt like he was at least holding. He wasn't afraid to have a pastry or a sweet drink like he had been at times. He was even eating the croissant, which was something he wouldn't have done before moving to Placencia. He was hopeful and relaxed about his weight, but knew he wasn't out of the woods yet.

And he felt like he had a lot more to do. The recycling project had come out of nowhere and had really energized him. He was mindful to keep it in perspective and to not abandon his Bible reading, swimming and intentional living. He was fearful of trading one difficult job for another. He knew there would be opposition to his plans. There would be stress and hard feelings. There always was when people were faced with change. He needed to keep his life peaceful in order to balance the external stresses. He was no Gordon Lightfoot who could just slip down that carefree highway, but he could definitely work on holding on a little more loosely to ideas and preconceived notions.

Sunday morning John talked to several people at church about plastic recycling. Tom was on board for sure, and there were four others who had expressed interest in helping. Living Water Church was certainly not a mission minded congregation. It was filled with nice people, but like the majority of churches, most people went to the service, ate a cookie and drank coffee, chatted for a few minutes afterwards then went home, not giving it another thought until the next Sunday. But there were a few that he clicked with, who knew that getting together to worship corporately was only one small part of being a Christian. That serving others, protecting the earth, and working for the common good was not just a Sunday morning fantasy.

So after church, he sat and talked to them. He was pleased to hear that two people lived in apartment buildings. When John described his vision of parking a large trash container there to collect plastic, they loved the idea. Each volunteered to be in charge of their buildings. They would meet with the manager, purchase and deliver the container, advertise it and then empty it into the dumpster when full. Tom and the other two would collect their own plastic and talk to their neighbors, encouraging them to collect as well. Everyone was up for helping more as plans solidified. It was truly turning into a community movement.

14

Monday morning he was to meet Bev at Holy Grounds. He showed up early on purpose, hoping to have a few minutes alone with Jessica.

He was in luck. There were no customers in line when he arrived. Her hair was down and she had on that "Mama ran off with the Drive By Truckers" t-shirt that he loved.

"Hi Jessica. Good morning!"

"Good morning John. How are you doing? How was your weekend?"

"Excellent. It really was. I got a few people from church signed up to help with the recycling."

"That's awesome."

"Yeah, only five but it's a start."

"For sure. Every little bit helps. Guess what I did?"

"Um. Fell in love with a cruise passenger and decided to move to Utah?"

"Close... I talked to a bunch of restaurant and bar owners around here about recycling."

"Really? I was going to do that this week."

"Well, I beat you to it. I didn't catch everyone, but did talk to quite a few. Everyone's on board."

"Really? Just like that?"

"Yep. They're going to save plastic containers from the kitchen, and if they sell drinks in plastic bottles they'll put out trashcans to collect the empties."

"That's so awesome. Thank you so much Jessica. I really owe you. That's going to save me so much time."

"Hey, we're a team. And you know how much I want to help with this. You need to let go of it a little. I know you're used to doing everything by yourself as a doctor and all. But these kinds of things work better the more we spread it around."

"You're right, as usual. And on that note, Bev from Friends of the Reef is meeting me, or I should say us, to brainstorm about how to spread the word and get more people involved."

As if on cue, Bev walked in. She and John ordered drinks and sat at a table to discuss strategy. Jessica joined them as she was able. Between the three friends they planned to involve much of the village in the recycling effort. Church helpers, Friends of the Reef volunteers, restaurant and bar owners, the friends and family of all of these people, it felt like they were really starting to get somewhere with this.

Bev and John spent the morning talking to apartment and condo managers about setting up recycle containers next to their existing dumpsters and trashcans. Most were receptive to the idea, especially if it didn't cost anything. When possible they tried to get the managers to commit to buying a canister.

Following what had been a successful morning, Bev had lunch plans so John headed alone to the office supply shop. On one of the computers he created a sign with the recycle symbol and examples of what types of plastic were accepted. He printed out five of them on eight by eleven inch sheets of heavy paper and had them laminated. Later he bought the trash containers that the hardware store had in stock and delivered them to five of the managers who had paid for them. He superglued a sign to each of the containers. Digging through the top of the trash at each location, he found several bottles to move over to the new canisters. At some of the places there were people around, curious about what was going on. When he explained the initiative, everyone showed interest in helping.

It felt good to get them in place and to start filling them up. To be making some visible progress. Back home that evening, John created a spreadsheet listing the location of each of the new trashcans and a column that indicated when they were emptied last. At that point, he stopped and thought a moment about the bigger picture. He had about ten days to get the dumpster full and yet was just now getting the system into place. It would be several days before the hardware store had new containers, and he wasn't sure if the reward was worth the cost of buying them for everyone. It was all a little overwhelming. He didn't want this to be a full time job and it would be very easy to turn it into one. He knew he needed to trust Jessica, Bev, Tom, and all the other volunteers.

That night John got out Dostoyevsky again. He had read almost nothing in the months since he had retired to Placencia. On one hand his mind was always moving, always thinking, and he didn't want to muddy it with stories and external thoughts. On the other, he was trying to be quiet and mindful and was worried that books would take him away from that. So he had read very little. But he loved the book. Father Zosima and his speech about how monks were no holier than those outside the walls really struck him. In fact, he said they were inferior and became more so the longer they lived in relative isolation. That struck John as he thought about his place in the world. Where he could be most effective. But after another ten pages he put it down again and simply watched the night pass from his balcony.

He sat and stood, thought and listened, planned and dreamed. And after awhile he lay in bed, reciting the Jesus prayer over and over until sleep came.

On the morning of the volunteer event, John started with a swim and then a visit to Holy Grounds. Jessica was ready to come help. She had her hair in a ponytail, which made that cryptic Chinese symbol behind her right ear visible, and her lovely sternocleidomastoid muscles more prominent. She was going to leave the shop in the hands of her employees for the rest of the morning.

"I'm excited about today," she exclaimed as John took the first sip of his decaf, having recently switched to coffee as his drink there.

"How do you think it'll go?"

"It's going to be great! I know so many people are coming to help. Probably twice what we had for the mangrove planting. This is a fun, easy project. It's right here so we don't have to travel up north and work in the hot sun. It's perfect."

They talked more about the upcoming day and about coffee and strawberry scones and the new Cloud Nothings album and how the sound of loud guitars and earnest voices filled their hearts with exhilaration and hope. It was a beautiful start to an exciting day.

Everyone gathered on the beach for instructions from Bev. John was there for support and to answer questions, but wasn't much of a public speaker, leaving that task to her. The plan was to split up and empty all of the recycle bins and trashcans around town into the dumpster, to pick up plastic trash in places were it was frequently dumped, and to gather recyclables from businesses that were saving it. They would work for about three hours and meet at the dumpster to wrap up.

John had supplied Bev with copies of his flow sheet so that she could send people to pick up containers. There were now fourteen of them scattered around the peninsula at hotels, apartments and condos. He had resisted the urge to check on them every day, knowing that awareness takes time and would grow.

John and Jessica went around to bars and restaurants and collected plastic. They dragged it behind them in big yellow bags. They were able to use and reuse just two bags all day, which felt like a minor victory. Bev's friend with a truck helped as well for the larger and further away collections.

It was another wonderful day: helping the environment, bringing the residents of the village together for a common purpose, creating community, it was all that was lovely and amazing about life. John and Jessica treasured their time together. They talked about Morrissey's rare and shockingly adept falsetto, their favorite spring flowers, Cesar Chavez, and the relative awesomeness of the various shades of green and black ink used in tattoo art.

All too soon it was over, another example of the extreme relativity of time. They arrived at the dumpster with a final yellow bag full of plastic water bottles, empty cooking oil containers, clamshell containers and other recyclables from a restaurant. There were about sixty people, a much larger crowd than John had anticipated.

As John and Jessica arrived everyone cheered and clapped, surprising and embarrassing John to the point that he froze in place. Jessica laughed and took the bag. With help she emptied it into the nearly overflowing dumpster. The cheers increased at that point, many people coming over to thank and congratulate John on a job well done.

Bev handed him a cookie and a paper cup of water saying, "You did it!"

"We did it," John replied with no hesitation.

He took the cookie and the cup, and when people had quieted down, thanked them for their help, for sharing this moment with him and with each other, for partaking of this communion of cookie and water. He asked them to remember this day, to remember the feeling that they had as they worked together for the common good, and as they gathered to celebrate and break bread together. He asked them to consider coming to help in two weeks as well, as this work takes many hands.

His voice was quiet but it was heard by all. And when he was finished Bev took over, giving more information about the project. While she talked, Jessica and John were able to sneak away, back to her shop where she talked him into an unheard of second decaf latte and a strawberry scone. She put on the Smiths, only playing the songs that featured Morrissey's brave falsetto. And they had no idea how brightly they were shining. And it was a magnificent day to be alive.

15

"I'm serious! There is no doubt in my mind. 'Hang Down Your Head' is the greatest Tom Waits song of all time."

John laughed at Jessica's pronouncement. "That's a pretty bold statement. I'll bet you haven't even heard half of his songs. And how many do you know well enough to pass judgment? How many can you name right now?"

"Okay. Those are two different questions. I know several albums: *Rain Dogs, Swordfishtrombones, Alice, Closing Time...* Oh yeah, there is also *Small Change* and *Mule Variations.* I can think of more if you give me a minute. I can't remember the names of many songs on the albums. Plus, I don't listen to them all the time anymore. I definitely went through a Tom Waits phase though."

It was late summer and they were on the balcony at John's apartment, eating a meal of rice and beans with fresh crusty bread and a pineapple. John standing, leaning on the railing as he ate from his bowl, was enjoying the time with Jessica, who was sitting in the plastic chair that was pushed up against the wall. The evening was beginning to cool a little. The sounds of the wind, the distant waves, and the people walking by were familiar and comforting.

"I actually agree with you. He has a massive amount of music and much of it's so amazing that it's hard to remember individual songs. I honestly don't know much about his personal life. Other than that he's married to Kathleen Brennan. But he's a hero to me. Someone who notices the margins. He looks at the human experience in its messy entirety and puts it to a soundtrack. He takes what is bitter and makes it sweet. He works up from the bottom, rejecting what is perfect or artificially clean or successful and finds beauty and hope in places where others don't bother to look. Like Kerouac or Burroughs or Bukowski or, going in a little different direction but really it's all the same, they loved the same people, Dorothy Day and Jesus… So why 'Hang Down Your Head'?"

"I just think it's the perfect pop moment from a guy who wrote a lot of them. It often took other artists covering his songs to get them radio play, but many of his songs have a pop feel. The melody, that crisp guitar, the perfect mix of gravely and sweet vocals. He usually does one or the other – on this one he blends them nicely. And the lyrics… so heartbreaking and universal."

John softly sang one of the verses and marveled, "Isn't that just amazing?"

"It is. And not a bad Tom Waits impression by the way. All right, I've got a couple for you. From the same album. Remember when Rod Stewart did that awful remake of 'Downtown Train'? It was perfect the way it was. But for a long time Rod's version was in my head instead of Tom's. Also 'Time'- it's hard to beat that song. In fact, *Rain Dogs* is by far his best album in my opinion."

"Probably. That and *Swordfishtrombones* are the two where he seems to have the balance just right. He uses his voice and that weird avant-garde sound in a way that is still accessible for most people. His earlier stuff feels like he isn't really being true to himself- or maybe hadn't found his voice. The more recent work is good but really, after forty years what else is there to say?"

"I disagree with you on that one. *Bad As Me* is one of his best. There are some really great songs on there. How cool is 'Get Lost' for instance?"

Jessica looked at him quizzically as he brought the song up on his phone. "Never heard that… not bad though," she nodded as her feet, which were perched up on the railing, started tapping to the catchy beat.

"I'm telling you- you should check it out. It's good from top to bottom."

"I will. Maybe tomorrow in the shop. We need to mix it up a little. We've been kind of stuck on New Order and OMD and that kind of eighties dance thing lately."

"Yeah, I've noticed... why do you think we're having this discussion tonight?"

"Why you! I should have known! You've probably got it written down somewhere don't you? 'Number one, work on Holy Grounds playlist. Number two, try to get Jessica to come to church on Sunday. Number three, meat is murder.' Am I right?"

"Pretty close," he grinned, sheepishly pulling out a small scrap of paper with the words 'music, plastic project, KC trip, church' written in tiny letters. He showed her the paper and she laughed like it was the funniest thing she had ever seen.

"You know I've been doing this for years. It makes me feel better to have an idea what to talk about. You wouldn't understand. It's an introvert thing."

"It's a crazy person thing. But it's actually really cute too. It shows that you've thought about me. About our talks."

"Of course I do. These times together are one of my favorite things. There's nothing better than talking one-on-one with someone. Really. Nothing."

She looked into his eyes for a moment then looked away. "So, how was your Kansas City trip, anyway? I haven't really heard. Are your children doing okay?"

"Everyone's fine. We really had an amazing time together. We stayed in a cheap hotel in the suburbs. We cooked dinner, went for walks, saw a Royals game, sat out by the hotel pool. You know, things like that."

"That sounds wonderful. You all get along so well."

"We always have. There were probably a couple years when they wouldn't have wanted to be trapped in a small hotel room with me for that long, but I don't know, we've always been close.

Probably more so since Ellie's death, which makes sense I guess. We share in those emotions in a way that no one else can."

"That's true... Did you see your sister?"

"I did. We got together at her house. My stepdad was there, nephews, some other family. It was a good time."

"How's your mom?"

"Not good. I mean I guess she's comfortable in that nursing home. I visited her twice while I was home. She recognizes me, but that's about it. We just talk about the weather, what's on TV, 'look at those pretty flowers,' that kind of thing. I don't attempt to see if she remembers anything... anyone. I don't see the point in it."

"That's so sad."

"It is. Dementia is such a strange disease. It makes you question what it means to be alive. If we don't have our minds, if we can't remember, if we can't compare things or pass judgment on them, if we can't pray, if we can't plan, are we really alive? We get so excited when she remembers something, has a little flash of recognition, says something about her parents for instance, or a friend from her childhood. But those moments are becoming less frequent."

"That sounds awful. And I know exactly what you mean, but I can see some beauty in it as well. I mean, she *can* actually pass judgment right? Not like she used to, not like we're doing with deep, thoughtful discussions and analysis, but it's a judgment nonetheless. Like a baby. I'm sure there's food that she likes and doesn't like. She may not like being too cold or too hot, maybe she prefers having her chair parked some places better than others. Those are all judgments and opinions. She just can't voice them anymore."

"Right. God is in the small activities of daily life. Bathing, being fed a meal, having a diaper changed or hair combed. All of it is holy. She can still enjoy these simple acts. Maybe it's just a smile or a comfortable feeling sitting near someone. I do try to be aware of this when I visit. She isn't really the person I remember, she can't play that role anymore. But when I simply sat there with her, staring at an arrangement of plastic flowers, one that had caught her eye for like the fifth time that day, everything felt okay. It happens to all of us. We either burn out or fade away. She's fading away. For the most part we don't get to choose."

"You know, I think Tom Waits would find a kind of messy beauty in a nursing home patient."

"I am absolutely sure you're right. I wonder if he's written a song about them. I wouldn't be surprised at all. Also, I keep thinking that I sure hope I don't end up there. I'll be a handful."

"You got that right. You'll be trying to escape!"

"They'll have to tie me to my chair. I'll try to start a rebellion, an uprising. Then I'll grab the cutest old woman I can find, create a diversion of some kind and we'll go over the wall, make a break for freedom."

"That sounds about right," Jessica said laughing, then looking at her phone. "Whoops, I need to go in a minute. Have to pick up Stella and get her to bed."

"Okay, thanks for coming over. It's been fun. Maybe we should do it again sometime."

"Yeah, maybe… how about Wednesday?" She said with barely a trace of sarcasm.

"Why yes, Wednesday would be lovely," John said somewhat theatrically, gathering up dishes and cups to take into the apartment.

"Do you need any help?"

"No, I've got it. You get home."

"All right, thanks again. I'll bring the food next time. You can start thinking about what sounds good."

"I will. Maybe something extremely complicated with difficult to find ingredients. Or maybe we could just make pizzas on flour tortillas. I'll see you tomorrow morning. Oh, I'm meeting Bev for coffee to talk about plastic."

"That's all you two ever talk about."

"Well, what do you expect? She doesn't know the first thing about Tom Waits."

Jessica laughed and said "Bye" as she got to the bottom of the stairs and turned towards her house. He watched her go, thankful for the hours they were able to spend together and already anxious to see her again.

16

Following his breakfast and daily Bible reading the next morning, John went for a swim. He had been able to get in the water nearly every day. On the very few days that the weather was stormy or the sea too rough he skipped it, but otherwise he was out there. By now he was much stronger than he had been the previous October. He swam parallel to the beach about two hundred yards. Back and forth was nearly a quarter mile. So, he figured eight round trips were about two miles. He would usually do nine just to be safe, and there were times when he would do ten or twelve.

Swimming was a time when he could think freely. Without a real job and with probably too much free time on his hands, he actually had trouble thinking during the day. As intentionally as he tried to relax and just exist, his mind was always working. He wasn't able to do anything for very long, and then would switch to something else. He was filled with nervous energy. But when he swam, because he was technically 'doing something', he felt free to let his mind wander. Some of his best ideas came while swimming.

He would watch the landmarks on the beach glide by- the kayaks at the surf shop, the different restaurants, a short pier, that big log, the grove of palm trees in the empty lot... He would be vaguely aware of these things, just enough to keep from drifting too far out. But mainly he would be thinking. Thinking about plastic, about Jessica, about his children, and about his future.

John had been kicking around an idea in his head for the past few days. It started as just that- a germ of an idea that appeared seemingly out of nowhere. And like a germ that leads to a systemic infection, it grew and multiplied. It began to require more of his attention.

These months in Placencia had been so good for him. He was mentally and physically much healthier. He could barely swim two laps when he had first arrived and now he was doing twenty with about the same amount of effort. He had been anxious, a workaholic, unsure if he even had a true self, much less where to find it. He wasn't even close to where he wanted to be yet, but felt like he was on the right path. He had turned back, which was the real meaning of repentance, and found what seemed to be a truer path and started again.

And then there was Jessica. She was such an amazing friend. He could talk to her about anything and he felt like she understood him. What's more, he actually listened to her thoughts and ideas as well. He felt like he knew her more deeply than almost anyone. Simply putting the time in, focusing on someone besides himself, had really paid off in a way that he didn't know was possible.

So why was he thinking of leaving? Why now, when everything seemed to be going so well? As he swam- four strokes then a breath, four strokes then a breath- he couldn't come up with a precise answer. One reason was that he didn't want to be one of those people who work out all the time, putting physical fitness in front of helping others. As good as it felt to grow stronger, have better lung capacity, bigger muscles, it also made him nervous. The ninety minutes it took to come down here, swim, and then dry off and move on to the next thing could be spent doing something else. He could be saving the world.

Another, more important reason was what he was doing with the other twenty-two and a half hours in the day. He was beginning to feel that he should still be working. He was perfectly capable of seeing patients, of doing surgery. And wasn't he obligated to continue doing those things while he still could? Especially now that he was stronger and mentally healthier. The plastic project was great, and he was sure that there was a lot more that he could do in Placencia to improve the ecological health of the area. It was easy and fun for him, but he was starting to think he needed more.

So, that was the idea that had been growing inside of him. He felt like it was time to go back to work. He wasn't sure what that meant yet. His old job in Kansas City was still waiting for him. But he didn't feel like he could do that. Working full time, taking call, trying to hit production numbers, sitting on committees, seeing wealthy, needy patients… none of it sounded appealing to him. He had talked to Michelle, his old secretary, when he was there the month before. They had a good discussion about everything, and at that time he wasn't really thinking about working as a physician again. But listening to her updates about the people there, some of the drama and just what seemed important to people with that type of job, didn't appeal to him anymore. No, if he did work it would have to be a different set-up. He wanted to work closer to the poor, those that really need a doctor, but who had a hard time finding medical care.

There were certainly people in Kansas City that needed help. People that had been effectively shut out of access to health care. Maybe it would be possible to structure a job there someday, he thought. But he wasn't ready to return yet.

Working as a physician in Belize would require moving to Belize City. It might be possible to do that. He would have to obtain a work visa and talk to people at the big hospitals there. But did he really want that? Living in Belize City would be a lot different than living in Placencia. He could visit the peninsula but would he? How often would he get on a plane and fly down here? Not very often. That idea didn't really appeal to him either.

Where else? The place that kept coming back to him was Uganda. Urologists were really in short supply there. And one advantage that Gulu, Uganda had over other locations that came to mind was the hospital. It was a huge complex with well-trained workers. There was both a nursing school and a medical school in town. There were residents to help and the staff had experienced everything, from AIDS to Ebola to the Joseph Kony years. He would be able to learn and teach, serve and receive.

He looked up and saw that he was veering a little too far away from shore so adjusted his course. Four strokes then a breath, four strokes then a breath...

However, Lacor Hospital in Gulu didn't really have supplies. They were always short and depended on donations from medical missions and philanthropists in order to keep the doors open. He didn't know if they would be able to support another full time surgeon, one who used resources yet didn't bring in much revenue. John started going through different scenarios in his mind, trying to find a way to make it work. One thing that swimming wasn't good for was detailed thinking. He needed a desk, pen, and paper for that. And eventually a telephone and the Internet. But he did have the start of an idea anyway. Next he would need to flesh it out a little, see if it was really feasible and desirable. Talk it over with his children... and Jessica. "Yeah, what about Jessica?" He didn't know if he could leave her...

He had lost count but knew he had swum at least sixteen laps, so headed for shore. He looked at his phone after drying off and discovered that it was later than he had guessed. Maybe he had done twenty laps after all. He hurried down the beach towards Holy Grounds.

When John arrived at the coffee shop, Bev was already seated, her computer open and papers spread out over most of the table. Coffee and a cinnamon roll took up the rest of the room. She looked up as John finished talking to Jessica at the counter. He walked towards her table with a mug of tea and a slice of carrot cake.

"Room for me?"

"I'll make room," she said as she stacked some papers and pushed her dishes closer to the corner of the table. "How was your swim?"

"Perfect as always. I sure love it out there. One of these days I'm just going to keep swimming south. See how far I can get. Maybe I can make it all the way to Honduras."

"Uh, okay, good luck with that. Swimming has never been my thing. I like being on a boat. Or looking at the water from the shore. Or occasionally scuba diving. But swimming? No thanks. I know it's good exercise though." Bev appeared to be in good shape. John wondered what she did to maintain her fitness. Of course, all of the walking required in Placencia may have been enough. Most people walked about everywhere in the small village.

"One of the cool things about swimming two miles is that I can eat this carrot cake with all of this amazing thick sour cream frosting and not worry about gaining weight."

"Yeah, I don't think you have to worry about gaining weight. So, have you heard anything from the city?"

"I was going to ask you the same question. Didn't they have a meeting yesterday? I haven't heard a thing."

"Well, you're in luck because I have. They finally passed it. They're going to place recycle containers next to all of the public trashcans. They'll be clearly marked with the type of plastic that we accept."

"That's great news! And who's going to empty them?"

"More good news- the city will. They'll sort them and put the plastic into the dumpster. They'll check them daily as they empty the other trashcans. It really won't cost anything after the initial investment. They're already emptying the trash."

"That is so cool! Thank you so much for your help with this. It's going even better than I ever could have imagined."

"It's been fun. And so rewarding. Haven't you noticed how nice it is to see less plastic around?"

"So nice. I noticed even this morning, when I finished swimming. The place where I lay my clothes is in kind of an open area that tends to have a lot of trash. But these past few weeks there's been less. People are starting to realize that plastic is recyclable. And it'll get even better once we have the city barrels next to the regular ones."

"We still need to stay on it, of course. It isn't second nature to most people yet. And new people arrive here all the time."

"Yep," John said as he took a sip of his tea. "My favorite thing to say, paraphrasing Catholic Worker Peter Maurin, is 'we must make it easier to do good.' Hey, do you want a bite of this carrot cake? It really is unbelievable. She makes it with finely chopped nuts and I'm telling you, this frosting..."

"Hey, isn't frosting against your religion or something? And the cake for that matter?" Bev said sarcastically.

"It is. I'll have to do penance, wear a hair shirt, that kind of thing... no, I'm vegetarian, not vegan. Although I guess I'm just about vegan. I don't make anything using dairy or eggs anymore, but sometimes I splurge. I'm not allergic to it. I just feel better with a plant-based diet and know that it's better for the world."

"You know I'm just kidding you. I'm basically the same way. I rarely eat meat anymore. Just fish a couple times a week. I avoid the others."

"Why can't everyone be as awesome as us?"

"Seriously! So, what else do we need to do?"

"Well, we had talked about trying to get the resorts on board. The ones up north. What do you think? Have you been up there? Had any luck?"

"I haven't really tried yet. On one hand it would be good advertising for them. Eco-friendly and all that. But on the other, their trash collectors and food deliveries and everything usually come to them. I'm not sure they would bring their plastic this way," Bev said, face frowning a little as she took a drink of her lukewarm coffee.

"Hmm. Yeah, we may run out of volunteers at some point and that job would be time consuming, driving up there in a truck or a golf cart to get their plastic, then bringing it back to the dumpster. Maybe. I wonder if someone from there comes down to shop. Perhaps to buy food at one of the fruit markets or use a bank. Something."

"Possibly. I think they're pretty self-sufficient at Maya Beach, but we could ask. If they do make a trip down here once a month they could drop off their trash then. We know they make it as far as the airport every day, but that's just an SUV so I suppose it wouldn't be very helpful."

"I think it's worth an ask. We should start at the resort hotels, especially the ones closest to the airport, and then work up from there. I guess a dream scenario is that we park a dumpster at about the eight mile marker and have the resorts and condos up there fill it up. I'm confident that they go through a lot of plastic at those places. Maybe more than we do."

Bev wrote some notes on a piece of paper then said, "Okay, you and I can figure out a time to talk to a few of the places. Maybe tomorrow? I think we can just show up and find someone to speak with rather than call ahead. I'll call Daniel's Grove at least."

"Sounds good. Sure you don't want a bite of this cake? It isn't going to last much longer."

"No, really, I'm good. I am going to get more coffee though. Do you need anything?"

When she returned she asked about the apartment buildings.

John looked at his papers. "We have twenty buildings now. Apartments, condos, other multifamily homes. You know what's great about that? I mean, other than the recycling. The volunteers. The way we've been able to involve so many people. Every single one of these twenty properties has a volunteer or two attached to it. Someone who has taken on the responsibility of keeping the area clean, of sorting the plastic, and of getting it to the dumpster. It's so heartwarming."

"It gives people a good feeling to help."

"I believe this project is beginning to change hearts. It creates community, makes people feel like they are a part of something bigger than themselves. The more of these kinds of things residents are involved in the better. It really does change lives. Before you know it they'll be helping install solar panels on apartment roofs and pushing to make the entire village vegetarian."

"One can dream."

"Yep, dreaming is one of my specialties. I believe in the inherent goodness of everyone. At our deepest level we're all peaceful and loving. It's competition and capitalism and the myth of scarcity that cause strife in the world."

Jessica walked up to catch the end of John's comment. "John! Lighten up a little, buddy. It's a beautiful day, we're sitting less than a hundred feet from the beach, and you don't have to go to work today. And what's more, you have me bringing more hot water for your tea." At which point she filled his cup.

"You always know how to put things in perspective, Jess. You're right. We're about finished here anyway. How's it going with the local restaurants and shops? Anything new?"

"Just more of the same. Slowly adding more businesses. They're either not selling plastic anymore or they're offering a place to toss the empties. Most are taking the full trashcans to the dumpster themselves. Not everyone is doing it, but a lot are. It makes me crazy. The stubborn ones who won't change, won't put forth a tiny bit of effort. Like they feel that they have a right to make as much trash as they want."

"It's all right. We're never going to catch every bit of plastic, or better yet, eliminate it. So we shouldn't focus on the holdouts. Who knows? They may come around eventually...Oh, by the way, I have a new favorite Tom Waits song. I was listening later and remembered how awesome 'Chicago' is. It's off of the *Bad As Me* record. Have you heard it? You know how he splits them into brawlers, bawlers, and bastards. Well, this is brawler all the way. It's just a monstrous song. It's full of movement and excitement and anticipation. It makes me want to move to Chicago just to see what the fuss is about."

"Well, with that endorsement I'll have to check it out. I'm a sucker for songs about Chicago. It's hard to beat his bawlers though."

John started to say something else when Bev cut him off. "Well, I think we're about finished with our meeting here."

"Oh sorry. Yeah okay, what do we need to do next?"

Jessica smiled, picked up the empty plates and went back behind the counter and into the kitchen.

"You two make such a cute couple," Bev said as John's eyes focused on the kitchen door.

"We aren't really a couple."

"Well, you could've fooled me."

John sat silently, his expression only slightly betraying his feelings.

"Anyway, it's none of my business. You asked me what was next. Next is we meet tomorrow morning to visit the resorts. How about ten? Do you want to drive?"

"Sure! Any excuse to take the golf cart out for a spin. It's ridiculous how much fun that thing is. I'll pick you up."

Bev had gathered her things and put them in her colorful cloth bag. She flipped the straps up onto her shoulder and, grabbing the coffee mug said, "See you tomorrow, John. Have a great day!"

She carefully balanced her mug on the dishes in the bin and left.

17

The next week John FaceTimed with Kate. She had just returned to school for her junior year at Grinnell. So far she liked all of her classes reasonably well. She was a little worried about physical chemistry but he assured her that was normal. He told her that everyone worried about p-chem. It was just something to get through.

"So… when are you coming to visit me?" Kate asked, half joking.

"How about in six weeks?"

"What? Seriously? What's going on?"

He let her in on his plan. He was going to leave Placencia and move to Uganda.

"Really? How long have you been cooking this up?"

"It isn't set in stone yet. I'm still working out the details, but I think it's going to come together. I'll be able to work at Lacor Hospital. They even have an apartment for me there."

"That's great. I think you'll like working again. I know you've been a little stir-crazy there."

"That's actually not true. It's been an amazing year. I really needed this time to think and to get reacquainted with myself. Something I've neglected for a really long time. But now I think I'm ready to move on. To do something that feels a little more useful to society."

"I won't argue with you. I'm sure you have perseverated about this for weeks."

"I prefer to call it discernment."

"Whatever you say, Dad. Have you told everyone there? What about Jessica? Aren't you like in love with her? Is she coming with you? Or maybe you broke up. That's it isn't it?"

"No, I haven't told anyone. No we didn't break up. I mean we aren't dating. Hey, I don't think it's appropriate for you to talk to your father like this!"

They were both smiling and laughing, enjoying seeing each other and being able to share this moment. John promised he would keep her and Sam in the loop and would come visit both of them before he left for Africa.

The thing was, he did need to tell Jessica. And soon. He had been working on this for the past few days and it had been difficult to keep it to himself. By now he was used to sharing everything with her. They had their standing dinner date tonight and he planned to tell her then. He was nervous but more than ready to get it off his chest.

He had been emailing back and forth with James, the chief surgeon at Lacor hospital. Like John had feared, they simply didn't have the resources to take on another busy surgeon. Short-term mission trips were fine. The visiting team brought most of their supplies with them and paid a small fee for every patient they cared for to help cover any other costs. This worked well as Lacor was not only dependent on funds from outside sources, they literally couldn't get many of the items that specialists needed.

So, what could be done? John didn't want to be a burden, but really at this point had his heart set on joining them in Uganda. He knew it was possible. He wouldn't be the first surgeon to move to Africa to work. In fact he knew several that had done it. People that had sold everything and moved to provide aid in locations where there was a real and desperate need.

After talking back and forth with James, it seemed like there were basically only two issues: money and a few pieces of equipment he needed that they didn't have. There was space in the operating rooms and in the clinics for another surgeon. There was a vacant apartment that he could stay in where some of the other medical staff lived. Most of the supplies that he needed could be ordered. In general they weren't any different than what was already being used.

He would need to bring his own scopes, and it wouldn't hurt to bring some other instruments if he could come up with them. Lacor's mismatched sets weren't ideal for bigger surgeries. So, with that in mind, he had been talking back and forth with a Kansas City representative that he knew from one of the urology specialist companies. The salesman thought there was a good chance he could get the cystoscopes as a donation. There was usually a long process with copious amounts of paperwork, but they were both trying to speed things up. The worst-case scenario was that the scopes would have to be shipped to Uganda rather than carried there by John. If he could have his own instruments it would take a huge burden off of Lacor and free John up to really be able to do the kinds of surgeries that he was trained to perform.

The other issue was money. He had decided when this idea started percolating around in his brain that money wasn't going to stop him. One option would be fund raising. And there was definitely a role for that in this case. He had some experience with raising money for nonprofits, and although it wasn't his favorite thing to do, he thought it would be possible to set up his move to Uganda as a mission. Medical rather than evangelical. But as important as God and religion were in his life, he still had issues with pushing his own ideas on Africans. Most people he had met there had a rich spirituality. He loved sharing and learning and was much less interested in lecturing and indoctrinating. But a medical mission nonprofit might work if he pulled some favors and really set it up in a way that was useful and engaging for the donors.

But he was leaning towards simply doing it on his own. He had run some numbers and it seemed feasible, if a little unconventional. He could donate the amount that the patient would have paid for a surgery. Lacor had already calculated these amounts. If he made the move to Uganda, he wanted to do everything he could to be a blessing rather than a burden. For a hernia repair he would pay three hundred and fifty thousand Ugandan shillings, which was about one hundred and five US dollars. For a larger surgery it could be as much as two hundred. It was still a bargain compared to the ten of thousands it would cost in the US. So, if he were as busy as he thought he would be and did a mixture of clinic and surgery, he would pay the hospital around twenty-five hundred dollars per week. Some weeks it would probably be less. That would mean ten thousand per month and somewhat less than five hundred thousand per year. He obviously couldn't afford that forever but he could for several years.

James had seemed happy with the arrangement. It was hard to know for sure. James had been through a lot and he kept his emotions pretty close to the vest. Especially with e-mail it was hard to know what he really thought. John would have to try to curb his anxiety and take the "yes" at face value.

He was so excited about the whole plan. About living in Uganda full time, rather than visiting one week a year. About staying right there on the hospital grounds. About being able to care for people at no cost to them. Taking money out of the equation was the most exciting thing. To simply see someone, diagnose and treat their problem, perform a surgery, give medications and then send them on their way with no bill, no debt, and no financial trade offs. What a gift to everyone involved.

Jessica was coming over tonight, and he would talk to her about it. There was still some little voice that told him he should just drop the idea and stay here in Placencia. It truly was paradise. Why was he thinking about leaving already?

He had read one of his favorite Proverbs that morning in his *One Year Bible*. For this day in August it was Proverbs 16:1-2. The second verse reads:

"All a person's ways seem pure to them, but motives are weighed by the Lord."

That was the verse he had written down, had prayed on and pondered. In his journal he wrote:

"Isn't that the problem with most people? That we do what seems right. We do what we want to do. What suits our interests at the time. Or the interests of our friends or family. How often do we take into account the common good? How often do we take a long view? The Lord weighs our heart. We can't hide our intentions from God."

He knew that as much as he loved Placencia, as much good as the plastic recycling program was doing, as much as he thought that he deserved to take it easy and simply enjoy life, his heart was being weighed and it was coming up short. It was time to get back out there. He was ready to physically and directly help them. He felt that old familiar clock ticking inside of him and knew he needed to get moving.

"I can't believe we haven't done the Replacements before," John said as he took a bite of the salad that Jessica had brought over for dinner. "We've done Soul Asylum, Husker Du, even Prince, but never the best thing to come out of the Twin Cities. This is really good by the way."

"I know. Weird huh? And thank you. I spent all day on it, can't you tell?"

"The best things are often the simplest."

"True, true. So, what are we doing? Best song? Best album? Worst album?"

"I don't like doing the worst of anything. Everyone has a bad day. Artists have to fill a whole album and they often don't have much time to do it. Or like on *All Shook Down* they were missing half of the band and it was just depressing. No, let's focus on the positive. There is absolutely no way you can argue with the fact that Tim is their best album. And not just the Replacements best album but also one of the best albums of all time. Probably top ten. And that is a perfect theme for a future discussion by the way."

"I agree completely. *Let It Be* and *Pleased to Meet Me* were almost as good. But they are merely the slopes of the mountain peak that is *Tim*."

"Should we do top five? Do you need to hear my 'there can't be a best song' opinion again?'"

"Ugh, no, but let's just start with one and go from there. All right, you go first."

They dove into the discussion. About the relative merits of "Kiss Me on the Bus", "Hold My Life" and "Alex Chilton." About "Answering Machine", "Kids Don't Follow" and "Unsatisfied," and all of the other songs of John's youth, the same ones that Jessica had grown to love years later.

Finally John said, "All of those are great. Amazing even. But I'm going to go out on a limb here and say that the Replacements actually do have a best song. 'Left of the Dial,' from *Tim* is not only their best song but is arguably the best song of the eighties. I know, a discussion for another night. But I'm serious. Think for a minute about how perfect it is. The middle of side B, in a position that no one would reasonably expect a great song to exist, it just comes out of nowhere. That first ringing guitar, the decisive drumming that enters with the second guitar, it's just the most epic beginning. Like they are truly writing for posterity and this is their last big chance. And the lyrics. They're so doleful and timeless and perfect. No one does melancholy like Paul. It's life on the road, it's long distance romance, and it's the heartache that always feels strongest in those years. Those years in your late teens and early twenties when everything was so profoundly important."

"I'm not going to argue with you, John. I love that song so much. The part before the last verse where it kind of switches gears and leads into those mournful words about a pretty girl in a bar. That whole bit there still gives me goose bumps no matter how many times I hear it. Didn't you see them play once?"

"More than once. Twice for sure. Maybe three times. It was a long time ago. My strongest memory of either show is during the *Don't Tell a Soul* tour. Paul was sitting on a chair onstage by himself with his back to the audience playing 'Answering

Machine.' I'd give almost anything to remember more. Maybe someday those neurons will reconnect. I feel like everything is still in our brains, we just have to find ways to access it. They had to have played 'Left of the Dial' you know?"

"Maybe. I know they were pretty erratic."

"I do remember standing right by the stage, basically in front of a huge speaker. How great is life? I mean truly? The things we experience that are just completely transcendent like that? Things that we'll never get back. A pearl of great price. Live music, spiritual moments in which God is nearly palpable, sunny days on a beach when we realize that we're alive, and moments like this, with you. Just sitting and talking in a way that's rare and wild and precious."

As John stopped talking he looked at Jessica, deep into her eyes. He could see her hair around her face, behind one ear. He could see her eyebrows, her clavicle, the small Marvin the Martian tattoo on her arm, and he knew he couldn't go through with it. He knew that he had to stay with her on this balcony eternally. Talking about nothing and everything.

He leaned in and kissed her. Anticipated for so long, filled with relief and desire, with both a blossoming and a fathomless history, it was the most beautiful, perfect kiss. Lost in the timeless moment neither wanted to stop. They would have given anything to continue it forever.

Jessica was the first to pull away. "John, wait...I have something to tell you. Really bad timing I know."

"No kidding," John said after a pause while he struggled to regain his breath. He was still staring at her lips as she spoke, the reality of the kiss more intense than the dream could ever have been.

"I've been wanting to tell you for the past week. I just couldn't do it. And now look at what we've done," she said, smiling sweetly.

The spell broken, John was listening now. "What is it? You know you can tell me anything."

"Oh John... I'm moving back to Illinois."

He didn't know what to say. He was stunned and relieved, horrified and confused all at once.

"You are? When? Why?"

"In about a month... I'm sorry... I should have told you as soon as I knew. But it's just so hard. I am going to miss you so much."

"Why are you leaving? And why now?"

"It's mainly Stella. She's getting older. I feel like I need to get her in a more traditional school. I mean, she's doing fine and it may not be the right thing to do but..."

"It's okay. I understand. You've told me about your concerns before. You're a mom. You get to decide what's right for your daughter. And she comes first for sure."

"Thank you. I knew you would get it. You're too nice to me you know? Aagh! You don't make this easy! But yeah, you know, the school is fine but I want better than fine for Stella. Plus, my mom is there. They're missing out on that grandma and granddaughter relationship."

"Do you have a job lined up?"

"Yes, that's part of the equation. I was offered the manager position in the x-ray department at the community hospital near where my mom lives in Decatur. My tech experience plus running the coffee shop helped. Also, I know the HR director. She and I went to high school together."

"Sounds perfect. What about the shop? Have you told Sandy?"

"I did. She's trying to figure out what to do. She had planned to be here in a month anyway, so she can run it for a while as she interviews and decides her next move."

"Wow...Well, I guess that makes what I have to say a little easier..."

"John, I already know. Or at least part of it. You're planning to move to Uganda."

"You knew? Is that why you...?"

"No. Believe it or not it wasn't directly related. But it made the decision easier. When were you going to tell me?"

"Well, my plan was to make out with you for a while, then ... No, I'm kidding. Tonight. It was going to be tonight. It all just came together in the past day or so. I wanted to be sure I had it all clear in my head. You know, to be certain I was making the decision on my own. With intention and mindfulness. And I feel like I have."

"So, tell me about it okay? So that I understand where you are going, what you'll be doing. Did you talk to your kids?"

John told her about the arrangement with Lacor, about the discussions he'd had with Kate and Sam. He told her everything with openness and she responded the same way, with grace and understanding.

"All of that sounds really good, John. I believe it's just what you need. You can't spend the rest of your life lying on the beach, listening to pop punk bands."

"Hey, watch it! That offends me. I think you know that I listen to a wide variety of genres. There's also a good amount of alt-country, post-hardcore, some Brazilian jazz, and what about the Malian blues?"

"Oh, yes, sorry, you can't lie around on the beach for the rest of your life listening to a wide variety of interesting yet obscure sub-genres of music that have a limited and yet somewhat nerdy appeal."

"That's more like it. Jessica, what will I do without you?"

"Let's not think about that right now, all right?" She leaned towards him and they picked up where they had left off, this time with no interruptions. What they had been carrying hidden was now exposed and they felt at peace, able to focus completely on each other, on what they had been anticipating, if only secretly, since the day they had met.

Late that night, with Jessica fast asleep, John quietly got up, opened his notebook and wrote one sentence under that morning's verse, tracing each of the letters over and over:

"It is so good to be alive."

18

The next several weeks were filled with a compressed version of life: joy, sorrow, rest and work.

Bev and John visited several resorts and new condo developments just north of the airstrip and most were interested in helping. They were able to add the initiative to their marketing materials, which helped them appear more eco-friendly. With the additional contributors, the plastic recycling project filled the dumpster every month.

Bev had agreed to continue the project once John was gone. Her Friends of the Reef group now spent much of their time working on plastic recycling. It had fit in perfectly with their mission and was something that was easy to plug volunteers into. Their mutual friend Tom from Living Water Church planned to take over the apartment and condo piece, making sure that there was a volunteer for every location. There was certainly room for growth, but they were elated by how much plastic was being kept out of the landfill in their little corner of the world.

The recycle bins that the city council had approved had yet to arrive. Island time was in effect as usual, but John had been assured that they would be in place within the month. There were already big trashcans for recyclables at the entrance to the cruise ship pier, which collected a large number of plastic bottles.

Everyone in town seemed to be aware of the project. Bev knew that John's ultimate goal was for people to avoid using plastic altogether. She promised that she would continue to work on that, holding up Holy Grounds as a model. The coffee shop no longer sold any liquid in single use plastic containers and used paper for both hot and cold drinks. A few other businesses had made the switch and several of the Friends of the Reef volunteers had committed to avoiding plastic containers. They drank water from the tap and from the big refillable containers, soda from glass bottles, and juice from cardboard boxes. There was some talk of making the whole village plastic free, but although everyone in town seemed to be aware of the project, John knew it was a long shot.

———————

John had called Kevin, the CEO with his old group in Kansas City, to let him know about the new plan. It was imperative that his medical license remained active. To that end, John had completed the continuing medical education requirement for the year and paid the fees. Kevin assured him that his license was current and not in jeopardy. The door was still open for him to come back in some capacity, most likely as an employee rather than a shareholder. He could possibly work at an outreach clinic in a nearby small town. John said he would keep that in the back of his mind, as he didn't know how long the Uganda experiment would last. In the meantime, they had hired someone to take his place. She was a young, enthusiastic woman that had grown up locally and who seemed like a good fit for the group.

He did learn that the cystoscope donation had been approved. He would receive two complete sets of scopes. This was a huge relief and a blessing. It guaranteed that he would be able to perform the kinds of procedures that he hoped to do there. He was always amazed and gratified by the way people wanted to help. Inevitably there was fear and defensiveness when it came to trying to level the playing field, or to decrease the vast inequality that exists in the world. But when concrete, one-on-one interactions were needed, people were generally giving and kind. If there were only a way to broaden that vision. Involving people in hands-on volunteer work seemed to be the best approach.

John's sister Deborah said that he was welcome to sleep in her basement guest room for as long as he needed. It would be for about two weeks, as he also planned to visit Sam at school in Texas. Luckily Kate was able to come home for a few days so he didn't have to arrange a trip to Iowa. The time would go very quickly there, but he would do his best to make the hours spent with his children as meaningful and special as possible.

The final piece of the puzzle was getting a work visa from the Ugandan Embassy in the US. It sounded like it all was going to work out. James said everyone was looking forward to having him there. He already had a list of over a hundred patients to see. As excited as he was to get started, John needed to tell himself to settle down. He was in this for the long haul and wasn't going to treat this like a one-week mission trip. On those he tended to stay up all night, sleeping only fifteen total hours during a five-day workweek. No, this was going to be his home. He planned to work, study and pray. To live a balanced life.

It was all so exciting that at times he even forgot that he and Jessica wouldn't be seeing each other any more. They had become nearly inseparable, determined to make the most of their limited time together. They chose to live vigorously in each instant. She had been able to push back her departure so that they could fly out together. From Placencia to Belize City. From Belize City to Houston. Then from Houston to... well, they tried not to think about that.

They had long talks at night and lazy mornings after Stella was at school. Jessica stayed over when she could, taking advantage of the goodwill of her friend who had a daughter Stella's age. John continued his daily Bible reading and journaling, but his entries became merely detailed descriptions of their days. Where they went, what they ate, what the weather was like, who they talked to... anything to help him cement the moments into his brain. He never wanted to forget those times. By writing them down it made everything seem more real. He did anything he could to slow the hours. And yet he knew that it was rapidly coming to an end.

"Do you remember the other night? When you told me your favorite Replacements song?" Jessica said as they sat on the balcony, during the final hours of their final week together, their emotions as thick as the salty evening breeze.

"How could I forget that night?"

"Why did you choose that song? It's because we're leaving, right?"

"No. Not really. I mean maybe. 'Left of the Dial' has always been my favorite. But maybe that's why. You know, that emotion of longing and loss. This emotion that we're feeling right now. I don't think there's anything stronger. Love, loss, missing someone, being so connected and integral to each other, it makes separation a physical event. Not simply emotional but physical. I'm going to miss you so much Jessica. It makes me literally sick to think about it."

"That's a strange thought, but I think it might be true. Love and loss are felt in different ways, but combined the effect multiplies doesn't it?… Me too. I think I'm going to be sick also. I must really be in love with you!"

"We're so in love that we make each other throw up. How pathetic is that?"

They both laughed. They laughed until they cried, cried until they embraced, embraced until they could speak again.

John said, "This is so difficult and ridiculous. Leaving each other right now. But it's necessary. We both are whole, real people. With whole, real lives. I mean we aren't sixteen. And who really knows what will happen right? On one hand, we had a great time. We have a wonderful connection, we had deep meaningful discussions, and we developed an amazing and rare friendship. And maybe all of that stands alone. A monument to the way life can be. On the other hand, it doesn't have to end. We can stay in touch. Maybe you'll decide to move to Uganda. Maybe I'll move to Decatur. Maybe we'll meet back here next year on this very same balcony. The world is a wonderful, surprising place and we still have all of our lives ahead of us, you know? We can still feel pain and love and sorrow and excitement and anticipation. Right? Your turn... what do you think? Is there hope for us?"

Jessica was watching him with amusement and familiarity and love. She looked into his eyes, ran the back of her fingers on his cheek and said, "I think you are awfully cute but sometimes you talk too much." She leaned forward and kissed him. And that was the perfect answer.

───────────

Three days later, in George Bush Intercontinental Airport, John, Jessica, and Stella had walked as far as they could together, they had gone through immigration, transferred their bags, made it through security, shared cups of frozen yogurt, but were now headed to different terminals. They stopped off to the side, out of the way of the rushing crowds. There were no more words. Jessica and John hugged tightly, kissing one last time until Jessica said, "We have to go. But quick, favorite Husker Du song?"

"It's the 'The Girl Who Lives on Heaven Hill'. Of course."

Her eyes wet and shining, she whispered, "I knew it."

19

Gulu, Uganda

One year later

There was never any doubt what verses John would focus on that morning. For September 24 there was a long passage from Isaiah, a chapter from Ephesians, a longish Psalm and the usual two verses from Proverbs. He read all of them carefully, thoughtfully and prayerfully. But it was Isaiah 43:18-19 that literally jumped from the page.

> *"Forget the former things; do not dwell on the past.*
> *See, I am doing a new thing!*
> *Now it springs up; do you not perceive it?*
> *I am making a way in the wilderness and streams in the wasteland."*

He had been awake for what seemed like hours the night before, repeating the Jesus prayer over and over. His mind wouldn't settle down and he wasn't sure why. He knew his mom would die one day. Obviously. She was eighty years old, had rapidly progressive dementia, hadn't been eating, and had been thin and vacant when he had seen her three months prior. What did he expect? But for reasons that he couldn't comprehend, the news had hit him hard. He had kept it together when his sister

Deborah called but as soon as he hung up, when he had a minute to process what she had said, he broke down.

John hadn't cried like that since Ellie's death. He couldn't figure it out. Ellie died suddenly and completely unexpectedly with decades of unfinished life ahead of her. His mom had passed away quietly and naturally, surrounded by people that loved her. It was a complex combination of guilt in not being around enough, and of simple fear about his own mortality. He no longer had a mother in this world. It was a surreal, dismal feeling.

He had been clarifying things in his mind all night, making plans and looking at different paths. And now, reading those verses from Isaiah, well, that had done it. There was no doubt in his mind. He was going home.

There was no hurry. Her body was to be cremated and the plan was to wait a while for the memorial service. His uncle was out of the country and most of the grandkids were in school and would have trouble getting home quickly. His stepdad was going to arrange the service for Thanksgiving weekend so that everyone could attend. So, John didn't have to decide anything right that minute. But he was pretty sure he already had.

He had spent a year in Placencia, a year in Gulu, and now it was time to go. He needed to face facts. He wasn't made to live anywhere else. He was no Wendell Berry, with an ancient patch of dirt that had been in the family for generations to which he felt tied. But he did agree that people were of a place. Their religion, habits, sense of humor, and pace of speaking were regional. Their bodies were accustomed to a certain climate and particular food. They were made of and for the local water. They were used to the way that people interacted with each other. They felt at peace with the scenery, the layout of the streets, the direction of the wind, the relative humidity, the natural landmarks, the pollen, and the sounds at night. All of these things and more were both genetically and environmentally ingrained. People who grew up in a place could live anywhere in the world and feel comfortable, do good works, make friends and assimilate to some degree, but it would never feel quite like home.

John had been thinking about it for some time now. As much as he loved living in Uganda, as much as he knew he was needed, as beautiful as the weather was with the year-round flawless temperatures, as lovely and gracious the people, he knew that he would need to go home at some point. Maybe it had been the brief trip to Kansas City that summer, spending time with the twins. Simply basking in their energetic auras had been so amazing.

He felt a tremendous amount of guilt as he thought about leaving. But it needed to be done. He decided not to tell anyone quite yet as he worked through the details and timing in his mind.

After he finished a breakfast of boiled millet and fruit with Ugandan tea, he left for the hospital. He strolled past the other apartments and the Ebola martyrs memorial, up the short drive and over to the surgical side of Lacor where he had his clinic. During the short walk, he almost changed his mind. Even with the unrelenting demands on time, the massive amount of need, and the brokenness of health care, he really loved it there. The thought of leaving was too difficult to deal with that morning.

Agnes was waiting for him in a hallway full of patients when he arrived. He wished her good morning and said he would be right back as he searched for Mary to round. This was the best time to see patients because the floors were being mopped, which meant that the family members, the mats, the food and assorted bags were all out on the veranda. He wanted to be sure that nothing severe had happened overnight. Often there were problems that weren't urgent enough to disturb him, but still needed to be addressed sooner rather than later.

"Good morning, Mary," John said when he found her adjusting a patients IV dressing.

"Good morning, Mr. John. How did you sleep?"

"Wonderfully, as always. How is everyone this morning?"

"No problems, Mr. John. Do you wish to see your patients now?"

"Sure, let's do it before it gets too hectic here."

The two of them went around to see the post surgical patients. He removed catheters, checked and redressed wounds, listened to Mary's report and made plans for the day for each of the patients. He found Fatima, the young girl that had the ectopic ureter repair two days prior. Mary brought her mom from the veranda.

"How are you?" he asked the girl.

She smiled shyly and nodded upwards a little.

"Have you been up out of bed? Have you walked?"

Mary translated back and forth, saying she had been out of bed and that she didn't have pain.

John looked at her wound and found it to be intact and dry, closed with dissolvable sutures and sealed with glue. He didn't use the glue on everyone. Everything was in short supply at Lacor. Nothing was used without a reason, without thinking through whether this patient needed it more than that one. But John treated Fatima a little differently than the rest. He had high hopes for her and wanted her recovery to go smoothly, with no wound problems.

"Everything looks perfect. Let's take her catheter out today. We'll see how she does."

Fatima and her mom had big smiles when Mary explained the plan to them. It was finally time to discover whether a miracle had occurred. They would see whether she could stop wearing multiple layers of rags to catch the constant stream of urine, and whether she would finally be able to go back to school.

John returned her smile and patted her leg. "I'll be back to check on you this afternoon, Fatima. Don't be afraid to move around today. You can wander the hallways all you want. You'll probably be ready to go home tomorrow."

More translation back and forth, more smiles and blessings as John backed out of the room, telling Mary he would see her later. He found Agnes at the nursing station and with a smile and a nod she indicated that he was ready to begin. She ushered in the first patient, a man with Down's syndrome accompanied by his father. He was carrying ancient appearing x-rays and dirty, crumpled medical records. David came in right behind them.

"Good morning, David. How are you this morning?"

"I am fine. A little tired but okay."

"Were you out too late last night?"

David grinned but didn't answer. He took the patient's records and handed them to John.

"Please, sit," John smiled and pointed to the chair. The father sat down while his son remained standing by his side. The boy had a large piece of fabric wrapped around his waist. He was calm but appeared wary.

John looked at the papers and the x-rays. The patient was thirty years old. He had been seen several times over the years at Lacor for the same thing. He spoke to the father. "Tell me why you have come here today."

"It is about my son. He has a serious problem. We have been seeing doctors about this for many years and no one has been able to help," he said in very clear English.

The man pulled the boy closer. He took off the fabric exposing a huge scrotum that hung nearly to the boy's knees. His legs were somewhat bowed, whether naturally or in response to the large scrotum, John couldn't tell.

He put on gloves and examined him. It was the size of a basketball and very heavy. Many enlarged scrotums are the result of a hydrocele, a fluid collection around the testis. But this one didn't feel like that. And an ultrasound report confirmed that there was no fluid inside. No, this was due to a blockage of the lymph channels. Not tremendously uncommon in undeveloped countries, it often caused elephantiasis of the legs as well. His legs weren't as obviously involved.

"How long has he had this?"

"Many years. I don't know exactly. Ten? Probably more."

"And you've seen other doctors? No one would help?"

"Yes, Marcus and I have visited many doctors. In Kampala a doctor agreed to remove it but we couldn't afford the price. I am a poor man. We have seen American doctors also but, again, no one could help us. Please. Can you make my son well?"

John had Marcus get up on the exam table. It seemed like the swelling stopped just before it reached the pubic bone. He was fairly confident he could remove nearly all of the mass yet leave enough to cover things back over without using skin grafts.

There was a chance that it would recur but it would likely take many years.

"I can do it," John told the man.

"Oh, that is wonderful! At last our prayers have been answered," he said. Then he paused… "But what will it cost? I don't have very much money…"

"It will cost you nothing. We will do it for free."

The man's face lit up with shock and gratitude. "Thank you, doctor. You have no idea how much this means to Marcus and me. We had heard that there was a chance that you could help. We traveled very far to come here to see you, praying that this would be the time that God blesses Marcus. My son doesn't like to come to see doctors, to wait at hospitals. He can't speak but he knows that people stare at him. That people make fun of him. He can't pass his urine normally and can't sit comfortably. He has this heaviness to carry around everywhere. It hurts me so much to see him like this."

Marcus was sitting on the bed with his legs bent in a frog like position, the massive scrotum filling the space between his legs. He watched his father with interest, seeming to understand what was being said.

"I will do it," John repeated. "Depending on what I get into he may lose a lot of blood so we will have some available. There is a risk of wound infection. This lymph filled tissue may not heal well. I'll leave a drain but it still may fill up with fluid. We'll hope for the best, keep him on antibiotics, have him wear tight underwear for a few weeks…"

"Anything doctor. I trust you. What day will this be?"

"Tomorrow. David can you help them get scheduled? I would like to do him first, so push back whoever's in front of him. Allow a couple of hours. Let's check his hemoglobin today just to be safe, and make sure we have a unit of blood available."

David had been listening to the exchange but now got up to lead Marcus and his father out of the room and down to the head nurse's desk to fill out papers and give more instructions. Marcus' father thanked John once more and then they were gone down the hallway.

John took a drink of water as the next patient came through the door, closed it behind him, handed John his papers and then sat in the single open chair.

His mind wandered as he waited for David to return. The patient, like many there, smelled like a wood fire. Like the small village that John had visited several years ago. On that trip he had been able to spend the night with a family in a traditional family compound. It consisted of five one-room mud huts surrounding an open area that was about the size of the living room in John's house. There was a hut for the father, one each for his two wives, and two for his children and the others that stayed there. There was a donkey behind a gate in the compound and several chickens running around. In the open area, food was prepared and laundry hung. There was an area for a cooking fire off to the side, and a place for a bigger fire for warmth in the center.

When John was there, the men sat on benches just outside the walls of the compound day and night, telling jokes, reminiscing, and at times just sitting quietly. They drank tea prepared slowly and methodically on a tiny coal fire, the little shot glass of strong sweet tea passed around in turn to everyone in the circle. John was included in the drink but not the conversation, missing most of the words due to the language barrier and the lack of context.

The women talked and worked. Pounding millet, making dinner, cleaning up meals, sweeping the dusty ground with a hand broom, and feeding the babies, the women were in constant motion. Bending, lifting, pounding, carrying, nursing, and sweeping, most of the work was done in community. The man's wives worked together, older children helped, other women joined in. It was difficult, unending work and yet there was fellowship.

At night a hut was cleared out, mattresses appeared, likely from their own sleeping areas, and the visitors were made to feel welcome. Where there was no room they made room. They literally had nothing. Nothing hanging on the walls of the hut. Although the women dressed beautifully, there was no closet or wardrobe for clothes. No extra food. No television. No books or magazines. No furniture besides a few chairs, two wooden benches and the thin mattresses. There were blankets, batteries and tools. For a family of at least eight people their belongings could have fit in the back of John's Chevy Cruze.

It was one of the most important events in John's life, seeing that for the first time. He had seen poverty before. He had worked in the free clinic, had volunteered at Loaves and Fishes many times, and felt like he had an idea how poor people lived. But this was a revelation. He felt so out of place and disoriented when he got home and when he looked at all of the things he and his family had accumulated. The house was utterly filled with things, ninety percent of which now seemed unnecessary and unfaithful. Paintings on walls, decorations and mementos on shelves, rooms with furniture that was rarely used, a guest room bed that wasn't slept in, boxes of things in closets, in the garage, and in the basement that were never looked at or enjoyed.

The clutter began to feel like a barrier to the way he wanted to live. There had to be a happy medium between the extreme abundance of unnecessary things throughout his house and the minimalism of a simple Ugandan mud hut. It was another turning point in John's life, and played a large part in what had caused him to choose Gulu as his new home.

By living simply, first in Placencia and then in Gulu, he felt closer to God. He wasn't distracted by electronics. He didn't feel guilty about a house full of unnecessary junk. He didn't have a refrigerator full of food that was going to have to be thrown out because he bought more than he could ever consume. Seeing that village had definitely changed him. He knew that if he did go back to the States he would have to continue to live simply. It was very unclear what that meant, but the last thing he wanted was to start accumulating things again.

David returned and John snapped out of his reverie.

"What has brought you to see me today?"

Another patient, another difficult problem. Most of the health issues he saw were a direct result of being poor. They had no preventative care and inadequate access to health care for acute problems. Many had ailments that should have been treated months if not years before.

He continued to see patients throughout the morning. After noon Agnes came by to tell him that it was teatime. He finished up with the final patient and walked him to the desk to schedule surgery before heading down the hall for tea.

20

In the break room he had a small ripe banana and tore off a piece of chapatti to have with his tea. He talked for a moment with Mr. James, who was leaving just as John arrived.

"You are working on Father Paolo today," James said.

"Yes. I think he's third this afternoon. He's most likely just bleeding from his prostate. That's the most common scenario in his age group anyway."

"I hope you're right. Well, let me know what you find and if you need anything from me."

John said he would. James dropped his banana peel in a box on the floor and left. John finished his tea, changed into the oversized communal green operating room clogs and headed to the preoperative area where his first patient was waiting.

"Mr. John! How are you? Are you ready to start?" asked the anesthetist. She was leaning over the patient's arm, taping a dressing on his hand to secure the IV needle into place.

"I am. I see you are about ready also, right? Have you seen Stephen?"

"Yes. I'm taking him back right now. Stephen is around."

That was always the answer. It could mean she had seen him two minutes ago or yesterday. When a person said someone was around it just meant that he was in the country. Around. Not around. Those were the only two categories it seemed.

"Okay, thanks. I'll be back there in a few minutes."

Stephen showed up just as the surgery began. He assisted John on that one and the next. After helping move the second patient to the recovery area, John walked over to Father Paolo who looked small and vulnerable in his thin pink and white striped hospital gown.

"Hi Father, how are you? Any more bleeding overnight?"

"No. None since yesterday morning."

"I'm not sure if I asked you, but any other symptoms with this? Burning with urination? Frequency? Slow stream?"

"Yes, I've noticed that over the past few months I have gone more frequently. And more urgently. It burns sometimes."

"Have you lost any weight?"

"I don't weigh myself so it is hard to know. I don't think so. Are you worried about what you will find?"

"A little. But we will know soon enough right? Are you ready?"

"I am if you are."

John moved out of the way to allow the anesthetist to come closer to start an IV and ask her own set of questions.

She took Paolo back to the theater, and once he was asleep, positioned and prepped, John carefully looked in his bladder with a cystoscope. He knew there was a problem right away. The prostate looked normal. It was short and not irritated or inflamed, but his bladder was full of cancer. The normal landmarks were obliterated. The ureteral orifices, from which urine drains in from the kidneys, weren't visible. Not a good sign. Stephen and Alice were watching on the monitor. Both remained silent.

John asked Alice to set up the resectoscope. With the cauterizing metal loop he was able to remove some of the tumor. It was everywhere and although he knew it wasn't going to be curable by removing it endoscopically, he did what he could. He cut out small strips of tumor with the device and then washed the bladder out periodically, catching samples of the tissue to send to the pathologist. He was able to do it in such a way that there was very little bleeding. He eventually removed enough tumor to fill a sixty-milliliter specimen container. John was satisfied that he had resected most of it around the bladder neck, which would help ease Paolo's symptoms for a while. He placed a big catheter and set up an irrigation system to have fluid drain in one lumen of the catheter, wash around his bladder, drain back out another lumen and then down into the drainage bag. The irrigant ran fairly clear when he finished. The whole process took about ninety minutes.

John helped Alice and Stephen get him moved over to the hospital bed, being careful not to pull on the catheter. Paolo was just starting to wake up by the time he was wheeled over to the recovery area. He tried to ask what John had found but was still too sleepy to focus. John went to change clothes and round on the inpatients while Paulo recovered.

———

After checking on everyone, giving a few orders, and saying goodnight to Mary, he came back to talk to Father Paolo. By now he was fully awake. The head of the bed was up a little. The bladder irrigant ran in clear and out a very light pink.

"Hi Father. How are you feeling?"

"Good. I feel fine. I don't hurt at all. I thought I would feel pain."

"No, this kind of surgery doesn't usually cause pain."

"So how did it go? What did you find?"

John carried one of the three metal chairs in the pre-op area over to Paulo's bed. When he sat down his face was a little lower than Paulo's so he found himself looking up at him.

"Everything went fine, Father, but I'm afraid that I have some bad news."

The priest's expression was serious. He appeared more anxious than John had expected him to be. "You can tell me."

"Your prostate looks fine. It's your bladder. I'm sorry to tell you that you have bladder cancer."

"…Oh. I see. Is it bad?"

John paused to find the right words. Paolo looked scared, even becoming a little agitated. "Aren't old priests supposed to be unflappable?" he thought to himself. Paolo had certainly downplayed his concern. He had put off telling anyone about the blood for at least six months. John was certain that the tumor had been there much longer than that. Probably for years.

The most common type of bladder cancer in Uganda differs from that found in the United States, where most of the disease is caused by smoking. Schistosomiasis is very common in Sub-Saharan Africa but virtually unheard of in the West. Infecting over two hundred million people, it is caused by a small worm that begins its life cycle in freshwater snails. The organism eventually becomes free swimming and penetrates the skin of swimmers and bathers in stagnant pools of water. From there the worm sets up shop in mesenteric veins. As it grows and matures it ends up in veins of the bladder, in time releasing its eggs through the host's urine. The chronic irritation of the eggs and the worms cause an inflammatory response that often leads to cancer.

While schistosomiasis itself is treatable with medication, the cancer it causes is not. It is often very advanced at diagnosis, a combination of the disease process itself and the inherent delay due to the scarce health care resources. Radiation and/or removal of the bladder are usually necessary. Neither of these was available at Lacor.

"Yes," John finally answered, "It's bad…I was able to remove a portion of it. Enough so that the pathologist will be able to make a definitive diagnosis. Enough so that you should be able to urinate more easily. I'm surprised you were able to go at all."

"It was difficult."

"Well, it should be easier now."

"Thank you for that."

"You'll wear that catheter overnight to let things begin to heal a little. If your urine is clearer tomorrow I'll remove it and we'll see how you do."

"Good. Thank you."

"You should be able to resume your usual activities after it's out."

"Okay…but what comes next?" Paolo's expression was frozen. He continued to look anxious and worried.

"Right. Well, I want you to get an ultrasound and a chest x-ray. Those can be done tomorrow. Ideally you will get a CT scan. Will you be able to return to Italy for treatment? That would be best medically. You could do your CT there. Or maybe in Kampala before you go."

"Yes. I will call my bishop and fly home to Verona soon. It will be nice to go home. It's been over five years since I have been there."

"You have family in Verona right?"

"Yes, a lot of family. Brothers, sisters, nieces, nephews, cousins… I miss them all terribly."

"I know you do. You have given such a large portion of your life to the people here. Your servant heart is such an inspiration to me. But right now it's time to take care of yourself. You know that it takes time to get a pathology report here at Lacor. I'm hoping it will all be back well before you get to Italy. You can bring your CT films with you."

"Thank you for your kindness, Mr. John. You are a comfort to me."

"I want you to get the best care available. And I'll help in any way that I can. Now, you get some rest. Can I get you anything? Do you have a way to get food tonight?"

"Yes, a brother will bring my evening meal."

"Okay, good. I'll check on you later. Have the nurse call me if you need anything, all right?"

"I will. Thank you."

John left to check on the inpatients. He found Mary and then they went to visit Fatima. She was fully dressed, looking happy and rested.

"Good evening Fatima. How are you doing?"

"She says she is doing well. She is very happy," Mary translated.

"So, everything is good? She hasn't leaked urine?"

"She says everything is fine. She is not having any problems urinating. She and her mother thank you for giving back her life."

"Tell Fatima and her mother that it has been my pleasure. That I want her to be joyful and successful. To go to school and get a good education."

"She says that she will. She wants to study to become a nurse."

"That's wonderful! That would make me so happy. It would be the best way possible for you to help others, to give back. You will be a wonderful compassionate nurse because you have been through so much yourself."

Mary translated John's sentiments back to Fatima. She looked shyly at the floor, smiling broadly. Her mother made a slight bow, holding her palms together.

John gave Mary some final instructions to pass along. She told them that she would be back to discharge Fatima in a few minutes.

Next they checked on a young patient next door. He was resting quietly following his bilateral hernia repair. His parents and three other family members were in the room. They were on his bed, and on his roommate's bed, and on a mat on the floor sharing a meal of millet ugali and what was probably a bean soup of some kind. Everyone was smiling and enjoying themselves in the tight space. Even John's other patient, being somewhat crowded out of his bed by the boy's family, was smiling. He was sharing in their dinner and their conversation.

"Good evening. How's everyone doing in here?"

The boy's father spoke for all when he said, "Everything is fine. Thank you for all that you have done for my son."

"You are very welcome. Is he having any pain?" John asked as he had the boy lie back so that he could look at his incision.

"No. No pain. He is doing well."

"That's great. And what about you?" he asked the other patient in the room. "Your urine looks clear. Are you doing all right? Need anything?"

The father of the boy translated back and forth from Acholi and told John that the man was fine. That he didn't need anything.

"Excellent, well, you all have a good night. I'll see you in the morning."

John left them to change out of his white coat and scrubs. The hours had slipped away from him and he was supposed to meet Stephen for dinner in less than thirty minutes. There was little chance he would make it in time, but he was going to try.

21

It was a treat to get away from the hospital occasionally. There was a surprisingly authentic pizza restaurant in Gulu. With the Italian influence at Lacor and all of the Westerners working at NGOs there must have been enough customers to support it.

Hurrying across the busy road outside the hospital complex, he approached the *boda boda* stand. The drivers were lounging on and around their bikes, talking and drinking tea. It was dark and he wasn't sure but thought he recognized one of the drivers. He had used him before and survived so he decided to go with that guy. The drivers had seen John come across the road for food before. They weren't shocked that this pale skinned fellow wanted a ride, but it was still a novelty.

He held on as the motorcycle sped across the still fairly new asphalt on the way back to town. The heavy rains that were a part of life in Uganda already had damaged sections. The driver expertly swerved at the right spots to avoid the big potholes. Sometimes he drove on the right side of the road if that was the more direct route, other times he stayed to the left.

In Uganda the larger vehicle always won. Pedestrians jumped out of the way of motorcycles. Motorcycles swerved off to the side for cars. Cars for trucks, trucks for busses, and the busses pulled over to the side to let big semis come through if needed. A friend of John's from Kampala who had visited the United States said that the thing that struck him the most about the country is how those on foot were treated. In Uganda they weren't even noticed by a driver, they were expected to stay out of the way of vehicles. "But in America," he said, "pedestrians are like kings. Everyone stops in their tracks if someone decides to cross the road." He laughed as he told the story, incredulous.

John's driver got him safely to the restaurant in Gulu. Stephen was already there at a table, drinking Coke out of a glass bottle. The same problem with plastic that John had spent so much of his time in Placencia fighting was in Gulu as well. Plastic everywhere. Those ubiquitous black bags that had been recently banned in Rwanda were still jokingly referred to as the Uganda state bird. Looking up, one could always see several floating in the sky. Thankfully there was still a strong market for glass soft drink bottles, just like in Central America.

"Hey Stephen, you made it! Have you been waiting long?" John asked as he pulled up a chair.

"No, not long at all. Do you want something to drink?" he asked, signaling for attention.

"I would like a large bottle of water please," he told the waiter. "And two glasses with no ice." As much as he disliked plastic, bottled water was still a necessity. Or at least he assumed it was. He wasn't going to test the Gulu municipal water supply tonight.

"I would like a margherita pizza please. Stephen, did you order?"

"Make that two. That sounds very good."

The waiter brought back a bowl of peanuts with the water and glasses, arranged everything on the table and left as Stephen and John resumed their conversation.

"I am so sorry to hear about your mother. So, she had been sick for a long time?"

"Yes and no. She had always been very healthy. It was just the dementia. It came on rapidly and relentlessly over about two years. She didn't even know me when I visited in the summer."

"That is sad. And you have one sister? There are such small families where you live."

"Not every family is small. But yes, much smaller than here. We're pretty close. Close enough. She lets me stay in her basement when I visit," John said, laughing.

"Family can always stay with family in Uganda. It is never a question. Distant cousins that we've never met will stop in for weeks sometimes."

"That's true huh? What do you think of that? Does it bother you? The big households. No privacy."

"It's just a way of life. We can always make room for one more. It isn't about what I think or what I want. It's just the way that it is, the way it has always been…. People that move to the city have smaller families; they have fewer people in their rooms. But even in Kampala, if I need a place to stay I could drop by the home of about twenty different cousins, aunts, uncles, and friends and they would squeeze me in."

"That's a wonderful thing. It's something I have seen many times here and is a much more authentic and healthy way to live. Something that has been forgotten in the US and we're definitely poorer for it."

Their pizza came as they continued to talk. Two friends some twenty years apart in age, but they had felt a bond upon meeting during one of John's earlier trips. That bond had only grown stronger this year.

"You are going back then? For the funeral?" Stephen asked. After finishing off over half of his pizza, he drained the Coke and poured water in the empty glass.

"Not right away. But yes, in a few weeks."

"How long will you stay?"

John paused before answering. Stephen looked at him differently now. He could sense by the pause that something was going on.

"Stephen, I think I'm moving back home."

Home. He had said it out loud. As much as he loved Uganda, it wasn't his home. It never could be. He could have friends like Stephen, James, and some of the others that he had met in the past year. He could be comfortable in his apartment. He could love his patients, the Lacor staff, the warm weather, the simple life, but it would never be home.

"Really? Back to Kansas?"

"Well, technically Missouri. Yes."

"How long have you known?"

"I think it must've been in the back of my mind for a while. It came to the front when Deborah called about my mom."

"You are sure?"

"Ninety percent sure."

"Who else knows?"

"You're the first."

"Wow, I hadn't expected this. Will you come back to visit?"

"Well, I'm still thinking this through. But yes, of course I would still like to come back on a regular basis. Maybe twice a year for a week or two."

"Can I ask why?"

"Of course. But, I'm not sure I can explain it. It just feels like it's time. You know, I moved to Belize in Central America to retire, to relax and get away from my life. To try to live simply and intentionally. Everything was just going way too fast and I needed a break. After several months there I began to miss work. Real work. The kind of work that I'm good at. Anyone can start a recycling program…"

Stephen looked at him questioningly. He hadn't heard about that yet.

John continues, "It's a long story…. The point is not everyone can do urology. And of the small subset that can, an even smaller subset would leave a profitable practice to care for the poor. So I felt like I might be spending too much time relaxing, wasting the few moments that I have on this planet when I could be helping people that really needed me. People that have no other hope."

"So you came to Uganda."

"Yes, so I came to Uganda."

"But that doesn't explain why you are leaving."

"Whoops, trying to change the subject. I just need to go home. I feel like I'm missing times with my family, with old friends, and with a new friend... I miss my church. I even miss the seasons a little. I'm crazy to want to go back in the fall. Maybe I should put it off until April..."

"That would be fine with me, but I understand. I don't know if I could move away from my home. Not permanently."

"People do it all the time. Some people never put down roots anywhere. But for those of us that do, it's hard to get the roots to grow anywhere else."

"Well, I will miss you. You have helped me so much. I have improved greatly as a clinician and a surgeon this year. It's because of you. You are a great teacher and mentor."

"Thank you Stephen. You're a good student. You learn quickly and have always been a joy to be around. And I want you to know that I'm not abandoning you. I'll be back and we'll stay in touch. It's not the same of course..."

"I know it's not. But I am glad to know that I can still contact you if I have a question or need help."

"Right. I'll do anything. When you finish your studies- and I know you will- and become a urologist it'll be the most incredible thing."

"It is my dream. Urologists are desperately needed in Uganda. As are all specialists. We simply don't train enough. Just a couple per year for a population of thirty-six million and growing. It's crazy. And the ones that are trained either stay in Kampala or move out of the country. They follow the money. Even Lacor, one of the largest medical centers in the country, can't afford to hire a specialist even if one did decide to come here."

"I know. It's a big problem. But you're part of the solution, Stephen. You just stay the course. Finish your training here in Gulu, return to Kampala for your specialty training, and we'll figure something out. Your dream is to become a urologist. My dream is to have you here in Gulu. To be able to care for your own people in your own town. To be near your family. To be an example to your siblings and cousins that achieving an education is important for a person's own personal satisfaction and growth but also for the good of the community."

"I would love to return here. It doesn't seem possible now, but you have taught me that all things are possible with God."

"That's exactly right. I want you to know that I'm committed to helping make this happen. That I won't let you fail for the sake of saving a few dollars. You do the work, study, keep progressing and I can help with the rest."

"Speaking of helping with the rest. Do you have money to pay for the pizza? I'm a little low," Stephen said, smiling.

"Okay, I see how you are," John motioned the waiter over to get the bill and to package up the leftovers. He had only eaten two slices. He gave his remnant to Stephen who would share it with his roommates. "I'm going to begin telling the others tomorrow, starting with Mr. James."

"So, you'll leave in a few weeks?"

"Yes, I need to let my sister know. Hopefully I can stay with her again until I figure out what I'm going to do. I have a couple ideas. I do want to work some. I've found that it's necessary. And I want to continue to live as simply as I possibly can. I suppose living in the basement of my sister's house is pretty simple. But it isn't a good long term solution."

"And your children?"

"I need to talk to them as well. They'll be excited to have me closer, I'm sure. We can see each other more often. Holidays, and maybe longer in the summer. Like I said, it's just time to get home, to get closer to everyone."

John paid the bill, and they left. They walked a block to the line of *boda bodas* on the corner. Stephen talked to the drivers in Acholi. Laughing at jokes that John wouldn't understand if he lived there another ten years, Stephen motioned to the driver that John was to go with. They sped off, leaving the dim glow of town behind in an instant, only the inadequate headlight of the motorcycles illuminating the night.

22

Upon returning, John sat for a moment and reflected on the day. He wrote a few lines under the morning's Bible verse:

"Once again I am ready to do a new thing. Not novelty for the sake of novelty. Not simply returning from where I came, but returning with new insight, fully restored, if not fully healed. Trusting that my instinct is right, that I am being guided by that flicker of spirit that is within me. Not my will but yours, oh Lord. Trusting that I can do good there, that I can stay faithful to my true self. I won't dwell on the past but I can't forget the former things."

He wrote a little more about the day, about Paolo, about his talk with Stephen. He listed the number of patients seen and the surgeries done.

John lay in bed for a long time before sleep finally came. When it did, he slept hard, sounder than usual and upon awakening, getting his bearings, he remembered that he was leaving. As that thought was solidifying, another rushed in at the same time: he should do one big thing before he leaves.

One final action. He would continue to see patients, to do surgery, to help train the medical students and residents, but he felt like he needed one more act to kind of wrap up his time in Gulu. Over a breakfast of millet porridge John began to formulate a plan.

Father Paolo had bladder cancer that was likely due to schistosomiasis. The disease remained common in Uganda despite efforts at prevention. Treatment was possible especially in the disease's early stages with a medication called praziquantal. World health initiatives had worked with governments and NGOs to treat populations in Uganda and other countries with a high percentage of infected people. Success rates had been spotty and depended upon how much money was allotted and who was in charge of distribution. John wondered if there was a way he could help treat a population in or around Gulu for schistosomiasis and intestinal worms.

He knew both diseases were a big problem but he didn't yet have a feel for whether there was anything he could do. He knew that it would likely be a one-time thing, and he certainly didn't want to cause more harm than good, or just throw his time and money away if treatment wasn't needed.

John finished dressing and walked over to the hospital, deciding he needed an expert opinion. He found Mary in the clinic and asked her if she knew where he could find Dr. Ernest, Lacor's infectious disease physician. She said he was around and that she would help John find him, but that he needed to see his patients first. And to also not forget that he had Marcus' surgery in less than an hour. He laughed and said she was right; he had duties to attend to before starting some new project.

By the time he finished seeing the inpatients, it was nearly time for surgery and there was no sign of Dr. Ernest. He asked Mary to see if the doctor could meet him later for tea. John went to check on Marcus in the pre-op area. He couldn't sit in a chair normally due to the gigantic scrotum, so he was sitting on the floor, his legs bent around it. The nurse had an IV in him already, and the anesthetist had prepared the room.

"Well, Marcus, are you ready?" said John.

Marcus smiled back as his father answered, "He is more than ready. Thank you again for doing this. You will be blessed many times."

"You're welcome. How could I resist such a nice looking boy?" He said as Marcus grinned up at him, his thick tongue perpetually out of his mouth.

"Okay, let's go Marcus."

John grabbed his hand and walked him back to the operating room where Alice helped him up on the table, speaking to him gently and kindly. He drifted off to sleep peacefully as John and Stephen scrubbed their hands.

Once they were gowned and ready, they went to work. The mass turned out to be very vascular, with countless small veins throughout the tissue. Every one of them required tying. Over the course of the next two hours they ligated probably two hundred veins and used over fifty silk ties. John always felt guilty when he used a lot of resources. However, there wasn't any other way to do it. The cautery machine wasn't coagulating them adequately and there were too many to clip. It was very tedious work, but they eventually finished.

There was quite a crowd of medical students, residents and even operating room nurses watching as the last attachments were freed. John had everyone give his or her best estimate as to the weight of the excised scrotum. The winning answer was 4.8 kilograms, over ten pounds, by a female medical student. John awarded her a cloth surgical cap that was covered with images of a Kansas Jayhawk.

When the incision was closed, the remaining scrotum looked fairly natural. They put on a fresh clean pair of white underwear to hold the dressings in place. Underwear is something that Marcus would not have been able to wear before. His thighs could now come together normally and he wouldn't be carrying around ten pounds of extra weight. A literal ball and chain. It was a satisfying procedure. One that, like many that he did at Lacor, would fundamentally change the course of someone's life. It was going to make Marcus more comfortable and it was going to greatly ease the lives of his parents and other family.

Stephen didn't mention the fact that John was leaving during the case but later, after John had helped transfer Marcus to the recovery area and had talked to the family, he asked if anyone else knew.

"Not yet. I'll start telling people today though… Hey, I had an idea this morning. You're from a small traditional village around here, right?"

"I am. It is about three kilometers away. In the bush."

"How many school aged children do you think live there?"

"Hmm…. I'm not sure. They walk to a primary school in a neighboring village. Between the two I think there must be over three hundred."

"That would be from first to ninth grade?"

"Yes. But, I can find out a more accurate number. My brother is a teacher there. What are you planning?"

"I wonder how many of those children have been treated for worms or schistosomiasis in the past year. If you think there's a need, I may be able to provide the medication for them."

"There is a great need. The government had a program when I was young. We were treated twice a year, but as far as I know that doesn't happen anymore. I don't know if the money ran out or if the politicians are just taking the money. It will be a wonderful thing if you can do that."

"I'm supposed to meet with Dr. Ernest in a few minutes. I'll get his opinion on it and then I want to tell Father Paolo."

"He will be so pleased. Okay, let me know if I can help."

"I will. I'll definitely need your assistance to make this happen."

The meeting went well with Dr. Ernest. He provided the correct dosage of plaziquantel and albendazole and felt like it was a very good plan. He wished that there was enough money and time to treat all of the schools in the area. The ones in town he thought had been treated, but those further out rarely saw doctors. They were dependent on traditional medicines that sometimes caused more harm than good.

Following the discussion with Ernest, John ran into James at tea. It was just the two of them so he took the opportunity to tell him the news about moving back to the States. He laid it all out, explaining that he would still like to return once or twice a year, continuing to help train young doctors and see new patients. James had seen many people come and go over the past twenty years and was neither surprised nor upset. His face was as calm as ever.

"We will be very sorry to see you go, but you are always welcome here, Mr. John. You are an important part of Lacor. We are so very grateful for the work you have done. For the commitment you have shown to the people of Gulu district. You have been selfless and devoted. You have blessed us beyond measure and we can never repay you. God will have to pay you."

John felt a little sick as he received the kind words, wondering if he was making the wrong choice. One of the things he knew, however, was that there was no right or wrong choice. There was prayer, discernment, and an intentional decision. And then there had to be peace and contentment.

He explained his plan for the local schools to James. The idea had expanded throughout the morning and now encompassed more schools and a wider area. James loved the plan and offered to help in any way he could.

By that afternoon as John saw patients in clinic, everyone had heard that he was leaving. Agnes, David and the others that he talked to were melancholy but supportive of his decision.

He checked on Father Paolo. His urine had about cleared up, but John decided to leave the catheter one more night. The ultrasound had been performed earlier in the day. It showed that his kidneys were draining well and there were no obvious masses in the liver or other organs. The outline of his bladder looked fairly smooth as well. He still needed a CT but that could probably wait until he returned to Verona.

"So, have you talked to anyone in Italy yet? Do you have an idea when you'll be able to fly back?"

"Yes, I did. I can go as soon as you release me to travel."

"That's great news. I think that you can fly about anytime. Three days... five days... whenever you're ready."

"Thank you."

"I've been thinking about you. About your cancer. About the life that you have lived here in Gulu. You have sacrificed so much to be here. You're no different than Dr. Lucille who developed AIDS yet continued to work, or Dr. Matthew who selflessly died of Ebola. You took the good with the bad here and have now contracted one of the diseases that affects the people of your mission field. The only difference is that you aren't going to die. We'll see to that. I really feel like you're eventually going to recover from this. Will you stay in touch?"

"I will. And you're right. I hadn't thought of it that way. I am in esteemed company! That is an awesome responsibility. I can't thank you enough for helping me. If you hadn't been here…."

"Well I was…but that brings up another matter that I want to talk to you about."

John told Paolo about his mother's death, the fact that he planned to leave Gulu, and about his internal struggle and feelings of guilt about the decision.

"Mr. John, you have prayed about it. You have practiced discernment. And now this is your path. You will certainly be sad and reflective about leaving, as will everyone here, but please don't have regrets. You have done so much. Lacor will be okay. Gulu district will be okay. The place and the people have a way of surviving. Even through European imperialism, Idi Amin, AIDS, Joseph Kony, Ebola and any number of other challenges they are still here. That's one of the reasons we love this place, no? We are here to help, but you know as well as I do that we are the ones who have gained. The beautiful spirit, and the welcoming and warm nature of the people here will sustain you in your new home."

"Thank you Father. You're exactly right and your insight is very helpful. One more thing. I'm planning to supply nearby schools with medications to treat schistosomiasis and intestinal worms in your honor."

"You are? That is amazing."

"Well, you know Stephen, David, and Alice, they're some of the young people that have helped me in surgery and in the clinic? They have identified ten primary schools outside of town. These are schools that draw from small villages, where the children are unlikely to have adequate health care. We'll visit

194

them, give a talk about hand washing and personal hygiene, and then we'll treat everyone with the two medications."

"That is a lot of work. When will you find the time to do this?"

"I'll make time. This is important and I want to do it. It sounds like we'll be able to treat three thousand kids this way."

"It's admirable and generous and it is an honor to me."

"You were definitely the spark. We'll see how it goes. If it's a success I can picture trying to do it yearly. This project will do just as well, maybe even better, without me. I am hoping that Stephen or Alice will take it over."

"I like that plan. But what about the government? Aren't they supposed to be doing this? ...Never mind, I think I know the answer."

John laughed, "Yeah, you know the answer. Yes, they are. My plan is to let the local Member of Parliament know what is going on. Give him a chance to get involved. The media will know about it as well. My goal will be to raise awareness, not to embarrass anyone. Ideally, the government would begin supplying the medications again. Hey, I should let you rest. Do you need anything? Food? Something to drink?"

"No, thank you. I am well-fed and watered. Have a good evening."

"You too, Father," John said as he closed the door to the private room behind him. He stopped for a minute on the veranda. It was dusk, a time that seems to go quickly in Uganda. One moment it was sunny and the next it was dark. The air was cool with a faint smell of cooking fires. Families of patients were bringing in dinner, getting settled for the night.

John was in his element and felt very much alive. These had been wonderful months in Gulu and he would miss nights like this. He was excited about the school project, anxious to get started on it. But behind that, he knew that his time here was almost over, he was going home.

23

Kansas City

It was the second week in Deborah's basement and it wasn't going so badly, all things considered. He had his routine and her family had theirs. They usually had dinner together. To keep himself busy, John had taken over the shopping. For the time being he was able to buy fresh fruits and vegetables at the nearby farmer's market. It was early October and barring a hard freeze, there would still be a market for another month. He loved being able to buy a sweet potato or an apple or a head of lettuce from a farmer with whom he had a relationship.

Because his schedule was more open than Deb's, he also did much of the cooking. He would prepare the meat separately from the rest of the meal and let the others mix it into their dish. While personally he ate a plant-based diet, and while he would passionately explain to anyone who would listen why it was critical to stop eating meat, he tried his best to keep his opinion to himself when he was living with Deb. After all, it was her house and he didn't want to create tension so soon after arriving. It was difficult enough adjusting to each other's schedule and idiosyncrasies. Besides, he had never won an argument with her. He was even more suspect in her eyes than he had been growing up. Now that he had years of odd counter-cultural actions and opinions behind him, she felt she understood him even less than when he had merely been a peculiar kid.

He didn't know what his next move would be exactly. He had returned home partly because his mother had died, partly because he felt like he needed to be closer to family. But much of it was that he missed community. He had always been an outsider, never really fit in anywhere, but that was literally true in Uganda. The color of his skin, his culture, the fact that he couldn't speak any language besides English, it all led to a sense of loneliness that he just couldn't get around.

When he had first arrived in Uganda all he could think about was Jessica. Their relationship had been so new and he realized it would take time for the emotion to begin to wane. But after weeks and months, after many cycles of sleeping and waking, by the time he had begun to come to terms with that loss, he still felt that something critical was missing. He made new friends and strengthened old ones. He had plenty of people to talk to and to share things with, but it just wasn't enough. He loved the work, loved that he was able to help so many people, to make the world a little healthier and happier, but he struggled with the lack of community.

On the other hand, in Placencia there had been community. The plastic project had brought a lot of people together. Everyone felt that they were a part of something bigger than themselves. Many on the peninsula had similar backgrounds to John, alike enough that he felt as if they were speaking the same language. They understood his dry sense of humor and his pop cultural references. The community was growing and was organic and open in a way that he hadn't felt in a long time. And then of course there was Jessica. But he had missed medicine. He had missed the specific, specialized work that he could perform and that few others could. It turned out that he needed to feel needed.

So here he was. Living out of two suitcases in his sister's basement with no specific plan. His mom's memorial was to be Thanksgiving weekend, but that really didn't require much from him. His stepdad Fred had made all of the arrangements. Most of her belongings had already been sold or given away months before and he had let Fred and Deb divide and sell the remainder.

He was the executor of the will but again there wasn't much to do. The small amount of savings that she had was enough to pay for the memorial and the nursing home with a little extra left over for Deb and him. John told Fred that he wanted him to have his half. He balked at first but relented in the end. Fred had taken care of Sara through the hard times, and it didn't seem right for John to take any of her money. It belonged to her husband.

He spent most of his days reading, writing a little, and cooking. He went for long walks in the empty streets. That was one of the things that was difficult to get used to again. In Uganda there were people everywhere. They were walking, sitting, working, herding cattle, and riding their bicycles. There was nowhere that a person could look that was free of people. There were people washing motorcycles and bathing in puddles along the road, people selling drinks and meat on a stick at every stop, children waving and carrying water, and women carrying long bundles of sticks on their heads. At Lacor there were people in every nook and cranny of the hospital and its grounds. Only when he retreated to his small apartment at night was he able to reliably be alone.

Here it was the absence of people that was striking. Everyone stayed in their cars or their homes. Sitting and enjoying coffee with a friend, watching the world go by at a table in a local coffee shop, reading up on the news and enjoying the company of others, all of that was missing in the perversion of the line of cars at a Starbucks drive through. Any chance of community was lost when people drove home after a day at work, pulled into the garage, closed the automatic door before the engine was even off, and went inside to watch Netflix or catch up on Facebook. It was lost even at work, work that was done for a paycheck without any real joy or passion.

He had moved back to the States in large part because of the lack of meaningful community and friendships in Uganda, but he was at great risk of not doing any better at home. The manner in which modern society had evolved made it difficult to connect with real people. He knew that he would have to actively seek out opportunities to meet with friends. So John began a series of coffee dates for fellowship and clarity.

One of these was mainly business related. He met Kevin, the manager of his physician group, one morning at a local coffee shop to discuss his future.

"Hey John, how are you? You're looking healthy and rested. I like the beard," Kevin said as he stood and greeted John, shaking hands with his old friend and colleague.

"Thanks Kevin. You're looking good also. How's life been treating you? How's your family?"

"Good. Everyone's healthy. The kids are both in high school now. Ben's driving."

"That's hard to believe. And even harder for me to believe is that I have seniors in college."

"That's nuts. I remember when they were little. You would bring them into the office sometimes. Hey, do you want anything to drink? Coffee?"

"Sure, I'll get it. I'll be right back."

John returned with his tea and they continued to catch up with what had been going on in their personal lives and with the physician group. The new hire that had taken John's place, the impending retirement of two partners, some realignment in call groups and hospital coverage and similar things that John had not been very interested in when he worked there, and had serious trouble focusing on now.

"So, what do you think, John? Can I interest you in coming back to work? You've still got a lot of good years left in you."

"I honestly don't know yet. I'm pretty sure that I do want to work in some capacity. Taking a lot of call doesn't interest me though. Nor does trying to hit production numbers. I worked hard in Uganda, but it was so nice to do it on my own terms. I didn't have to worry about maximizing charges, or about no-shows, or about taking time for tea. I just had to practice medicine."

"Yeah, I understand what you mean. But I don't know how you're going to replicate that here. One way would be to put you in an employment situation. Not as a full shareholder. We could then structure it however we choose. Maybe you wouldn't have to take call. We could set lower production goals…"

"I don't know about that either. I'm aware of how that plays out. Those kinds of things always come at great cost. Like I said, I can still work hard. Harder than most. What I'll need to do is to limit the amount of stress outside of work. Yeah, like no call. And maybe instead of working shorter days or taking a three-day weekend every week, I could do something like two months on and one month off. That would really give me time to get away from it all. It takes a few days to relax and settle down. It isn't something that a three-day weekend really helps."

"I'll bet we can work something out. And if not, just between you and me, there'll be some hospital or other group that will probably jump at the deal. Do you want me to take something specific to the board?"

"Sure. I guess it wouldn't hurt to do that. Let's start with kind of what I just said. Two months on and one month off. No call. Some additional paid vacation as well. That gives me enough time to go to Africa to work if I decide to do that. I don't care where they put me. Back at a big hospital- a small town- it doesn't matter. When do you all meet next?"

"In about two weeks. I'll keep you appraised okay?"

"Sounds great. Thanks for meeting with me Kevin."

"No problem. I'll see you later."

Kevin got up to leave while John stayed behind to finish his tea and think about his future for a little longer. He really needed to work soon. Placencia had proven that. He just wasn't ready to give up all that he had gained from the years away.

Deb had an average-sized house with a medium-sized lawn on a typical suburban street. The grass was still green and growing in mid-October and the oak trees had just begun to shed their leaves. Looking for something to do, John offered to mow the lawn. Since moving from Placencia to Gulu he had lost all of the conditioning that he had gained by swimming. The little bit of walking he did there and simply standing all day had been the only exercise that he received.

It had felt nice to be in shape, but in general John wasn't interested in working out. He didn't want to run, bike, lift weights, or do anything in that regard. He just could never devote the time to it. For the same reason he watched movies standing up in twenty-minute increments. It usually took several days to watch a whole film. He simply couldn't justify devoting so much time to something that wasn't producing anything, wasn't changing the world.

Mowing a lawn, however, was more like work. And bonus points that it wasn't even his yard. And if it helped him stretch his legs a little, made him take deeper breaths well, all the better. Deb had a simple gas-powered mower, not self-propelled. She mercifully wasn't one of the people on the block with a huge riding lawnmower. Why anyone needed a riding machine to care for a few thousand square feet of rye was beyond him. It took away the exercise component, which was nearly the only positive thing about a manicured lawn.

He looked up and down the street and saw green yards all uniformly short and tended. No doubt they were all helped along with herbicides. The whole point of having a well-kept, beautiful lawn had been lost, he felt. Rather than creative uses of native plants and maybe some well-chosen exotic ones to make soft turf of a combination of soft, green plants, everyone had the same monoculture of bluegrass (which was native to Europe, not Kentucky, despite its name) or rye. There was an occasional zoysia lawn, which was native to East Asia.

The amount of fertilizer, water, and herbicides used on single-family homes' lawns was staggering. Following Ellie's death, he had quickly lost any slim remnant of interest in having a grass lawn. He mowed occasionally but had stopped watering or adding amendments or reseeding. It all seemed pointless and even unfaithful. Definitely reckless and egotistical. The corn monoculture in the United States, grown on farmland that if put together would take up an area the size of Germany, was a serious enough problem. Corn that was grown for an inefficient, ultimately doomed, form of energy, and to feed farm animals at least was used for something. Lawns were used for nothing. Peer pressure, the dominant culture, and restrictive covenants perpetuated the maintenance of what was by far the largest irrigated crop in the country. There had to be a better way.

John filed this in the "major problems that I can't do anything about right now" file in his brain and continued to push the mower back and forth. There was only so much time and he had only so much energy. He no longer had a yard of his own which he supposed was a minor victory.

Deb's front yard and those of her neighbors looked nice and had a pleasing aesthetic quality. After all, that was the point. People no longer had front porches and yards were too big and houses too far apart to easily communicate with neighbors or the infrequent passersby. At least one could stand at her street corner and look straight through five yards on each side of the road to the next corner.

The backyard was a different story completely. Everyone had fences. A few were of the low, chain link, see through variety. But most were six-foot tall, continuous wood privacy fences that did their job very well. Or at least they did when people were outside. John doubted that any of the fences eliminated neighbors from peering into their backyards from a second story window. So if people couldn't suntan naked, or do whatever else that was so private that they needed a tall, expensive fence, what were they for? Dogs were probably the most frequent answer. To give the dogs a place to run around and to be able to use the bathroom in a place that didn't require the owner to go for a walk with a plastic bag in their other hand. Whatever the reason, it had to be important enough to shut out contact with the neighbors.

While John pushed the mower back and forth through the yard, listening to Ringo Deathstarr in his ear buds, he had a utopian vision. Maybe it was due to the fuzzed out guitar sounds, but it seemed to make so much sense that he was amazed that this wasn't already happening all of the country. He dreamed that people would take down their fences.

203

This would create an open field of gardens, trees, and recreational areas. Ten yards seamlessly connected side-by-side and back-to-back would provide room for a huge communal plot of land. Shared tools would be stored in a shed. There would be a large garden that everyone could take part in, helping to tend it and then sharing in the bountiful harvest. Playground equipment would be used much more frequently than the private sets in fenced backyards. There could be a small orchard of fruit and nut trees. There would even be room for a small dog run. All of this would be visible and accessible from everyone's back porch.

He thought about how amazing it would be to join ten families together in that way. Exclusive homeowners associations would become co-ops. Anyone who moved in would be included and welcomed. They would have an instant community. The care of different areas could be rotated among different families. As much as possible, the area would be self-supporting and low maintenance.

Alas, because the dream hadn't become a reality he still had work to do after all the grass was cut. He found a handheld clipper and began trimming the weeds and tall grass on the edges of the yard. An unseen dog barked aggressively on the other side of the fence, proving the point that neighbors didn't know each other. Or at least neighbor's dogs didn't know neighbor's brothers.

Finishing his brand of exercise and his utopian daydream, John went inside to get ready to meet Jacob from Loaves and Fishes Catholic Worker. They hadn't seen each other since John had returned and both were anxious to catch up. They decided to meet at a local bakery. It would have been called a patisserie in France or a konditorei in Germany. And in either of those countries there would have been a similar wonderful shop on nearly any block that hadn't been swallowed up by chain restaurants. A place where someone could sit at a tiny table eating a beautiful pastry and maybe even a light sandwich or slice of quiche. The coffee would be wonderful and there would be a large selection of teas. If the treat were for takeout, it would be carefully placed in a decorated box and tied up with a ribbon.

These kinds of shops are one of the joys of Europe. There were a few that came close in Kansas City, and these were the places that John and his sweet tooth often went when he had time. And right now, he had nothing but time.

24

So with a flaky, creamy, chocolaty pastry in one hand and a decaf coffee in the other he joined Jacob at a table in the busy shop. Jacob was tall, with bright kind eyes, loose second-hand-clothes and a resonant, preacher's voice.

"John, how are you? Wow, it's good to see you," he said, giving him a big hug. That was something that John could never quite get used to. Not very physical by nature, hugging women was difficult enough, but men...well he tried his best, but a firm handshake felt more than sufficient as a greeting.

"How's your family?" he continued. "You're staying with your sister, right? How's that going?"

"Well, how long do we have?" he joked. The two friends caught each other up on what had been going on in their lives. They were truly brothers, with similar spirits yet different specific experiences. They understood each other on a deep level, intuitively and spiritually.

"How has the adjustment been without Ellie? Has it been difficult coming back? I can't even imagine..."

"Thank you for asking about Ellie. That's a topic that most people try to avoid. It's been hard, of course it has. We were together for well over twenty years. A lifetime. We grew up together, really. She allowed me to become who I am today. You know, put up with all of my craziness.

"After the accident I was just in shock. I stayed busy at work and was simply trying to keep going. It was the kids' freshman year in college. It was all a big mess. Then there was the trial. I wasn't super involved with that but it did act as a distraction. What helped more than anything was forgiving Jarius. I've stayed in touch with him, you know? We've written letters back and forth. When he gets out next year I'm going to be his number one advocate. I want to help him get a job. A real job. Something that leads somewhere. He wants to be a physical therapist. How cool would that be? It won't be easy with a felony conviction, but I think it's possible if he works hard. Maybe I can pull some strings. I know way too many lawyers. Maybe one of them can help."

"That would be amazing. Forgiving Jarius has contributed so much to your healing. It's a monument to your love for Ellie. Your Taj Mahal."

"That sounds a little hyperbolic, but I'm sure it's been helpful. It's always true right? Focusing outward helps us heal inward. Of course Belize and Uganda helped as well. A change of venue. Staying busy. I sure miss her, Jacob. We were together a long time. I see her in the kids of course, so she lives on in many ways…"

He ate a little of the pastry, sipped some coffee as they sat quietly for a moment. Jacob finally broke the silence.

"Tell me about Jessica. Have you seen her since returning?"

John smiled at the sound of her name. "Not yet. That was so difficult also. Our relationship was brand new. And then to suddenly and painfully end it. It all seemed like a dream after a few weeks in Africa. A wonderful hazy tropical dream."

"Have you stayed in touch?"

"Kind of. I tried to avoid spending a lot of time on the Internet when I was in Gulu. Long distance relationships are difficult under the best of circumstances. But eight time zones, thousands of miles, very little spare time… so I guess a more honest answer is no. We didn't stay in touch. But I've called her since returning. We're slowly working through everything. I'm still hopeful. It'll be hard to replicate what we had. I mean seriously…the beach, nothing to do all day…"

"It sounded like you had plenty to do. That big recycling initiative. It's amazing what you were able to accomplish."

"Yeah, but first of all, it wasn't just me. That thing snowballed. The whole town got involved, which really helped share the load. My mind was as relaxed and open as it's ever been. There are times when I feel a little guilty about that year. But other times I believe it was the most important period of my life. I've never felt more alive and real and true to myself. Anyway, seeing Jessica here, now, would be a completely different thing. I'm not a hundred percent sure our relationship would be the same. Maybe. I'd certainly like to try."

John's voice faded, and for a moment his eyes unfocused. He quickly recovered, saying, "And what about you, Jacob? How's Rachel? The kids? Who's all living there now? Do you have interns?"

Jacob updated John on the news of the house. They often had interns living in the community with them for months or even a year at a time. They were often college students, but could be older as well. They were immersed in the life of the house, working on shower mornings, helping in the garden, preparing meals, participating in political actions, and just living very simply. For most, it was a happy interlude on the way to somewhere else. Occasionally someone would stay on and become a full member of the community. Currently there were two living with them: a young woman who was a sophomore in nearby Avila College, and another who was a student in one of the local seminaries. Jacob spoke very highly of both of them.

"How was the garden this year?"

"It was really good. Not perfect. We had almost too much rain. And then in August it got really hot and totally dried up. But overall it was successful. You need to come visit. We pulled up some more asphalt. The chickens have a much larger area to roam around in now. And there's even more room for the garden. The front and back yards we've always used, of course. But now we've expanded out along that back fence behind the other building. In that far northwest corner we have some fruit and nut trees. Also the bees."

"A lot of people probably refer to you all as fruits and nuts."

Jacob laughed, "I wouldn't be surprised. We have our fans but we have plenty of the other. Especially people that are trying to gentrify the neighborhood. We want it to be safe and friendly. We want everyone to know and to love each other. But we don't think that buying properties cheap, fixing them up and selling them for three times the price, or worse yet, tearing them down and putting up higher priced condos, is helping anyone except the developers. Anyway…you need to come out and see."

"I will. In fact I want to start coming down to volunteer at the shower house again. How about Tuesdays? Is there a need that day?"

"That would be great. We can often use an extra body on Tuesdays. I work outside the house that day, but Rachel and some of the others will be there. Any day is fine really. And next Friday we're having a clarification meeting about white privilege. It's a subject that we can't talk about too much. The manner in which we keep others down by our actions, laws and attitudes is subconscious but very damaging."

"My social calendar is pretty empty. I'll be there for sure."

"Great! Then I'll see you soon. Take care my brother," Jacob said as they got up to leave, giving John another hug whether he wanted one or not. They left the bakery together into the dry, bright October day.

———————

The next few weeks became a comfortable routine of reading the Bible, writing reflections, volunteering at Loaves and Fishes once or twice a week, preparing meals, and simply enjoying the slow days. Initially the hours seemed to drag, but after a while it became hard to believe that there had been enough time to work. Once again, as in Belize, he had discovered the holiness found in a simpler, slower life. He prayed, recited the Jesus prayer while raking or going for walks. He was at peace, while realizing that this was just an interlude prior to the next phase of his life.

Thanksgiving dinner was at Deb's house. Her family, Fred, his daughters and their families, John's two uncles, and the twins were all there. In the greatest of family dinner traditions, people brought dishes to share. Deb's husband Bobby had smoked the turkey. There was cheesy rice with broccoli, mashed white and sweet potatoes, vegetarian stuffing, salads, and three kinds of pie.

John was so happy to have Sam and Kate home from college for the long weekend. It had always been Kate's favorite holiday as there were no gifts to buy and no distraction from the food and the company. One of her favorite hobbies was watching people, and large family gatherings were one the best places to do so. She would observe and store away everything, from the way that her uncle's full belly moved when he slept, to Deb's crooked grin, to the way that her cousins held forks. She wasn't making fun, she simply always had an interest in the anthropology of her family. She would provoke her grandmother. She would call her Sara instead of Grandma, make a provocative comment, a dramatic eye roll, anything to get her started. When she took the bait and snapped at Kate with an acerbic comment, Kate would take great perverse joy in it. John's mom had always been tense at family gatherings, making it almost too easy for Kate to push her buttons.

"I miss messing with her," she told John.

"I know you do. You're kind of a mess yourself."

"I mean, it wasn't fun after she lost her memory. That would have been cheating. Plus, she mellowed a lot. But remember her? She was something else! She sure liked us grandkids though. Took us to every G-rated movie that came out. Bought us school clothes every fall and she and Fred made peach ice cream in the summer."

"She sat through ballets, baseball games, and school plays, about everything you invited her to."

"I know. She really had a big heart inside that little body. Hey, why are we moping around? We can do that all day Saturday if we want. Let's go play Rock Band with everyone else."

"First of all, we aren't going to be moping around on Saturday. It's a celebration of her life, not a funeral. It will be a lot like this- food, conversation, laughter, and some reflections. There'll just be more people. She had a lot of friends before her dementia hit. Many of them are still around." John's voice dropped to a whisper. "Look over there, slowly, quietly…"

Uncle Alex was sleeping in a recliner with a half eaten slice of pie balanced on his stomach, his chair facing the muted football game.

Kate laughed at the perfect Thanksgiving image. Then said, "Speaking of pie… how are you doing, Dad? Have you gained any more weight?"

"I'm not sure. I haven't weighed myself in a long time. I feel good though. And I'm pretty sure I'm close to one thirty. I feel like it anyway."

"What does a hundred thirty feel like? You actually need to weigh yourself. What did you eat today?"

"I ate a ton. I'm stuffed," John said, sounding somewhat vague, even to himself.

"You did have pie right?"

"I did. Seriously, I ate a lot. Pumpkin pie, apple pie, lots of salad, pickled okra…"

"So, sweets and raw vegetables. I see that nothing has changed. Dad, you need to eat more. You look too thin."

"Hey, let's stop talking about me. Where's your boyfriend? I thought you were going to bring him home this time?"

"Uh, nice try. If I have a boyfriend, and I'm not saying I do, I don't think a funeral would be the best place for him to meet everyone. I thought we were going to play Rock Band," she said and headed downstairs, leaving John to watch the slow rise and fall of the pie on Alex's stomach.

The party had moved into the basement, which also happened to be John's apartment. Deb's big television was there, along with their Wii. He went down to join them, the sounds of "Mr. Brightside" by the Killers rising to greet him. He watched as Kate sang, Sam played the drums, and Deb's children played bass and guitar. Other family members rotated in as songs ended and others began.

John took his turn at drums and guitar but had to play the game on the simplest level. Even then, he felt his muscles tense and his eyes glaze over as he tried to stay with the music. After two songs he remembered why he didn't ever play video games. He developed a headache and was in a worse mood after finishing it than when he began. He continued to watch though, singing along and laughing with the others. It really was a nice day and he knew his mom would have enjoyed it.

Fred seemed okay. His girls were there, and John was sure that helped a lot. He only had about ten years with his wife, but they were good years. Even the difficult ones had moments of grace. Fred had been through this before. His first wife had developed ovarian cancer, dying at a relatively young age. He had raised his girls through their teenage years on his own. A feat that John couldn't quite imagine. As well as he got along with his children, being the only parent, the only decision maker, food preparer, taxi driver, clothes washer, grocery shopper, homework helper and rule enforcer...it made him hyperventilate a little simply thinking about it. Yet Fred was laid back and easy going. His children were well-adjusted, sweet, self-controlled, and they sure loved their dad unconditionally.

John took time to talk to Fred that day, as he knew they would both be busy at the memorial. His stepdad was really doing fine. Sara's passing had certainly simplified his days, freed up several hours. But it sounded like he had managed to fill many of them. He was busy preparing for the memorial, selling and distributing his wife's things, talking to family and his friends. He was also playing more golf. This was an activity that John could never completely understand. He couldn't justify the three hours spent walking around chasing after a ball. Probably for the same reason he couldn't watch a movie in more than thirty minute increments. But Fred loved it and it was good for him right now, those long walks with his friends.

John knew that days could be filled with nothing much and time could slowly slip away. But as an interlude, a transition, times like these were necessary. Playing golf, going for a walk, having coffee with friends, working in the yard, and cleaning the house were as important to a healthy life as one's vocation.

So taking his own advice, he stealthily gestured to Sam and Kate and led them out of the house. They walked through the quiet suburban neighborhood, talking, catching up, and getting reacquainted once again. Facebook status updates, texts, and forwarded emails could never get to the heart of things. Only eye to eye, voice to ear, hand to hand could do that. So as the day's last rays of sunlight shone through the nearly bare maple tree branches, as they watched their step on the uneven and cracked sidewalk, and as the cool dry air with a hint of fireplace smoke filled their lungs, they talked and they walked. They lingered outside until many of the guests had gone home, until it was dark and their skin had cooled to the point that they knew they had to return to the world of other people. But those moments were magical and eternal.

———————

The pastor from Sara's church spoke at the memorial service. Pastor Ron was a good guy and his church was still vibrant and alive when many weren't. A local Methodist church in an age when many either didn't attend at all, or drove miles to one of the megachurches on the outskirts of town, it still attracted families from the area. Ron was just liberal enough, just progressive enough. He could speak to the people who longed for inclusivity and reconciliation, making them feel like he understood and valued them. But he could also retain the more conservative members, the ones who clung to the old hymns, the pews, the choir, and the "family values" of their youth, or maybe their parent's youth. Either way it was religion as nostalgia, a sort of egalitarian country club.

John's mom had always gone to church. She taught Sunday School for decades which was surely one of the reasons that John started teaching. She never really liked Paul, but loved the Old Testament. Sara was an independent thinker who wasn't afraid to argue with ordained and lay people alike.

Like Pastor Ron, whom she adored, she fell to the left of middle, but not far enough that she would side with John if he began talking about immigrants, or prison reform, or a single payer health care system, or the endless wars that have defined the United States since it's inception. She believed in "common sense", not facts that she had learned in books or seen on TV. In fact she never watched television and rarely read the paper. But that didn't stop her from expressing her opinion about the way things ought to be, or the problems with the world today. She was short of stature, but a giant in the eyes of her children and grandchildren. Usually fearsome but occasionally soft, she was a parent of her times- strict and decisive.

John thought about all of these things and more as Pastor Ron gave his sermon. It was the same message he delivered at funerals at least once a month, sprinkled with anecdotes given to him by Fred, Deb, John and Sara's brothers. Everyone was listening with somewhat glazed but thoughtful eyes. There were few tears, which wasn't surprising. It was a blessing that the stroke had occurred when it did. She had only been a shell of her former self with the personality-stealing dementia.

When the service was finished, everyone met in the fellowship hall of the church for coffee and cookies. Old friends, cousins, nieces, nephews and everyone else traded memories and stories about Sara. The time she forgot to turn the oven on to bake the turkey, the time she poured too much salt in the potatoes, how she loved to burn trash. It was all done with a sense of respect and was a part of the healing process. She was still there in everyone's heart.

People live on in that way for one or two generations. They are important to their family and their friends and maybe to a few co-workers by the time they pass away. For the most part, by the time people live a long life, there simply aren't many people around who remember their youthful energy and their productive vital years. This made John a little melancholy as he sat and watched everyone. But the purpose of life isn't to create memories for others, to live on for decades in any kind of qualitative way. Life is for living. It's to make the world better, to make others more comfortable, to give much more than we take, and by and large his mom had done a good job. She had two thoughtful children, four grandchildren that seemed to be doing okay, a husband who was grateful for his years with her, but was going to be all right without her. It had been a good life.

As everyone drifted away, John put four soft, homemade chocolate chip cookies into a Ziploc bag to take home for later. He talked to Sam and Kate and discovered that they had things to do and people to visit. He didn't have a car but didn't want to slow them down, so he told them to go on, that he would catch a ride with Deborah. On the drive, Deb and John reminisced about their mom, laughing at moments and feeling comfort in each other's company. By the time they arrived home, they had put her to rest.

25

By early December John still hadn't come up with a plan. He was sure that Deb was wondering when he would arrive at one. Her whole family had been so accommodating. If they were sick to death of him, they sure didn't show it. He helped around the house as much as he could and stayed out of the way the other times. His next move had been slow to arrive. The short intermission was stretching into an actual phase of his life.

He thought he wanted to work, but he couldn't decide what that would look like. Kevin had offered him a nice part time job in a nearby town. It was about eighty minutes away if traffic was light. He wouldn't have to take call and could work three or four days a week. The pay was good but not great. Ultimately, though, it felt like a big step back and he just couldn't commit to it. He was sure the patients were nice and the hospital staff and administrators would be appreciative and gracious. But after working the way he had in Uganda, with no money involved, strictly volunteering his time and expertise to the poor and desperate, even small town Missouri seemed too capitalistic for his taste. Kevin told him that the job would still be there when he was ready. No one else was beating down the doors of the hospital trying to take the job.

So he drifted, or that's what it seemed like to his friends and family. He still felt at peace with his move back from Uganda. Remaining open and faithful, he was confident that God had plans for him. He continued reading his Bible every day and taking note of the verse that had spoken to him most clearly. He really studied that book and had read it enough times that he felt like he knew it. He didn't memorize verses but understood that it was a complete story.

John was most interested in the prophets and the Gospels. He felt that Isaiah, Ezekiel, Amos, Jeremiah, and the others really understood what was happening and what needed to happen. They spoke out with fiery words and actions. They were harassed and ostracized, and yet their words and their examples remain. Their form of protest against the oppressors of the poor lived on in Jesus. John especially tried to understand and to live the Sermon on the Mount and Matthew 25. The woes of Matthew 23 and the entire Gospel of John with its high language of love also spoke to him.

And although his zeal may have diminished a little from the days when he would listen to the AM radio preachers and only play Christian rock music at home, his faith had become much deeper. It was a part of him, in the air he breathed and all around him. "The kingdom of God is within us," Tolstoy wrote and it was true. He didn't have to go to a church building with uncomfortable pews and tiny Tic-Tac sized communion bread pieces on a velvet-lined brass plate. He didn't have to recite a specific creed or exclude entire categories of people from the joy of God's love. As much as loved his church and Ann's amazing sermons, God was here and God was everywhere.

Although he felt aimless at times, he knew he was only resting up, learning to be faithful and patient instead of relying on his own will to decide what was next. Intentional and mindful, he waited.

────────

It wasn't as if John never thought of Jessica. It wasn't that he had forgotten her, or that their time together in Belize was a fling or a lark. In the many quiet moments of his slower life, she filled his thoughts. He could no longer clearly remember her face, at least not the way she appeared in person. The way her eyes changed when she laughed or when she was serious or was about to kiss him. The few pictures on his phone didn't come close to capturing those eyes. The static, flat images out of time and context were a poor substitute. The times they had talked on the phone he had heard and remembered the way she put sentences together, her funny way of saying certain words, with just a trace of a northern accent, the clichés and phrases that they had begun to share. But there was a vast difference between talking on the phone and being with someone in the same space. The mysterious aura that people emanate, that is real yet as elusive as peripheral vision. It's not sensed by looking at pictures, talking on the phone, reading emails, or using Snapchat.

But they did, in fact, talk. She was enjoying her job at the radiology center, although running the coffee shop was much less stressful. Stella liked her school. She made friends easily and hadn't really missed a beat socially. Jessica could already see an improvement in Stella scholastically. She had been doing okay in Belize but seemed to be learning more quickly at her new elementary school.

"So, when are you going to come visit me?" John asked, probably for the tenth time in as many conversations.

"When are you coming to Illinois?" was her standard answer.

It wasn't easy either way. Of course he could rent a car, drive to Decatur, and stay in a motel. It was certainly tempting, but for some reason it just didn't feel right. Jess was living with her mom and her daughter, so it would feel disruptive to have him there from out of town. The first time anyway. They hadn't seen each other in over a year and both wanted to simply spend time together, not with family.

For the same reason, Kansas City was out. He supposed they could stay together in Deb's basement, but he didn't think that would go over very well. The option that seemed the most natural was to stay in a hotel on the Plaza for a long weekend. They could sit in cafes, walk in the nearby parks, visit museums, and just hang out together. They both liked this idea the best. There was still an underlying anxiety that after so many months apart, they might not feel the connection that they had in Placencia.

But in the end they decided to just go for it. She would have her mom watch Stella some weekend soon when the weather was nice enough to drive.

"You should see if there are any good bands playing the weekend I come," she said. "No one ever comes to Decatur."

"Most of them skip Kansas City too, but I'll check. There are a few places to see music here. I mean ones that a fifty year old man can enter without feeling like a grandpa."

"Nothing wrong with grandpas appreciating good music is there? So what have you been listening to lately? I know you don't listen to anything for very long."

"Umm… a lot of Tinariwen, you know that band from Mali? Even though I can't understand the words, I know the meaning is so peaceful and profound. They simply want to be able to go back home. The music is hypnotic and just really amazing, and the guitarist occasionally breaks out a really cool solo. It's excellent walking music and it was always good operating music."

"Cool. I think you've shown me before, but I'll check them out."

"I can't do a top five favorite songs with them though. They have a ton of records but they all kind of sound the same to me and I don't know any of the titles. We'll have to pick something else for that."

"Right. I've just been listening to old Drive By Truckers lately. Nothing better than that, you know? Hey, speaking of OR music, have you made a decision about work yet? Are you going to take that job with your old group? Or have you thought of anything else? I told you that Decatur could probably squeeze in one more urologist."

"Nope. No decision yet. It feels like time has really slowed down for me here. I'm just volunteering at Loaves and Fishes, thinking, writing… I'm not ready to give up my freedom yet."

"You don't have to give it all up you know."

"I've never done it any other way. I'm afraid if I just work three days I would worry about all of my patients the other four. I'm about ready to try it though. Somewhere. Who knows? I miss you enough, I might look at that Decatur job."

"Well, there's no hurry right? Hey, I need to get going. Not all of us have a life of leisure you know?"

"All right, if you insist. But first... favorite Truckers album?"

"That's too easy. *Decoration Day.* The Jason Isbell songs alone make it the best. Plus you've got 'Sink Hole.' 'Do it Yourself,' and that one about the brother and sister and their four little babies. Good stuff."

"No argument here. Although its hard to beat *Gangstabilly.*"

"Yeah, the first one's awesome, but I don't think it's their best. Okay, I really need to go. I'll see you soon!"

"Finally! All right, I'll talk to you later."

John hung up and started researching hotels for that weekend. He was nervous, excited, and nauseated all at once as he thought about it. But he knew that they needed to see each other soon if their relationship had any chance.

It was during showers at Loaves and Fishes that he made the decision. It had been a challenging morning due to a conflict between two of the guests in the clothing closet. One man was taking a really long time trying to choose his clothing. With some people, it didn't speed things up to try to help them, and Manny was one of those. He was in there for much of the morning. Only two people were allowed in the tight space at a time to pick out clothing, so that obviously slowed things down a little. But everything still seemed to be calm. Both guests and volunteers were patient and kind. Everyone had a bad day now and then.

But when Bob tried to go for the same pants that Manny wanted, pants that Manny had looked at and rejected thirty times before throughout the course of the morning, it got a little rough. There were words, there was a shove and then Manny got even more agitated and started threatening Bob. The two volunteers in the closet were doing their best to handle the situation. The main goal was always to defuse the conflict and to keep anyone else from being drawn into it. With John's help, they got the two guys outside and let them talk it out. Manny was really not in any condition to reason with. He was more confused than usual. Off his meds, hung over, on drugs, who knew? But he was still a human being and deserving of love and respect, so everyone gave him both that morning.

Manny never got his shower but he did have breakfast, and what could have been a violent encounter turned out fine. After the twentieth and last shower of the morning, John gave the entire bathroom a thorough, final clean. The toilet, the mirror, and the sink were scrubbed. He emptied the trash and mopped the floor. The other volunteer in his area deep-cleaned the other bathroom. When they were finished, they took the last baskets of dirty clothes to the basement to be washed.

When everything was finished, after the others had cleaned their areas, they all gathered around the table in the dining room. Eight people, a mix of volunteers and community members sat with their Bibles and reflected on the morning. They re-read the morning's verses, this time a passage from Leviticus about leaving the land fallow on the seventh year. They talked about faithfulness and trust. About sharing and sustainability and working for the long term. About not trying to squeeze every last bit of profit or production out of a plot of land, but letting the poor come and take what they need.

It was a message of abundance and grace and it was something they all needed to read. John and the others lived in a culture where a feeling of scarcity was the rule. Where everyone worked as hard as they could to get what they wanted right then, not worrying about leaving enough for their neighbor. In fact, people didn't seem to be happy unless they had more than their neighbor. If they didn't have a bigger house, nicer car and clothes, a more interesting vacation, Royals seats that were closer to the field, and children at more expensive schools than their peers, they felt inferior. Or if someone didn't have the top yoga instructor, the special chef's table at the new restaurant, and the board position on the correct number of civic organizations, they would be embarrassed at the next fundraiser.

Everyone seemed to worry that there was only a limited supply of food, leisure time, security, lakeside property, and really everything imaginable, so they lived their lives in a state of anxiety, competition and fear.

John talked in the circle about how rare it was to see that at Loaves and Fishes. People who were at the very bottom of society, who had every reason to worry and to push for what was theirs, seemed more content than the rich people he knew. People there tended to share well. They didn't fight or push or raise their voices to be the first in the clothing closet. In fact, they probably should worry that the one pair of gloves for their cold fingers, or the one pair of shoes in their size for their bruised and tired feet would be gone, but calm usually prevailed. He was afraid that he wouldn't be as magnanimous if he were in the same position. The situation with Manny and Bob that morning had been due to Manny's mental illness and the fact that he was having a bad morning. Any other day the two of them would not have fought over those pants.

Rachel agreed that she had learned so much from her friends that live on the streets. They took turns using the house phone, were patient when waiting for breakfast. They often gave away their last cigarette to anyone who asked and even lit it for them. They lived from day to day, and yet knew that there was plenty, that God would provide what they needed. A warm place to sleep, safety from drunken violent people, enough food for the day and a private place to use the bathroom. Maybe if they were lucky there would even be a smile from a friend or a passerby and warm sunshine on their face.

Following their discussion, they began to disperse, going about their days, Rachel to work on laundry, the volunteers to return to their regular lives. John, however, stayed seated. It wasn't anything he had planned or thought through, but when the others left he didn't move. Jacob came into the dining area from outside a few minutes later to find him still seated, seeming to have a conversation with himself.

"Hey John, what's going on? Everything alright?"

"Oh, hi Jacob. Yeah, I'm okay. Just thinking a little. I wasn't quite ready to go home yet."

"Okay, stay as long as you need to. The morning went well?"

"It did. Nothing too out of the ordinary... Hey, Jacob?"

"Yeah? What is it?" Jacob stopped fiddling with the coffee maker and came to join John at the table.

"Do you think I could move in here for a while? Is there room? I wouldn't be much help I know, probably get in the way, and I'm not very strong nor a very outgoing person, so I'm not sure how I would do with the guests. I'm not really a voice of authority, but I've just been thinking..."

"Hey. John. Slow down. Yes. That would be great!"

"Really?"

"Sure. One of our interns is leaving this weekend so there'll be room. You'll stay in that apartment upstairs. You'll do fine and I'm not worried at all. You already know how to do everything on the mornings that we offer showers. And the rest, well, that's why you'll be here. You'll be an intern. You'll learn how to care for the chickens, help with community meals and the upcoming clarification meeting. You'll be completely immersed in the dirty water of Loaves and Fishes."

John's face had gone from one of concern and anxiety to one of calm and trust. He had been thinking about it for a long time. For years really. But for whatever reason he had never made the leap. Now, with the Placencia and Uganda experiences behind him, or more accurately, inside of him, he felt that he was ready.

Years ago, when he had first met Rachel and Jacob, he dreamed of moving his family there. He regretted not doing it at times, but he knew that he had done his best. He had tried to be a good example and to raise the children to know that there were many people that live in poverty. They had fed the hungry and had been on mission trips with their church group to Central America, and with John to Africa. But now that everyone was gone, now that he wasn't making decisions for anyone else except himself, he felt that he was ready. Now was the time.

26

Selena had been coming to Loaves and Fishes for years. She had bad times and good times. There were days when she needed constant direction and help picking out clothes and toiletries. On these days she was agitated and didn't make sense, her vaguely Caribbean accent taking over. Other times she was sweet, coherent, and giving. Today was one of the latter. After choosing clean clothes, a towel, and a new toothbrush from the clothing closet, she came in to wait her turn for a shower, sitting down heavily on the couch.

"How are you today, Selena?" John asked as he came back from cleaning one of the bathrooms. "You're up for the next shower. It shouldn't be long."

"I am blessed," she smiled.

"We're all blessed aren't we? We woke up this morning."

"Praise Jesus, I know that's right! Every morning when I wake up I just lie in bed for about fifteen minutes. Just praying and giving thanks for another day. I am truly blessed. See what I have? You're looking at it. This backpack. These clothes. That's it. This is all I have in the world and yet it is sufficient. God provides and is faithful. I am happy and content. When I go to bed I fall right asleep. Sleep like a baby. And yet there are people who have everything. A big house. Anything they want, they just buy it. But they're miserable. Truly. I've seen it. I pray for people like that. That they can know the peace that I have."

"That's wonderful, Selena. You are an inspiration to me."

And she was. As were most of the guests that came to Loaves and Fishes for showers, a hot meal, clean clothes and a peaceful place to rest and use the toilet without being harassed or scared. It was so counter intuitive that he could learn more about God from a homeless person than from a seminary-trained pastor or from an endless stream of inspirational memes on Facebook that it still surprised him.

"I tell the truth. Jesus' truth that is inside of me."

"Thank you for telling the truth. That truth inside of you needs to get out."

"Oh I let it out. Every chance I get."

"Hey it's your turn for a shower. Give me just a minute to clean it up for you."

When she had gone in, John set the timer for twenty minutes. Most people didn't take that long, but if she was still in after fifteen minutes he would give a knock. Then another knock when the timer went off. It was rare that anyone stayed in the bathroom longer than that.

He saw that Betty was about ready. She was a big woman. Big stomach, big legs, big personality. She told John that she didn't need a shower that day. She just needed a bathroom so that she could change her shirt and redress her wound.

"What happened?"

"I had surgery. They fixed a big hernia," she said, pointing to her belly.

"When was that?"

"Uh… Thursday. I remember because it was the day before my birthday."

"Wow. Are you doing okay? Does it hurt?"

"Not too much."

"Is the wound all right? Do you want me to take a look at it?"

"No. It's okay. It isn't really draining anymore. It isn't red. I go back next week so they can take the staples out."

"Well, you look pretty good for someone who is only five days out from surgery."

"Yeah. It was a big one. They took out eight inches of my colon also. Said that it was in danger of strangulation. Said I was lucky. They used mesh to close it."

"That's amazing. When did you get out?"

"Sunday. I was only there for three days. You know what the worst thing was? I was there over my birthday. I had wanted to go to Denny's to get my free meal. I look forward to that all year long. Denny's is my favorite place and on your birthday they give you the food for free. Anything you want. Now I missed it. I was so mad. But I had to go to the hospital. I just got too sick."

"That's terrible. I wonder if you can get a note from your doctor. Have it say something like, 'Please allow Betty to have a late free birthday meal as she was in the hospital.' Then you could get that dinner."

"No, they don't work that way. It has to be on the exact day."

"Are you sure?"

"I'm sure. You can't do that."

"Well, there's always next year I guess."

"Yeah, it's okay. Hey, do you have anymore of this gauze? I think I might need more than two."

"I'll go check for you," John said as he went into the closet to search through the drawers. He found more and brought them out, saying, "Here you go Betty, bathroom number one is ready now. The far one. Let me know if you need anything, all right? I'll be right here. And I don't mind looking at your wound if you need me to."

A few minutes later Terry was over in the corner, weighing himself with all of his clothes on. Boots, heavy coat, light coat, sweater, two shirts and who knew what else.

"How much do you weigh Terry?"

"One hundred forty five. I've gained."

"Well, you can take off at least five pounds due to those clothes. Maybe ten. Are you trying to gain weight?"

Terry had a large distended stomach but a very thin face and neck.

"Yes, the doctors say I need to eat more."

"You have liver problems, right Terry?"

"Yes, it's from too much drinking. I quit it though. Two weeks ago. No more. I'm through with it."

"That's great. I'm proud of you. It's not easy, I know."

"Yeah, well, it was killing me. They said I can't drink anymore or I'll die. I was in the hospital for two weeks. Very sick. Jacob took me. He knew I was sick so he drove me there. I couldn't have done it without him. He helped me fill out the forms. Everything. I was so confused. I didn't know what I was doing."

"You were at St. Francis? Did they treat you well?"

"Yes, fine. They poked me right here in the side with a needle. It's still sore when I touch it. They took off three bottles of fluid. My stomach was smaller for a while. It all came back already though. Also my feet hurt."

"Are they swollen? Let me see."

Terry pulled up his pant leg and down his sock to expose his lower leg. John pushed his finger in nearly a half-inch and the indentation stayed behind.

"You really are swollen. Are you taking your medicine? I'll bet you have a water pill. Lasix? It's also called furosemide. You need to make sure you're taking it. Also, you need to keep your legs elevated as much as you can."

Terry looked with some concern at his legs, but seemed noncommittal about the medicine and self care. John couldn't tell for sure whether he was taking his pills. He asked in a couple more ways. Sometimes it sounded like Terry had his medicines and was taking them. Other times it didn't.

After Terry's shower he was back on the couch with his shoes and socks. He struggled to bend far enough over his stomach to reach his feet. John stooped down to help. He carefully pulled the socks over his swollen feet and as far up his calf as they would reach. Then he put his boots on, lacing them up with Terry's instruction. He wanted to get it just right for him.

"Thank you for your help."

"No problem. Hey, make sure you take your medicine. If you're having trouble figuring them out then bring the bottles tomorrow and we can go through them together."

"I will. Thanks again. God bless you."

Terry left to get breakfast, probably hoping to gain another pound or two. John didn't realize it then, but he would be seeing Terry again the next week. He was admitted to St. Francis in liver failure and fluid overload. He was intubated and sedated when John came to visit. John sat next to his bed for over an hour just talking, reading scripture, and praying quietly. At the time he thought that would be the last time he would see him, but people have an amazing way of rallying. With the help of many health professionals he eventually recovered, feeling better than he had in a long time.

Despite his impending hospitalization, Terry had seemed much more hopeful than his medical condition should have allowed, and so John was also. After he left the room John turned to help the other man sitting on the same couch.

Vaquero wasn't his real name, it may not have even been his street name, but it was what everyone at Loaves and Fishes called him. It was because of the hat of course, which was the defining, unique characteristic of the man. He was an older Hispanic man who always seemed calm and in control. He wore an old crumpled leather cowboy hat. The brim was rolled and the crown was a little crooked. There were about ten metal buttons pinned to the crown. John had often wondered about the hat, so he took the opportunity to ask about it.

"It's my granddad's hat. He was in the war."

"What war? Korea? World War II?"

"World War II. He was a marine stationed in the South Pacific. This is all I have of his."

"Well, it's a nice hat and a wonderful tribute to your granddad that you wear it."

John thought it was remarkable that this man, who was either homeless or nearly so, had managed to hang on to the hat all these years. Amazing that he wore it every day, pins and all, and that it was still in such good shape. Of course, it was possible that he was making up the story. John tended to let people believe what they wanted. It was their story and their life and he wasn't going to gain anything by checking out the veracity of the guests there. Their lives were complicated and what mattered was that they were loved and accepted.

Two people worked in the shower area at a time. His helper this day was Vicki. Speaking of stories, he didn't really know hers. Something about being homeless at one time and wanting to give back. But he was pretty sure she was just couch surfing at this point. Living with her daughter sometimes, friends or a boyfriend others. She was a high-energy extrovert and that day even more than usual. She told John that she didn't usually drink coffee, but had drunk four cups so far. She didn't get much sleep the night before and was trying to keep moving. And move she did- from cleaning a shower, to drinking more coffee, to eating breakfast, to going outside to smoke.

She had cleaned all her life- her own home, other homes, restaurants and hospitals. Cleaning was her specialty and she was an expert. She wore an apron stuffed with gloves and rags. She sprayed, wiped, scrubbed, swept and mopped so quickly and efficiently it made John feel completely inadequate. Luckily, at Loaves and Fishes all talent levels were welcome. It was the thought that counted.

Vicki loved candles and if she wasn't talking about food, her daughter, or her hair problems, she was talking about candles. Scented candles. John had this vision of a cloud of vanilla doing battle with the pine and the autumn spice all in a small apartment. For someone who was sensitive to any smell that wasn't natural, it made him a little nauseated, but it was still fascinating. How someone could talk for five minutes about a new candle was beyond him, but it happened more than once that morning. She was a joy to be around, though, and knew a lot about the guests. She certainly knew much more than John.

He had been living there a week and was getting a crash course but still had a long way to go. It took time to develop a history with people. People on the street tended to be more open in some ways, but more secretive and private in others. There was always pain and sadness and hurt and loss, despite the optimistic front that many put up. More than most people, they had compartmentalized lives.

Vicky knew the guy who was telling stories about snakes. He said that on three different occasions he had come upon a dangerous snake. Each time he was either fishing or on the way to his fishing spot. All three times, he luckily saw the snake before it saw him. Twice he killed it and the other time it got away. On every occasion he had great success fishing, as if the pond was thanking him for saving them from the serpent. It was an interesting story. Possibly another tall tale, but John was attentive and appreciative of it.

Vicky also knew that this man beat his girlfriends. A woman had come in with him one morning for food and clothing, her face swollen and bruised. He had been banned from Loaves and Fishes for a while. There were some behaviors that just weren't overlooked there. But he had repented, and a few months later he was back again. For now. John looked at him carefully. He knew that people couldn't be defined by their best acts or by their worst. Everyone is multifaceted and complicated. But that type of abuse was disturbing and difficult to reconcile with the guy sitting there, smiling and waiting for a shower.

When everyone was out of the showers, and the bathrooms had been cleaned a final time, the rugs removed, the floors mopped and the walls wiped down with a homemade soap solution, Vicky and John joined the others in the dining room for reflection. As they gathered, they talked about how the morning's scripture passage had paralleled some of their experiences. They talked about technical issues, how they could have done things better. These points were helpful for John as he was still feeling his way from occasional volunteer to full time house member.

All of the people that they saw, all of the health issues, substance abuse, and mental illness, the cold weather, the poor nutrition and the bad shoes, the loneliness and the sadness, all of it was too much sometimes. Voluntary poverty is a long way from involuntary poverty. A relatively rich, healthy, well-educated white male can't really understand what it's like to be homeless, any more than he can understand what it's like to be a Syrian refugee or an Asian sex trade worker. But he was trying to come closer to that understanding. He felt that there was nothing more important than putting oneself in another's shoes. Or lack thereof.

After reflection, Vicky and the other volunteers left, but he and Rachel and the other intern still had work to do. He let Summer, an intern in her first year at the local seminary, feed the chickens and gather eggs. He would finish the laundry. Rachel had mom things to do.

So far, he liked everything about life there. He enjoyed the daily routine. The schedule was predictable even if the details were unpredictable. As interns, John and Summer were there all four mornings and handled a lot of the day-to-day chores.

There was a mountain of laundry to wash every day. Someone had donated brand new commercial sized machines but it still took a long time. When it was warm they could hang the clothes outside to dry, but not in January. He had washed and dried several loads, folded them, and put them away upstairs in the clothing closet when he felt his phone vibrate with a text. It was Jessica.

"Passing the stadium. See you soon!"

27

"I'll be watching for you," John texted back.

This was finally the weekend that Jessica was coming to visit. Even though Jacob had assured John that it would be okay, John still felt a little badly. He had just begun his internship the week prior and here he was, leaving for three days. He hurried to finish the laundry and checked with Summer to be sure she didn't need any help. He apologized again for having to leave, and she once again said that she could handle what few chores there were to do.

Jessica pulled up a few minutes later. When she got out with a big smile, John's heart skipped a beat. She was more beautiful than he had remembered. Her Belizean tan faded to smooth olive skin, her hair even darker than before and those eyes...

"Welcome to Kansas City. Was the drive alright?" he finally spit out, hugging her awkwardly and tentatively.

"It was fine. I-70 is a little bumpy and boring, but I made it," she returned the hug, neither wanting to let go.

"I'm so glad you did! I'm incredibly happy to see you."

They separated and she said, looking around, "So this is it huh? Looks pretty cool. Love the chickens. Where do people take showers and have breakfast?"

"Here, I'll give you a tour. Ready? Do you need anything first? Bathroom? Something to drink?"

"No, I'm good. Lead on."

He showed her the building with the showers and dining room, the chickens, the gardens that were resting for the winter, the house and his tiny one room apartment.

"It all suits you, John. Pretty sparse in your room, yet there is enough space for everyone in the common areas."

"Exactly. I think of monks or nuns in a monastery with just a change of clothes and a Bible, a few toiletries. Really very little is needed privately. Everything has become so out of control. People want everything to themselves. Just piles and piles of stuff. Things on the wall and on shelves. Electronics. So many clothes, shoes, and closets to hold it all. And for what? Why does anyone need more than one spare change of clothes? Maybe something nicer if someone has to dress up for a meeting or a wedding. But really? Walk-in closets?"

"I understand what you're saying. And I don't require a walk-in closet. But I do need more than one pair of shoes. It's a constant battle though, you're right. Consumerism is the most common religion in developed countries."

"So, I'm helping to prepare the community meal for tonight. The main dish is ready. It only needs to be heated up. I just have to make a salad and set everything up. You'll like this dinner. There are usually about fifty or sixty people. Volunteers, neighbors, friends, community members. You can meet some people and then we'll be out of here by about eight. Does that sound all right?"

"Sure. It all sounds fun. I can help you cook. Just tell me what I need to do."

They worked the rest of the afternoon, getting the meal ready. Summer and the others pitched in as five o'clock drew near.

It was something they did every Thursday night. A volunteer usually prepared the main dish and everyone chipped in to help with the rest. The meal was served by homeless guests, Loaves and Fishes members, and volunteers. It was fresh food and conversation and bonding and community integration at its best. Usually, someone grabbed a guitar or played the piano and a singalong ensued. In nice weather, people would spill out onto the porch.

John introduced Jessica to everyone. Jacob especially had been anxious to meet her. John talked about her often and he wanted to see what the fuss was about.

"So you're sure you can spare him this weekend?" Jessica asked Jacob after John left them to help serve dessert.

"Oh, we'll make do. I'm so glad you were able to drive over for a visit."

"Me too. It's weird though. It feels like a lifetime ago that we were in Belize. I mean I think we'll be fine, but you know, when you see someone out of context it takes a minute to get your footing. Back then I was working in a coffee shop and John was just messing around. Well, I guess that part hasn't changed," she said in a good natured, sarcastic kind of way.

"Yeah, you've got to watch him- he's a bit of a mooch."

"Right? Hey, this whole place is amazing. John tried to explain it to me, but it's even more impressive in person. I love the shower idea. I can't imagine what it must be like to not have a hot shower every day. I know that after camping or something, being dirty and smelly and sticky for a couple days, a shower always made me feel human again. There probably aren't many places for a homeless person to wash off, huh? Maybe a sink at a gas station or something. Or the library. Anyway, it's a genius idea. You should be up for the Nobel peace prize or something."

Jacob smiled a little and began to protest, "It's not just me. Rachel actually initially came up with the idea."

"Really? Okay, you both deserve prizes. How long have you been at this?"

"About ten years now. Hard to believe. I think John's been coming out here almost that long. We're really happy to have him here on a more full-time basis."

He told her about the beginnings, about how Loaves and Fishes had evolved. He talked about Dorothy Day and Peter Maurin. Jessica had heard most of this before, but it helped to hear it from a different source, a different point of view. Jacob was a preacher and a teacher and really spoke like one once he got going.

"Thank you Jacob. It's all so amazing. This place is an oasis of peace in the city, isn't it? I want to hear more. Also I really need to read that Dorothy Day book. I'm not sure why I haven't yet. I'm just lazy I guess."

"You really should. How long are you going to be in Kansas City? Can you come with us to the minimum wage rally on Tuesday?"

"No, I wish I could, but I have to leave on Sunday. I've only been at my job a little over a year and haven't built up much vacation time yet. I know I need to start participating in things like that though. Thank you for doing so much." She looked around, "Hey, where did John wander off to?"

She finally made eye contact with him on the other side of the room. He worked his way over to her. They said a few goodbyes as they sneaked out.

"I'm just glad you have a car," John said as they got into her blue Focus. "One of the requirements of being an intern here is that we aren't allowed to have a car. Of course, I don't own one so that part was easy. But I was used to borrowing Deb's whenever I needed it. I even took a bus here for my first day."

"A bus? What was that like?"

"It was a great exercise, not really bad at all. I've taken public transportation on the east coast, in Europe, Canada and even Africa, but never here. The Midwest isn't made for public transit. The suburbs are far away and really spread out. Also people are suspicious of it. They worry that the wrong sorts of people will get out or get in, depending on their point of view."

"Well, you're in luck. Or maybe I should say, we're in luck. We don't have to figure out a bus route to the hotel. Just point the way."

They made it to the Plaza and had a great night catching up with each other, which turned into a wonderful weekend. They found out that their connection wasn't solely dependent on the

Caribbean sun. They talked about music, of course. But also about books, movies, and sit-coms. They talked about their families, where they've traveled, about life and about God.

John told her all about his year in Uganda. The people he met. What the days were like. The food, the way everything smelled, the crowded patient rooms, and the long clinic lines.

She did the same- telling him about her year in Illinois. Her job, her mom, about Stella and how big she was getting.

"So, what do you think? Are you going to stay in Decatur? You feel comfortable there, it sounds like," John said over breakfast Sunday morning, knowing that their time together was now very short.

"I think 'comfortable' is a very strong word. Illinois is where my mom is. It's where my job and my daughter are. It makes sense for me right now... but wow, this has been a great weekend. Really great. So, do you think you're going to stay there for a long time? At Loaves and Fishes?"

"It's hard to know. I want to give it a shot. You know I've always wanted to do it and now is my chance. It's only been about a week but I can picture myself living there long-term. Over the last two years, I've proven to myself that I don't need much. In fact, too many things gunk up our lives. And private ownership creates conflict not peace. So, really it's perfect for me."

"But you want to work too, right?"

"Yes, I definitely need to figure something out there. Once I get settled, maybe get a few weeks under my belt, I'll begin looking at my options again... So you liked it there? I saw you talking to Jacob for quite a while."

"I was really impressed with him. I didn't get to visit with Rachel as much, but she seemed amazing too. Yes, I can understand why you like it there so much. It's Christianity at its most authentic and simplest level. Love God, love your neighbor. That's church, if you ask me."

"Maybe the next time you come back to visit we can stay there. It would be a different experience for sure. You could stay for a Monday morning and help with showers."

"I would really like that… I'd better get going. I need to be back by late afternoon. My mom has to go somewhere tonight. A place she can't take Stella. Girls night out or something. So, what should I listen to on the way home?" she said, trying to lighten the mood a little.

"You'll need something to keep you awake right? So maybe Cloud Nothings or Superchunk? On the other hand, I feel like something with at least a little country twang is best for driving across Missouri. How about Uncle Tupelo or Whiskeytown?"

"I like that direction. What else?"

"Oh, John Moreland and Sturgill will sound good I'll bet."

"I don't know John Moreland, but I'll check him out. Quick, favorite Sturgill Simpson song?"

"I don't even have to think about it. 'You Can Have the Crown' with no doubt," John said. "I love the way he literally growls that first word. He takes a flying leap at that song and never slows down. It's self-deprecating, fun, catchy and clever. All the things I love about him. Are you sure you have to go now?"

"I'm sure. But I'll tell you what- if you're nice to me I'll give you a ride home."

"Okay, you've got me. I guess since you have the keys you get to decide when it's time."

"Sounds fair to me. Come on."

Jessica drove him back and they lingered as long as they could, the cold January wind whipping at the car while they kissed and talked and planned and dreamed. With a promise that they would see each other soon, they finally parted. John watched her drive away and then went in to find his housemates to see what needed to be done.

───────────

They gathered outside a Taco Bell on the Missouri side of State Line. It was one in a series of protests in which fast food workers and their supporters were raising awareness about the low wages they were being paid. Fifteen dollars an hour is what they were aiming for. It had already happened in some settings in other states but seemed a long way off in the Kansas City area.

The mainly twenty and thirty-something workers, many were women with children, picketed and sang and chanted, as the media filmed and reported. There were perhaps seventy-five people there, including several Taco Bell workers.

This was the first of this type of demonstration that John had attended, but it was an issue that was close to his heart. During his college years he had worked several minimum wage jobs, and he had barely made enough to pay his share of the rent on a cheap apartment, gas for a car he rarely drove, and a diet of hot dogs and mac and cheese. Luckily he was still on his parents' health insurance plan. Most of his income at the time came from school loans. There was simply no way a person could survive on six or eight dollars an hour. Not in the early eighties, and definitely not now.

Food, shelter, and transportation alone would eat up all of the paycheck and then some. Insurance, clothing, and a phone bill would be nearly impossible. Add in a child or two and all of the extra expenses that comes along with life, and pretty soon it becomes apparent why John and the others were picketing.

He understood the owners' arguments about staying competitive, about keeping prices low, about how it would put them out of business to pay fifteen dollars an hour. But he had seen the numbers. Numbers and calculations run by real think tanks at universities and foundations, and he knew that getting workers up to fifteen dollars would raise the price of a taco maybe eight percent.

Like everything else it came down to greed. Watching out for oneself rather than caring for one's neighbor. The gap between rich and poor had never been wider. The voice of the working class remained silenced. Not only national, but also state and local elections were decided by those with the most power and money. The shrinking middle class was subsidizing the fast food industry by paying for food stamps, subsidized housing, Medicaid, disability, and other safety net programs. One way or another, people would pay. It would either be at Taco Bell or with their taxes or their insurance premiums.

The tide had begun to turn in some places. In Kansas City there was some support for at least a slow phasing in of a higher minimum. So here they were in the cold, holding signs in the rapidly fading sunlight. There was a sense of camaraderie and common purpose among the people. There were fast food workers present, along with their families, community organizers and openhearted sympathizers. It was serious business, but there was laughter, a matter of human dignity, but there was joy and hope.

John was happy to be able to help in this way. With his previously busy life he always longed to put his body out there more. To vote in a physical sense for justice. His mouth was there and sometimes his pen, and definitely his heart. But being on call, worrying about his professional reputation, doing activities with the twins... he had so many excuses for not standing up for what he believed. To literally stand was a revelation. It was physically doing something that truly changed people, not writing a check or sharing a post. This was something he knew from his time at Loaves and Fishes over the years, and from working in Uganda, and even to some degree by working towards plastic recycling in Belize. Hearts and spirits are changed by our physical activities. It's what we do that matters.

And not only our own hearts. The hearts of those around us. The fast food workers that met John, who discovered that he was standing in the cold with them in solidarity, their hearts were changed also. It legitimized their action. They faced fear, misunderstanding, resistance, and even hate for the simple act of voicing their concerns. It was so meaningful to have others stand with them. Even if that was all they did. Even if they never wrote a letter, called a congressman, or emailed a CEO, it made their spirits lighter and their work easier.

After a final round of "We Shall Overcome," hot chocolate and coffee were distributed, the media dispersed and people began to leave. Rachel, Summer, and John drove back home to Loaves and Fishes in the community car. They were in a peaceful, content, reflective mood, talking a little about the event. They were optimistic that the tide was turning as the minimum wage issue continued to be a top story in many media outlets.

In their dreamy state they almost didn't notice in time. There was a figure curled up in the parking spot next to the building. Rachel parked and they all got out to investigate.

28

They were able to awaken her with some effort. Once they had her inside the shower house, Summer made coffee while Rachel found a warm blanket. She wasn't someone they had met before. The lady said she hadn't been in town long and was trying to find her daughter. She was scared and alone. Someone on the streets had directed her to Loaves and Fishes, and she was hoping someone could help. When Rachel explained that they weren't a shelter and don't typically take people in, but would see what they could do, she was grateful.

Her name was Carla and she was originally from the area. Her mental illness or the drugs she was on, or both, caused her to ramble on with stories that didn't have a point. They had no beginning or end and the middle went on forever. The main themes were her daughter and her time on Broadway. She said that years ago she had been a singer and dancer in musicals.

She had a fading bruise under her left eye, rough and wrinkled skin and her fingers had cigarette stains. Despite all of that, she still had a spark of beauty. Her thin coat, silk scarf, slender frame, and the way in which she sat straight in the chair made her seem somewhat regal. When she flashed a smile during a long nonsensical speech that included a mention of possible grandchildren, her eyes came to life and her whole face glowed with charisma and vitality. Just as quickly, it returned to a flat, confused expression.

They talked about calling the local women's shelter. They

usually had room on a temporary emergency basis. But it wasn't clear that Carla was in danger. The bruise under her eye was greenish yellow in color so it had likely occurred over a week ago. She denied remembering what had happened, and in fact seemed surprised when Rachel asked her about it. In the end they decided to let her sleep there.

One of Dorothy Day's ideas early on in the Catholic Worker was that everyone should have "Christ rooms," kind of a guest room for anyone who needs it. At the height of the Great Depression, there were thousands of homeless people in cities and towns. They may have been passing through, or may have been in town for a long time looking for work, or just aimlessly wandering. She felt that if everyone opened up his or her house to even one person in need, it would alleviate much of the suffering that was present at the time. It was also consistent with the servant mentality of the movement. Once again, it was a Sermon on the Mount way of life, in which everyone shared what they had, whether an extra coat or an extra room.

Catholic Worker houses since then have focused on different things. There was no singular way of setting one up. Some were mainly shelters, but many weren't. Rachel and Jacob had always maintained two small one-room apartments for whoever needed them. They were for short-term relief while more permanent solutions were found. Sometimes there were Somali or Sudanese immigrants. Sometimes it was a person who needed to get up early for a job interview and wanted to be sure he had a good night's sleep and a warm shower with clean clothes. And at times a woman who felt unsafe on the streets was given a place to rest in peace for a few nights.

It was a wonderful idea and one that John had felt guilty for not doing in his own home. He had plenty of guests over the years, but not a single homeless person or refugee. Of course the pool of immigrants and mentally ill panhandlers was not as large in the suburbs. That was his excuse anyway. He was just happy at this point to be in a place where there was an extra room, someplace a person in need could find safety and rest.

Whether from years of being a busy doctor or maybe just an

innate gift, John had always had a talent for remembering faces. He couldn't count the number of times he had walked into an exam room to see a new patient and recognized him or her from ten years prior.

The problem came when he saw someone out of context. A nurse away from the operating room. A cashier out to dinner with her friends. A patient at the grocery store or at a baseball game. He knew the face but couldn't place it. That is what happened with Carla. He knew her face- not in the very beginning but later, as she talked. When she smiled. When her eyes opened wider and squinted a little. The way she sat and the way she moved. That straight back and the grace. He knew her. But from where? It was distracting enough that he didn't hear Rachel the first time.

"John. Will you please go downstairs and get me another blanket for Carla?"

She looked at him strangely, trying to figure out where his mind was.

"Sorry. Yeah, sure. It's been a long day. I'll be right back."

When he came back with the blanket, Rachel and Summer had already begun moving her to the apartment just outside the door. He thought it would be best for them to do this themselves, to give Carla some privacy. He handed Rachel the blanket and said he would see them in the morning.

That night as he wrote in his journal, reflecting on the Bible verse and about where he had seen Jesus in others, he wrote mainly about Carla. There were thousands of people like her in every major city in the country. They were confused, addicted, scared and tired. They were also lovingly created with special gifts and for a purpose known only to God. It was sickening how these fellow citizens from this rich country fell between the cracks. Cracks that were far too wide and easy to disappear into.

Funds for those with psychiatric issues had dried up over the past forty years. Institutions weren't ideal. The conditions were often substandard and treatment wasn't regulated like it should have been. But with no treatment beds, more and more people were on the streets. It was the same for those addicted to alcohol and drugs.

It was another case of living for the moment. Not worrying about the long-term sustainability of the country and society. By ignoring huge populations of people, those in power stayed in power. By dehumanizing immigrants, undocumented workers, prisoners, and homeless people the decision to cut funding and avoid any long-term solutions became much easier.

That wasn't what Jesus wanted. It's not what Martin Luther King Jr. or Cesar Chavez or Dorothy Day had wanted either. They dreamed of a society in which everyone loved and was loved. Where there was no differentiation between the haves and the have-nots. When it is Christians that are fighting hardest against immigration, against inclusiveness, and against reconciliation, when it is Christians that are holding tightest to their guns and making it impossible for poor people to have basic medical care, that is when we know that something isn't right.

John found solace in the fact that Carla had found them, and that she was now sleeping soundly and warmly. He put away his notebook and got into bed, reciting the Jesus Prayer as he quickly drifted off to sleep.

———————

He woke up with a start and looked at the clock. It was only three thirty. He had been dreaming of Loaves and Fishes and of high school and of Carla. It was all mixed up in his mind. She seemed so familiar. It was one of those vivid dreams that was more like a prophecy or a memory. He tried to shake it off and relax but couldn't. "Who is she?" he thought as he tried to put himself back into the dream.

He had just about fallen asleep when it came to him. Her name wasn't Carla. It was Kristin!

Kristin, the girl from high school with whom he had made a fool of himself at the Lionel Ritchie concert. Kristin, who had come to watch him swim at that high school dual meet, so beautiful with the same straight back and dancer's grace that he had noticed tonight. Kristin, who he had last seen that sad, embarrassing time at her friend's house when she was on break from touring with Cats. Kristin, who he had often wondered about, who he had been subconsciously watching for without really understanding why.

He knew it was Kristin. Of course it was. It totally explained that strange feeling he had when he looked at her. It wasn't the feeling that he had when he looked at a patient or someone he had seen at a store or at church, but someone he *knew*. It was all he could do to keep from going down to her room to wake her up, to find out what happened and see if there was any remnant of the old Kristin left inside. But he resisted, reminding himself that she wasn't the same anymore. That she had been through a hard night, and probably a hard decade, and was likely still sleeping soundly.

About the time he fell asleep again, he was awakened by his phone alarm. Five seventeen of course. It took a few minutes before he recalled his early morning revelation. It was Wednesday, so Loaves and Dishes didn't offer showers. This made for a more leisurely morning. As they gathered for breakfast and reflection, John chose not to make his suspicion public about Carla/Kristin yet. He wanted a chance to see her again and determine if his intuition was right. They decided to try to contact her daughter and see what they could learn.

Later that morning Summer brought Carla to the kitchen to eat breakfast. John came down as they were finishing. She looked more coherent after a good night's rest and a hot shower. They were trying to figure out what to do. Carla didn't have a correct phone number for her daughter and she wasn't even entirely sure she lived in the Kansas City area. She thought it was somewhere in the Johnson County suburbs, but it had been years since they had seen each other.

They had Summer's laptop out and were searching for the daughter using Facebook, the white pages, and anything they could find. She had a common name, which wasn't helping anything.

John wrestled with himself, trying to decide what to do, what to say. As he watched her, he became convinced that it was she. As dim as the thirty-five year old memories were, it wasn't as simple as looking and remembering. It was subtle, more like the recognition of an aura. It was wordless, instinctual. It didn't seem like she saw anything familiar in him. He wouldn't expect her to. It had been a long time ago and she had obviously been through so much, had experienced so many things and her mind wasn't functioning normally anymore.

Summer found a phone number that looked promising. She called it and got voice mail. She left kind of a vague but hopefully intriguing message so the woman would call back. John decided to at least verify his suspicions.

"Are you from Kansas City, Carla?"

"No. Not originally. But I did live here for a while. I went to high school in Johnson County for two years."

"Why did you move?"

"I got a part on Broadway. Cats. It was wonderful! I was on top of the world. Singing, dancing."

Even without the details he knew without a doubt that it was Kristin once she started talking. That squinty-eyed grin with the arched eyebrows when she spoke excitedly hadn't changed across the decades. It was like they were in high school again. At one point she looked at him, into his eyes and he was sure she recognized him. She paused for a fraction of a second, almost with a surprised look. John noticed the look but decided not to test her in that way.

"Did you do any other shows?"

"Oh I did them all- Chicago, All That Jazz, West Side Story, My Fair Lady. Being under the lights, performing, becoming a different character for a few hours, it was magical. We were on the road for months at a time. I never wanted it to end.... But then..."

Her face changed. She appeared to lose her train of thought. She suddenly looked very sad and confused.

"I need to go," she said. "I have to find my daughter. She's not far from here."

"Let's wait a little bit, Carla. Remember we left a message, she might call us back any minute," said Summer.

"No, I need to go. Where am I? Am I anywhere? Can you

even see me?"

"We can see you Carla. We're all right here in Kansas City. You're safe here. Do you want some more coffee?"

"I feel like I'm not really here. Like I'm speaking into a vacuum. I need to go. I'll be okay, don't worry, they can't find me. I'm invisible!"

Summer held her hands and leaned over to speak softly to John. "Go find Rachel. I'm not exactly sure what to do here. I think we should call crisis intervention, but I want her to talk to Carla as well."

John looked over at Carla/Kristin again as she continued to mutter words that were increasingly nonsensical. She no longer looked like his high school friend. He went upstairs to Rachel and Jacob's room and found her there, folding clothes. He explained what was going on. She told him to go ahead and call as she headed down the stairs to try to comfort Carla.

Within the hour, a policeman arrived and two people came in an ambulance. They talked to Carla for a bit and then cajoled her into coming with them. They planned to take her to St. Francis Hospital for evaluation. Summer and John said they would visit her as soon as she was allowed company.

After they left, John told the two women about Kristin. About how important her kindness and maturity had been to him as he looked back on those times with her. That he had often felt guilty about how he had treated her. That it really wasn't an excuse that he was young and naïve.

"Yeah, I think that is an excuse. A good one," said Rachel. "You were a seventeen-year-old shy, sheltered, white suburban boy. She was an actress. Already a woman. An extrovert. I'll bet she could have held her own with someone ten years older."

"Maybe so. I still feel awful. I really feel like I owe her. She showed me what it was like to risk something for love, whether for a person or a career. How to follow and nurture your gifts and your dreams. But, I don't feel like there's any sense in trying to jog her memory of me. She has enough going on without that. But I do want her to do well. I'll go visit her as soon as I can, if you all think that is wise."

"I think that's a great idea, John," said Summer. "She'll need an advocate as she tries to get better. And you two go way back. It's perfect. I'll go with you the first time. It'll be interesting. I haven't ever been on a psych ward."

"Now that surprises me," joked John.

"Hey, maybe you'll run into another old girlfriend up there!"

"Ouch. I deserved that."

They went out together to start on the short list of Wednesday chores that needed to get done. Living in community, the work was split up so that everyone helped. Interns learned how to maintain and care for every area of the organization. They worked on things that came easily to them and things that didn't. The idea was growth in knowledge and a deeper spirituality. Work as prayer.

It was a few days later when Michelle called. She had friends and contacts all over the city and had heard from a secretary at St. Francis that they were in dire need of a urologist. Theirs had retired after a long busy career and his practice was being held together by a patchwork of residents and attendings from the local medical school. That was the rumor anyway. She knew John was looking for a job that would meet his fairly strict criteria and suggested he check it out over there.

"Thanks Michelle, I'll do that. How are you doing? Boyfriend treating you right?"

"He is. We have a good time together. He's kind and very funny. He even introduced me to his parents over Christmas, so I guess that's something."

"Yeah, I saw that on Facebook. That's always a little tricky. Did they approve?"

"I'm pretty sure. His mom and I made pumpkin cookies together. That was interesting."

"I'll bet. Did Kayla go with you? How is she?"

"No. She stayed with my mom. I'm trying to shelter her a little from all of that until I'm sure that our relationship is going to stick. She's doing great. Still dancing. And now she's in middle school. Can you believe it? We get along most of the time. It's just been the two of us for so long. We depend on each other for support. Maybe a little too much."

"She's a great girl and you're doing a wonderful job. Hey, thanks for the tip. I'm going to follow up on this. We should get together for coffee sometime and really catch up, okay?"

"I'd like that. Take care, John."

When they hung up, he lingered for just a moment on the thought of Michelle. The last time they had seen each other was when he was getting on the plane to fly to Belize. That was a bittersweet memory. He had always felt that they had a strong connection. It was another instance of people being in different places and different times in their lives. Everything in life seemed so random. Relationships lived or died largely due to events beyond anyone's control. He wasn't a strong believer in fate, rather he felt that most events in our lives simply happened. It was up to us to bring something positive out it, to determine how to use these fairly random occurrences to make our lives and the world a little better.

There were multiple nearly impossible circumstances that had brought Ellie into his life when he was in medical school. And there was no way to determine the odds of meeting Jessica in Belize. Or even more incredible, the chance that he would have his very specific and very unique children. Or the fact that he was now living at Loaves and Fishes with such amazing people who were also there through an extremely unlikely course of events.

John's mind quickly got carried away in the wonder of it all. What were the chances that the earth was tilted on its axis just so, and that there was a moon controlling weather and tides placed exactly that far away, and that our planet was this distance from the sun? It was all too much. All he could do in that moment of expansive wonderment was pray and thank God for all of the happy circumstances that had brought him to that point right there and then. It was times likes these that made him realize how truly blessed everyone was.

He knew a few doctors that worked at St. Francis. He resolved to call them soon and see what their opinion was about the hospital. Although he had worked in Kansas City for years, he had never practiced at St. Francis. He knew that they tended to get the bulk of the poor patients, the unwanted and uninsured, the ones that no one else wanted to see.

It sounded perfect when he thought of it that way. These were his people, the ones that God had been calling him to care for.

One of the things he liked about his church was that he could ride his bike there. It was less than three miles away. On cold, snowy, or rainy days he could borrow the community car or hitch a ride with someone. That afternoon he had ridden his bike to the service. Ann's sermon was uplifting and encouraging. It validated and mirrored John's thoughts as her preaching often did. She always had a little different angle, something surprising that he carried with him through the week.

She preached that life was about change, taking risks, following one's heart and not taking tomorrow for granted. They were thoughts that John had been having for the past three years and he was ready to take another chance. He was anxious to go back to work- a real job after being an unpaid volunteer for the past two and a half years.

On that mild evening in late winter, anything seemed possible. He talked to Ann for a few moments after the service. As always, she was supportive and agreed it was a perfect fit.

"Have you talked to anyone at St. Francis yet? Do you think it will work out?"

"I have. And I do. I'll be able to work twenty hours a week. The rest of the time will continue to be filled with a mix of doctors from the med school. I won't have to take weekday call but will work every fourth weekend."

"That sounds great. Twenty hours a week. How does that work? Not four hours a day, right?"

"Basically two and a half days. It won't be exact, it's more of a goal. I'll have two full clinic days and a half-day of surgery. I'll guard the other two days so the job doesn't seep over into them.

I'll have health insurance again, which will be nice. The best thing is that I'll be able to take care of patients. Just like in Uganda, I'll be able to do what I'm good at. Jacob would tell you that I'm adequate at cleaning showers and gardening, but I'm much better at being a urologist."

"It all sounds perfect. When do you start? Is there anything I can do?"

"Pray for me. A new job! I don't think anyone ever gets used to that. I'll have to train on a new computer software system, learn the culture, how to find my way around. I'll be fine but it's still a little daunting."

"You will certainly have my prayers. You'll be wonderful. When do you start?"

"In about six weeks."

"Okay, I'll put you on the prayer list. Hey, you look great by the way. Healthier. Have you been eating better?"

"Thanks. Yeah, I think so. At least I haven't been worrying about how much I weigh for quite a while. I rarely think about it now."

"Well, you seem at peace. Whatever you're doing, keep it up."

"I think that's it. I've been at peace…Well, I'd better start heading back home. Thanks for the encouragement."

"Anytime. Be careful."

John rode his bike home to Loaves and Fishes. He sped by renovated buildings and dilapidated ones. A new Tesla drove past, but a moment later he waved at homeless friends who were walking towards their shelter for the night. He was glad to live where he did. As he neared home, he was filled with hope. This new job was going to be perfect for him, another piece of the wondrous puzzle that was his life.

29

Jacob had made the eggs that morning. Usually community members were on their own. They would help each other out if they were in the kitchen at the same time, but for the most part breakfast was a do it yourself, informal process.

However this was a special day. John was becoming a full member of Loaves and Fishes. He had been living in the house for over six months and had enjoyed his time there as much as the others had enjoyed him. Like any family, there had been adjustments. Everyone came with his or her own brand of brokenness. But for the most part it worked.

It was Thursday and they planned to celebrate that night during the community meal with cake and an embarrassing skit. That morning Jacob had volunteered to make breakfast, so they were all up a little earlier than usual, gathered around the table in the dining room of the main house. There was a little grumbling and sleepiness and good-natured sarcasm as he worked away. There were sounds of dishes, silverware, pans, laughter, and the creaking of chairs and footsteps on the wood floor. All of this echoed more loudly in the early morning atmosphere.

"Thanks for doing this, Jacob. It's nice to be together for breakfast," John said as Jacob placed a plate of eggs and vegetarian lentil cakes in front of him.

"You're welcome. It's been kind of a tradition."

"Really? I don't recall this tradition." Rachel said lazily.

"Yeah, remember? When Dan joined? We had breakfast then."

"No, you are thinking about when he left. That was when we had the celebration," she joked. Dan had been with them for over five years, but moved out when he got married. They still lived in the neighborhood and were an important part of the extended family.

"Oh yeah…you're right. Here, I'm sorry. I'll need to take that back," He reached for John's plate, who laughed and pretended to smack his hand with his fork.

"Too late, Jacob. It's mine now."

It was a really pleasant morning. Jacob and Rachel and their two children were there. Steve and Diane, who had both been a part of Loaves and Fishes for years, and Summer were there as well. It was a small but close group. Their numbers waxed and waned at times, but they always seemed to have just the right number to get the work done.

John enjoyed his breakfast. The thin lentil patties were home-made. The eggs had been gathered the day before. The bread came from a local grocery that donated outdated baked goods to Loaves and Fishes, who in turn gave them away or served them to their guests. The honey was courtesy of the beehive right outside the door. The tea was made from peppermint and lemon leaves that they grew as well. There was even a slice of fried tomato that came from the garden.

At Loaves and Fishes, they strived to live in a way that was an example to others. Sustainably and faithfully. While not everyone was vegan or even vegetarian, they were all engaged in the discussion of livestock agriculture and its effects on the health of the planet and its inhabitants.

John himself had been vegetarian for so long that he rarely noticed meat even if it was on the table. And when it was his turn to prepare a meal he simply left it out. He became another strong proponent of a plant-based diet and believed that unless everyone fairly quickly phased out meat, that it wasn't too strong of a statement to say the entire planet was at risk.

For some reason, the discussions about food didn't affect John's ability to at last dine without anxiety and guilt. He continued to eat simply and sustainably as he had tried to do for years. Maybe it was the supportive people around him. Maybe it was the fact that his life was finally structured in a way that felt authentic now that he was living in community and working with marginalized people on a daily basis. He felt closer to God than he ever had. Whatever the reason, his weight had come up over ten pounds and he finally felt peace at the table.

She brought her cat to the first appointment. John was allergic to cats, but he didn't flinch. If she felt more comfortable with it in her lap, who was he to judge? She had seen another urologist but wanted a second opinion. Kelsey had trouble urinating. She just couldn't get a stream started. She would sit and sit and nothing would come. From the sound of it, the problem seemed to be worse with stress.

She knew how to catheterize herself and it actually sounded like that was going fine. She did occasionally get infections. Mainly, she wanted someone new to talk to about her problems. Someone who had enough time to listen. Kelsey was forty years old and lived with her mother. She wasn't able to drive, so was dependent on others to take her to doctor's appointments or anywhere else she wanted to go.

During the discussion she talked about all the things she would like to do. She wanted to go to Disney World and ride Space Mountain, she wanted to hike in Colorado, ride a horse and even sky dive. She wanted permission from John to be able to do those things.

He listened to her complaints, her hopes, fears and dreams for over thirty minutes. He would never have had the luxury of being able to do that in his previous job, or in Uganda for that matter. He heard her out and took time to mourn with her about her condition and dream with her about all of the things she could still do. He went through her records and couldn't find a cause for her bladder problems. She had already had a complete work-up including examinations and x-rays. It didn't seem like she wanted more tests. Her psychiatric problems and possibly the medications used to treat them were the likely source, as he couldn't detect anything physical.

More than anything she wanted someone on her side- an advocate and a confidante. She may have had this already. Certainly her cat was one. Maybe her psychiatrist. He hoped she had friends and family members she could talk to as well. But John knew as well as anyone that people need a village. They need multiple sympathetic ears. People to whom they can tell their story. The world is lonely and pointless unless we are able to share disappointments and triumphs. We need someone who will listen and laugh or cry or express indignation. Someone who will encourage and celebrate.

So, he listened. They talked about how to carry her catheter discreetly. About how she wasn't going to worry if she had to catheterize, because it was all just part of what made her special. She was happy with the plan and knew that she could come back anytime she was worried or needed to talk.

His first weeks at St. Francis had been great so far. There was the usual anxiety of learning a new hospital. He discovered where the back stairs, the operating rooms, and the patient floors were. He took time to meet OR staff, floor nurses, secretaries, other doctors, and patients. Every patient was new to him those first few weeks. It is much more time-consuming and difficult to meet new people than to have a familiar patient following up for the tenth time. He had to learn a new electronic medical record system as well, which was also a challenge.

None of this was really any different than what he had done in Uganda, or what he did every time he went somewhere for a short-term mission trip. He learned the new system as he dove right in to see patients. And really, people are the same everywhere.

A doctor's office is not typically regarded as a blessed meeting place. But amazing exchanges occur there, such intimate sharing. What makes it work are the gifts of trust and connection that form in the room. In an average day in John's practice he saw a wide variety of patients: old, young, rich, poor, white, black, brown, gay, straight, Christian, and Muslim. He saw triathletes and those with Parkinson's disease, new patients and familiar ones. All arrived anxious, apprehensive, tender, and yet mostly optimistic.

He had learned many things over the years by simply opening the door and entering the microcosm of the exam room. He learned that black lives matter because the young paraplegic black man in front of him mattered. He learned that love wins because the two women in front of him showed love and concern for each other in their every word and expression. He learned that we are a land of immigrants because the Latino father and roofer in front of him was a recent immigrant. And he learned that our prisons were full of people that desperately needed rehabilitation rather than warehousing because the prisoner in front of him was lonely, broken and not defined by his worst act.

Jesus knew that the essence of all life is goodness. He stayed among the poor and marginalized, touching and teaching people. He didn't spend time on church boards. He didn't ask people to recite creeds nor pay lobbyists to push through laws that excluded the vulnerable. He resisted and criticized the dominant culture, proclaiming a God of abundance, never scarcity. He preached love, not fear. He taught that when we personally know someone, we experience the web of life. He enjoined us to love our enemy and to pray for those that persecute us. He healed the blind, the lame, the mentally ill, and the anemic without questioning their ethnicity, gender or economic status. He healed their disease even if it was at an inconvenient time, and then extended an extravagant welcome into the Beloved Community.

John still had dark corners in his soul. There were times when he reverted to small-mindedness and bigotry. And yet, he constantly prayed for a merciful heart, and he thanked God for the grace that allowed him to keep trying to get it right. He knew that ultimately all he had was that moment. The Jesus that presented herself or himself to John right then in that space. This person who needed John and who in a sense was John. Small talk in an exam room or over coffee or sharing a crust of bread becomes holy when people find common ground.

John knew that everyone had opportunities for this type of connection. Moments when it was apparent that we all have the same needs and desires, that we are created and loved. The truth is we are all wonderfully made, unique yet universal. More and more John was able to see the radiance in others, to appreciate the beautiful aura that surrounds and connects everyone.

At the end of the workday, John rode his bike back to Loaves and Fishes. After months of coming home to an empty house in Uganda, Placencia and even in Kansas City following Ellie's death, it was nice to have people around. He still enjoyed his privacy when he could get it, but there was a nice mix of community and alone time at the house.

With everyone's help he had been able to carve out time to think, write and pray. Time that had been missing and hurried past in his previous life. Moments that were so necessary in order to have any semblance of an intentional life. It was certainly tempting to go from activity to activity with no break. There were chores without end, especially in the summer. The garden alone could become a full time job. The mountains of laundry and dirty dishes, maintenance and handyman work throughout both buildings, talking to people that stopped by, helping the homeless and others that came with a constant stream of needs, some just wanting to find a friendly person to talk to, all of this plus his part-time job could easily have smothered out any spare time for himself.

So instead, he began with his private time, his time alone with his thoughts, time in which he could hear God and speak with God. He rose, as always, at five seventeen. This gave him over an hour to read the Bible and write down his thoughts for the morning. Days in which he wasn't working at St. Francis he also took an hour in the afternoon to retreat to his room to rest, meditate, and sometimes write a little. Most evenings, except

Thursdays, people did their own thing, so he was able to have at least two hours to himself, reading a book, or writing in his journal or for church or for the Loaves and Fishes newspaper.

All of this contributed to John's piece of mind. By creating a more sustainable rhythm, periods of interaction with others, mixed in with moments spent alone, he felt whole and real. By talking about this need and faithfully making a schedule to fill it, the other people in the house grew as well. Not everyone was as organized or even wanted to be. But by creating an example of this kind of day, by making time for each component, much more was getting done. The paper was getting written and published on time, the clarification meetings were being scheduled, the community meetings and even neighborhood nonviolent actions were being done in a way that the others hadn't been able to pull off in years.

In community, everyone contributes what they have. Each individual has unique gifts and talents. What John lacked in handyman skills, he had in organization and motivation. He felt obligated and honored to be able to share those for the common good. Like the followers of Jesus in Acts 2, everyone worked together and shared all they had.

That applied to money as well. They had traditionally put all income into a common pot. Dorothy Day had also stressed voluntary poverty, partly because of the manner in which it brought people closer to God. Trusting in God to provide what was needed.

Members received a couple hundred dollars a month allowance. Enough to go to a movie or out on a date. To buy clothing or something that hadn't been donated. They didn't have cable television or Netflix. They had very basic phone plans and all shared an inexpensive Internet plan. They didn't use an air conditioner and rarely used the furnace. Power came mainly from the solar panels.

This particular day was payday, which always made John joyful. Everyone liked to get paid for her or his work. John loved it even more these days because he was able to give it all away. It never even made it into his bank account. Even the income generated as a part time doctor was considerably more than everyone else's combined. It made a huge difference towards the financial security of the house. They had many friends and donors, and John had always written a fairly large check monthly. But even that amount was small compared to what he was able to give now.

This was one of the things that John had dreamed of doing one day. To be able to use his entire paycheck to help others. Previously he had helped his own family, given ten percent of his gross income away, and saved the rest, but it was all discretionary. The decisions were his. It certainly was the most common arrangement and sounded appealing on the surface, but once John started making more money than he needed, it was a source of stress. He felt guilty that he was saving too much, not being faithful in the belief that he would have enough for the future. He knew that he spent too much. It was ridiculously easy to go out to dinner, or buy a new shirt, or a new phone, or remodel the kitchen, or landscape the backyard, or take another family trip to Europe, or buy a new car. It was all absurd but surprisingly difficult to resist, even for someone who, in theory, was opposed to consumerism.

Uganda had helped. While there, he had no income except for a small amount from investments, and yet he gave tens of thousands for the opportunity to help sick and needy people at Lacor. However, it wasn't a sustainable situation. In another four or five years he would have spent it all. He had certainly thought about doing that. Just work and work and give away every last cent. Then he could live on the tiny hospital salary and try to fundraise enough to continue there in some capacity.

But he knew now that he had made the right choice. He would continue to visit Uganda at least yearly, but his home was in the States, in Kansas City. Proud of the place or not, in agreement with much that went on there or not, it was his home.

So now with St. Francis Hospital linked to the Loaves and Fishes bank account he was able to have the dollars completely bypass him. Everything went into the common account. And all the community members had an equal vote as to where the money was spent. It was liberating.

They had decided to buy a second car. It would be an inexpensive used sedan like the other one. Jacob had some skill as a mechanic, and there were plenty of people around that had even greater skill if needed. With the extra member, and the fact that Jacob and Rachel's children were old enough to drive, it was becoming too difficult to organize the schedule for a single car. When John was on call and he needed to go in to the hospital after hours or at night, he liked to take the car instead of a bike when possible.

With the extra money coming in, they could easily spend five thousand dollars on an adequate car. They also planned to replace the leaky roof on the main house. This was something that the members and friends could probably have done themselves and saved a little money, but they weren't experts and it would take them away from their real work. Much of life is deciding where to spend time. Is it spent on our family or ourselves? Is it spent doing household projects? Is it spent working in a job that brings everyone closer together? Time is money for sure, but time is time also. We only have so much of it and John knew that every hour was important. He had to weigh moments like working on a roof all summer with all of the other things he could accomplish in that time period.

That was one thing that he had learned and that he was still learning- the closer a person lived to a minimal subsistence level of income in the developed world, the point where food, shelter, transportation, clothing and, these days, a phone were taken care of- the happier a person was. If a person was striving for more and more money, with no clear purpose as to what the money was for, unhappiness was sure to follow. There was unhappiness for the entrepreneur, businessperson, doctor, attorney, real estate developer, and certainly unhappiness for all of the people that were in his or her way.

John knew that there was never enough in this world. Many people never learn that truth. They buy new kitchens on credit, they trade in perfectly functional cars, phones and houses for new ones, they divorce for vague reasons, they marry for even vaguer ones, they travel to look at new things, and buy new clothes when their closets are full. People buy things to put on their walls and on shelves. They have a hundred times more earrings, bracelets, and rings than they have ears, arms and fingers.

There will never be enough. And John had known the truth of that for years. He knew that only God could satisfy. That everything else is a distraction. A momentary pleasure. That the best remedy for the feeling of emptiness and loss that we all have is not more but less. Less stuff, less noise, less clutter, less of oneself. Happiness is found in more time in nature, more quiet talks with friends, more love, and more moments spent helping others.

So, when payday came and he didn't see one cent of it, he felt a joy that no object could ever match. He had all he needed in his small room. Just like in Placencia and at Lacor, he had a few simple pieces of furniture, a Bible, three changes of clothes, a wooden cross and a couple framed pictures. Books were in the common library. Food was in the common kitchen. He owned very little, and yet had more than he needed.

30

A small challenge when living such a simple life, it was a little tricky having visitors. Both children had graduated college in the spring. Sam had landed a job as a high school math teacher in Tarrant County. He could stay in his apartment in Fort Worth and could keep dating his girlfriend, who planned to work on her masters at TCU. Being a teacher hadn't been his initial plan, but he was happy with the idea now. Sam took the job with the understanding that he would also be the assistant baseball coach. He loved kids, math, and baseball and was really looking forward to getting to work, earning a paycheck, and seeing what it was like on the other side of the classroom.

Kate had been accepted to medical school everywhere that she applied. It was least expensive to attend Kansas University School of Medicine due to the instate tuition and a nice scholarship. She was following in her father's footsteps like she always said she would. She planned to keep her mind open as she went through school, enjoying each of her rotations, but said she wanted to be a surgeon. She was happy to be home and looking forward to moving into her new apartment near KU Med soon.

In mid-July the showers closed for a week while several community members traveled on vacations or to visit family. That left room for Kate and Sam to stay at the house with John. They had a great time catching up. John brought Kate to work one day and showed her around. He introduced her to the operating room staff and took her to the doctor's lounge. She had always loved visiting doctor's lounges.

"So, are the cookies any good here?" Kate asked as they looked at the small, somewhat sad assortment of treats.

"Well, you know I'm pretty particular. They don't look that appetizing to me, but be my guest."

"I think I'll pass. Maybe I'll just have some tea," she said, opening a tea bag and draining hot water into a paper cup. She bounced the bag up and down absentmindedly. "I remember that other hospital. Where was that? The one with the amazing snacks?"

"North Kansas City. I went there occasionally."

"Yes! That's it. I think I only went twice but I still remember. There were so many drink choices. There were chips, donuts, cookies, containers of candy... I remember a little bag with an egg in it. That was weird. I always wondered who ate those."

"You missed the good old days. I caught just the tail end of them. In Nebraska there were two hospitals that had a whole buffet brought in every day. Free food. Big desserts. Nice looking fruit. For a poor surgery resident it was heaven to have all of that free food. I wasn't really supposed to eat it but some of my attendings let me sneak in."

"Do any hospitals offer that anymore?"

"I honestly don't know. Maybe. The model has certainly changed. Hospitals are here primarily to make money. The physician feels like a cog in the wheel. If they think it helps them retain good doctors they might offer some perks like that. But many hospitals see doctors as just another commodity. We're interchangeable and expendable. I said I would never work for a hospital, but now look at me!"

"This is different though, right?"

"Yeah, it is. In several ways. For one, I don't really need the money. For another, I'm not on any kind of production quota. I have it set up so that I work my hours, show up dependably, do a good job, see who needs to be seen, and that's it. So it seemed like the best fit. I'm so happy to serve the poor here. These people need a doctor.

"Anyway," John continued. "The whole thing is probably better in some ways. Doctors aren't on a pedestal anymore. They're 'providers' like anyone else. The days when nurses stood up when doctors entered the room, when they could yell and throw fits with impunity. Luckily, those are things of the past."

"Maybe because more women are physicians."

"I think you're right. It's such a good thing to have more equality in that way. Thank goodness for people like you that are crazy enough to still want to become a doctor. Oh by the way, you remember where the best snacks are, right?"

"Umm… St Lukes?"

"Nope. Lacor. In Uganda. Remember that time you came with me? Those warm oily chapatti, the milky tea, and the sopapilla things? That was all so amazing. They served the cabbage at lunch as well. And back when I used to drink soda that ginger drink in a cold glass bottle was so good!"

"You and your glass bottles! Have you heard anything about that by the way? The plastic recycling in Placencia?"

"Still going strong. They're capturing more and more plastic. Keeping it out of the landfill. And the tide is slowly turning there. More stores and restaurants have stopped using plastic bags and selling plastic bottles."

"I'm proud of you for doing that. What a great legacy. You weren't even there a year."

"I can't take much of the credit. The idea mainly. The initial push. But the town must have been right at the tipping point. That's all it takes sometimes. It's so cool that it worked and that it continues to grow. What a great project. It involves a lot of people, which is always the best kind of action. Hearts change in community."

"Hey, you know what? I think I'll try one of these cookies. What do you think? Good idea?"

"You're on your own kid. So, excited about med school? You start pretty soon."

"I am so excited. And scared. It's hard right? I was a little spoiled at Grinnell. Small classes, everyone was so nice and wanted to see me succeed. It really wasn't too difficult. High school was actually tougher."

"Yeah, I think pretty much everyone is challenged in med school. But it's in the school's interest to keep everyone in the program. They can't really add people later. You'll be fine. You're smarter than I was. I just want you to study hard. Keep your heart and mind open. Find out what it is that speaks to you. Hopefully you'll land on a specialty that really helps others. Something that would be useful in a medical mission or in an underserved area somewhere. ER, medicine, surgery… something broad enough that it's needed and adaptable in the smallest, poorest of villages."

"I'm still thinking surgery. Although I'm not convinced I want to work in a developing country or out in western Nebraska or somewhere."

"You don't have to. Seriously. This is your deal. Your life. And obviously if a urologist can figure out a way to work in a small town in East Africa or wherever, so can anyone."

"Well, it still feels a long way off. First I have to pass anatomy…Wow, these cookies are actually terrible," she said as she dropped it in the trash. She drained the rest of her tea and said, "I am hungry though. What's for lunch?"

John laughed. "Hey, what do you say we pick up your brother and try that Indian buffet that we used to go to?"

"Sounds good, but are you allowed to eat at restaurants? Isn't that against Catholic Worker policy or something?"

"I'm not a cloistered monk, goofy. I can go where I want."

"Okay, just making sure," Kate laughed as they headed towards her car.

There were four varieties of tomatoes in the garden and they were all growing well. It had been dry the past two weeks, so John was out early watering and weeding them. The July days were hot and humid, and he tried to get things done in the mornings when he could. But even at ten o'clock the sun was blazing and he was sweating profusely.

Working hard in the yard or garden had never bothered John. In fact, it was his favorite type of exercise. To have something to show for the sweat and sore muscles always made a lot more sense than simply running or biking in a big circle. Or even worse, running or biking in place. There was something holy and soothing about pulling weeds and tending a garden. About creating order out of chaos.

He spent well over an hour pulling weeds around each plant and picking the ripe tomatoes. The smell of the earth, the tomato plants, and the weeds combined in a way that was intoxicating. In the summer, everything had an odor. It smelled so alive out there.

The water for the garden came from huge interconnected rain barrels that caught runoff from the roof. John carried a bucket back and forth, watering each of the forty plants. He supposed he could have hooked a hose up, but this seemed just as easy. Plus, he didn't have to worry about the hose tearing up the plants. One bucketful per plant. Forty trips. When he was finished he sat down in the shade of a walnut tree and admired the tomato plants. They really did look nice.

Now he needed to do something with all of the tomatoes. He had probably thirty or forty pounds between what he had picked today and what he had from two days prior. He decided to make pasta sauce, saving three of the ripe tomatoes to eat raw with dinner the next couple nights. He found basil and oregano from the garden. Someone had recently donated onions and garlic, so he had plenty of those.

John spent much of the afternoon making the sauce. He let it simmer for over an hour, reducing it down until it was dark red and thick. The kitchen smelled heavenly. Summer had walked through at one point and marveled at the aroma coming from the kitchen.

That evening he and Summer, Kate, and Sam had spaghetti out on the porch. There was just enough of a breeze that it felt nice to be out there. It wasn't Placencia, but it was home. They ate and laughed and talked. Everyone competing to tell Summer a more embarrassing family memory than the previous one. The morning's vigorous work in the garden, followed by the preparation of a fulfilling meal to be shared by friends and family- it was truly a day to remember.

———————

John was on closet duty a few days later when he saw Terry's name on the list for the first time in several weeks. He was anxious to get a look at him. It wasn't unusual for people to disappear. They might have changed their routine, or ended up in jail, or in the hospital, or been taken in by friends or family, or drifted away to another town, or sometimes they had died and it could take a long time for word to get around. He had been busy enough that he hadn't seen Terry until he called his name.

"Terry, you're next!" John looked around the dining room and finally saw him in a soft chair at the back, his head back against the wall, sleeping.

"Hey man, he's calling you. Wake up," a helpful guest said as he elbowed him in the stomach.

Terry looked around sleepily, then slowly rose to his feet. He sort of shuffled to the door and into the closet.

He had steadily declined since they had first met six months prior. John could see that Terry's legs were even more swollen, his stomach protruded even further, his chest, cheeks and eyes were even more sunken in. Mercifully, he was as optimistic as ever and pleasantly confused.

"Hey Terry, how are you? Do you want to shower today?"

"Sure. I'm going to need some help though."

"No problem. Here, let's pick out some clothes for you."

Terry put down his backpack as John started pulling out clothes- a shirt, pants, underwear, socks, and a towel. He noticed Terry was wearing huge slippers.

"Are those shoes okay? I'm not sure we have any big enough for you."

"Yeah, they're fine. My feet are so swollen. I can't wear regular shoes anymore. Just like house slippers and flip-flops. Do you have a belt?" He showed John his waist. His pants were being held up by a piece of thick string.

"I'll look around. We'll come up with something. I'll check downstairs while you're cleaning up. Hey Vicky?" John called into the next room. "Will you help Terry a little? And let me know when he comes out of the shower. I can help him get his shoes and socks back on."

"Okay, you've got it," she said cheerfully. "Come on, Terry. Let's have you sit down over here. Do you need anything? Coffee?"

Terry said yes to the coffee and slowly moved over to a chair. He gingerly lowered and then dropped himself into it. John watched from the doorway and saw that he was breathing heavily. He gave Vicky a look indicating that he would be there if needed. She nodded and went to get Terry his coffee.

When he was finished in the shower, he came out to the sofa barefoot, holding on to the waist of his huge pants to keep them from falling down. John and Vicky changed stations as John came in with a long belt.

"Hey, look what I found, Terry. This thing would fit around a redwood!"

Terry managed to smile a little as John handed him the belt. He threaded it through the loops of the jeans with some help. John then kneeled down to look at Terry's feet as he had done months before. This time they were nearly twice as big. They were weeping clear fluid and there were ulcerations above the ankles on each side.

"Do your feet hurt Terry?"

"Not too bad. Why? What do they look like?"

"They don't look very pretty. When did you see the doctor last?"

He didn't know. He was confused and couldn't remember if it was last week or last month. After John dressed the wounds and got his big house slippers back on, he looked through Terry's backpack for clues. He found medicine bottles with an assortment of physician names on them. He recognized one as a GI doctor at St. Francis.

"Do you remember Dr. Gupta? Is he someone you've seen for your liver problems?"

"Sure, I know him. He's a good guy."

"I'm going to give him a call okay?"

"Why? I feel fine."

"You may feel fine but you don't look fine. You're having trouble breathing, your feet look terrible…You need some help, my friend. I'll call him and take you over there, okay?"

John went outside to call the hospital, asking to speak with Dr. Gupta. One of the greatest things about his new job was his access to everyone at the hospital. He could directly help his friends at Loaves and Fishes in a way that he had only dreamed of before. When previously he would see someone with health problems, all he could do was empathize, take a look, or give a brief opinion. But now that he was working at both St. Francis and the Catholic Worker house, he could see people over time. He could watch their progression. He could find them more specific and useful medical help. It was something he hadn't thought completely through before taking the job, but it was turning out to be such a gift.

He was able to get the doctor on the line and explain the situation. Dr. Gupta knew Terry well. He said that he sounded much worse than he had been a few weeks ago. He asked John to try to get Terry to the emergency room so that he could take a look at him there.

By the time John had driven him to the hospital, had waited with him for hours as he was examined, as blood was drawn, as x-rays were performed, as the doctors conferred and then determined that he needed to be transferred to the ICU, it was well after eleven. John was scheduled to work the next day, so he felt like he needed to get home and try to get some sleep. He hesitated to leave Terry, but knew he was in good hands. With the hospital blanket pulled up leaving only his head and upper chest exposed, Terry looked very thin and frail. John whispered goodnight, walked through the quiet hallways that just for a moment reminded him of Lacor, found the car in the nearly empty lot where he had left it, and drove home.

The next day John checked on Terry as soon as he arrived for work. He didn't look any better. His breathing was labored. His catheter was draining dark brown urine. He was more out of it. John talked to the nurse and found that they were trying to find next of kin. Terry was too confused to make decisions for himself, and they needed to know whether to intubate him or not. No one wanted to put him on a ventilator if they didn't have to. He was in the very end stages of his liver disease and there was no chance of a cure.

John called Jacob to see if he knew of any family. He didn't. Terry never talked about children, siblings or parents. John sat next to his bed and talked to him for a long time. He faded in and out, but occasionally was lucid. By coming at the question in several different ways, by asking him to tell stories of his childhood and having him reminisce, he finally came up with a name. Linda was his sister. She was married and probably lived in Dallas. He even had her number on his phone.

So he called Terry's sister. He explained the situation, how sick he was and had been for so long, how there was really no chance of significant improvement. She hadn't seen him in over five years but she knew her brother. Knew that he was chronically depressed. That he definitely wouldn't want to drag things out like this. John had a social worker talk to Linda as well. She knew how to make her the power of attorney in a tough case like this.

By the time John had finished his day, had seen all the patients, done all the tedious electronic charting, had operated on a few people and rounded on his patients in the hospital, Terry was near the end. It had come quickly. His breathing had slowed dramatically. He had been unresponsive for several hours and his blood pressure was very low.

John sat with him. He held his hand. He read several Psalms and the first chapter of the Gospel of John to him. He talked about anything he could think of- the Royals, the garden, even the pretty nurse that had just come in to check on them. Terry's eyes were open and focused on a spot on the ceiling. Or maybe something beyond that. His breathing became more infrequent.

John prayed for an easy transition. He told Terry that it was okay. That he would feel much better in a few minutes. That his parents were waiting for him. And his grandparents. That there was no hurry but when he was ready, he could just go.

And all at once he did. He suddenly sat up. His eyes opened wider and his mouth formed a faint smile. He kind of gasped as his shoulders twitched, and then he fell back and was still. John continued to hold his hand. He watched his chest for at least a full minute. It didn't rise or fall. He checked for a carotid pulse for another minute. There was none. He said a silent prayer of thanks for Terry's life and just sat there by his side, thinking and praying. When the nurse came in on her rounds she found John in the same position. He looked at her as if he was emerging from a dream.

He said, "He died at ten forty-nine. I'm not exactly sure why, but I'm really going to miss him. He was important, you know? Something about him. I felt like he was ministering to me more than I was to him."

She patted John on the back, straightened the blankets around Terry and quietly left to call his sister, leaving John alone once again.

31

It was only a few days later that John became certain. The idea had been percolating for months. That morning upon waking, after making tea and standing in the warm shower as he continued to live in that half-awake, half-asleep state that is one of the greatest gifts to all of us, when we often think more clearly than when the day is in fill swing, it became obvious. He was in love with Jessica.

He quickly dressed, placing a few things in a backpack and went to explain his idea to Jacob who graciously offered to help out. He said that he didn't have plans that morning so would be happy to cover his shift at shower hospitality and that he could have the car for a few days.

He filled his Swell bottle with peppermint tea, tossed his backpack into the trunk and was on the road, headed north by seven thirty. He took I-35 to Cameron and then US 36 to Chillicothe before stopping to stretch his legs.

Chillicothe claimed to be the place where sliced bread was first mass-produced. It was 1928 when the Rohwedder Bread Slicer that was actually invented by an Iowan farmer was put into practice by the Chillicothe Baking Company. John was mildly disappointed that he had just missed the Sliced Bread Saturday festival, but did take a moment to be thankful that someone had figured out how to make those conveniently perfect little slices. Rather than bread however, he bought gas and M&M's and then continued on his way east.

He stopped again in Hannibal, famous, of course, for being the boyhood home of Mark Twain. There were Tom Sawyer and Becky Thatcher and Huck Finn buildings, street signs, restaurants, and statues all over town. There were riverboat tours and even a Mark Twain cave tour. Although John skipped all of that, he did listen to "Tom Sawyer" by Rush on Spotify as he slowly rolled through town.

One of the things he had always wanted to do was wade in the Mississippi river. He had waded in the Nile, the Niger, the Missouri and the Colorado rivers. He had driven over the Mississippi in several different areas but had never put his feet in it, and this felt like the perfect day to do so.

After stopping at a gas station and splurging on a Green Machine Naked Juice he worked his way down to Glasscock Park. It was a pretty area, but he couldn't really see a place to get in the water without attracting a lot of attention. Across the river, however, he could see people on the edges, maybe even swimming.

Highway 36 gave way to I-72 as he crossed over to Illinois on the (what else?) Mark Twain Memorial Bridge and found a little road back down to the river. It didn't appear to be an official park but there were no posted "keep out" signs, so he parked in the dirt and walked another hundred feet to the soft sandy soil on the edges of the water. He kicked off his sandals and waded up to mid-calf, thankful that there was no risk of schistosomiasis in the Midwest. The water was cool and, of course, muddy. He could barely see his feet less than a foot below the surface.

He took a selfie with his phone to commemorate the moment and then texted Jessica. She was eating lunch, and had a meeting after that. She would get off work at four. He was vague about his morning to that point and said he would talk to her later. He ate some M&Ms, drank some of the juice and got back on the highway. It was only about two hours to Decatur from there. It was amazing to John that he was able to leave at a comfortable time in the morning and arrive by early afternoon. She had always seemed so far away, when in fact only Missouri separated them.

He arrived in the birthplace of Abraham Lincoln at two thirty and drove around a little. He learned that the town motto was the amazingly concise and understated phrase, "Decatur, we like it here." Also that a good portion of the town's seventy-five thousand residents worked for the huge, troubling agricultural conglomerate Archer Daniels Midland.

As he drove through the middle of town, he found the perfect spot. Krekel's Kustard on Wood Street was one of those old burger and ice cream shops that everyone loves in theory but not enough people actually visit. He pulled up next to a Cadillac that was painted like a US flag in the front and a chicken in the back. It had a big rooster head attached to the top and a tail on the trunk. He decided it was time to call Jessica.

"Hey, guess what I just discovered?"

"Um… honey cures cancer!"

"Nope. Although it wouldn't surprise me. That stuff is amazing. I am fully confident that it cured my allergies. But that's not it. Do you know what the first song off the first record by Seam is called?"

"I can't remember who Seam even is."

"Really? You know: shoegazers, Sooyoung Park was the guitarist and songwriter. Mac from Superchunk played drums? Anyway… the first song is 'Decatur.' I have no idea why. Although Park is from Chicago so maybe he had relatives in Decatur or something. Cool huh?"

"That's cool. I'll have to check it out. So what led to that discovery?"

"I'll tell you in a minute. Hey, are you off work yet?"

"Yeah, just now. I need to run some errands before going home."

"Oh okay. I was hoping you could meet me for ice cream at Krekel's. You know, the one on Wood Street."

There was silence for a few seconds while she processed what John was saying.

"You're here? Why? Are you kidding me? How do you know about Krekel's?"

277

"Because I'm sitting right here in the parking lot watching a lot of happy people coming out of it. Here look," he said as he sent a picture, leaving no doubt that he was there.

"Oh my… John! I am so excited! I'll be over there in five minutes. Bye."

"Be careful, I'm not going anywhere." So far, so good, he thought. In the very back of his mind he was a little worried that she wouldn't be happy to have him drop in like this. They hadn't seen each other since that time in Kansas City. They talked and emailed and texted often, but for whatever reason the weeks and months had been piling up.

When she arrived to find him once again unsuccessfully attempting to finish Dostoyevsky, they went inside and had a shake and fries, and it was like they were never apart. They got caught up in a way that is impossible without physically talking to each other. Good friends by email and on the phone, they were two halves of a whole in person. They couldn't stop looking at each other. Time went quickly and pretty soon Jessica looked at her phone and saw that it was nearly six.

"I need to get Stella from my mom's. Come with me. We'll explain what's going on. Wait, what is going on? When do you have to go back?"

"The day after tomorrow. Is that okay? I can entertain myself while you're at work. We can meet somewhere for lunch."

"No way. I'll take tomorrow off. They'll live without me. It'll be like old times. You're kind of a bad influence on me you know? How many times did I leave early or skip work in Belize?"

"A few maybe," John laughed. "That would be awesome. You can show me around Decatur. Let's go. I can follow you there, but give me the address in case I get lost."

They picked up Stella who was excited and surprised to see John. Jessica's mom was friendly, but somewhat wary and protective. He knew it would take a little work to win her over.

They got Stella fed and to bed and then stayed up talking things through. He laid out the case for Jessica and Stella to move to Kansas City. It felt sudden to Jessica, something she hadn't completely expected. She had thought about it, of course. But

Stella's school? And her mom? And her job? It was a lot to give up. A lot of change once again.

"We aren't moving to Belize. I got here in a little over six hours. It's even the same time zone. Your mom could still see Stella often. But yes, I know. It's a big change. I don't expect her to like it. Did you see the way she looked at me?"

"She looks at every guy that way. She knows every man that I introduce her to could potentially take her girls away. Again. But she likes you. I could tell. I've built you up a lot, you know? Laid a lot of groundwork over the years."

"Wait. Every man...?"

"You know what I mean. There haven't been any since I've moved back. No one but you John."

"Okay, just checking. So, would it help if I told you that I think I've found you a job? Two of them maybe. There might be a job if you want to work at St. Francis with me. Or I know someone at a stand-alone radiology place that's interested as well. And I found just the place for Stella to go to school. It's really good. It's nearby, very diverse and has good teachers. I know an administrator and he assures me that there's a spot for her."

"Hey, I thought you said all of this came to you this morning in the shower or something. It sounds like you've been scheming for a long time."

"Not scheming, but definitely dreaming. You know I'm always thinking. I've been scared to take this step. It felt too soon, too reckless... Well, I'm not scared anymore. Everything has become crystal clear. What a journey this has been. Think about it... Belize, Uganda, Loaves and Fishes... I feel like it's been a progression. You've seen it, right? I was still a mess when I met you in Placencia. I was searching, but directionless. It was you, Jessica, who put me on the right path. The one I had been searching for all of my life."

"That's a little dramatic..."

"No, it's true! I was able to finally relax. To find that balance between contemplation and action that had been missing."

"You did all of that yourself. The plastic project was you and Bev, not me at all."

"Not true. It was you who first believed in me. The way we were able to make Holy Grounds plastic-free. It was something I had just been dreaming about. I think about a lot of things, but when we did that together it encouraged me to push harder. And you were with me every step of the way."

"Okay, I'll go with that. But then we went our separate ways. You took off to Uganda and I moved back here. How is that encouraging?"

"Don't you see? I had to do that. It was part of the journey. I had only done mission work for a week at a time. Those weeks were difficult and rewarding but I wasn't risking anything. A couple of weeks of vacation time a year is no way to transform a life. To go back and actually live there, to not be able to escape for months at a time, to not have any of the luxuries of home, to be totally immersed in their culture and day to day lives, it was an amazing experience."

"Why did you leave? It seemed perfect for you."

"I think you know. We've talked about it. I missed community. A community that I could fully belong to. I had the contemplation component, the work piece, but I didn't have any real, deep friends… and I was missing you."

"You had Stephen."

"True, I did… I mean do. We're still friends. He's doing great by the way. And I'll continue to work there at least two weeks a year. That place is a part of me now, but I can't live there any longer."

"And now? Now you think you're in a place that you can stay? How do I know you won't decide to move to India next year? Start an orphanage or something?"

"Now I'm home. Over the past three years I've learned to be content with very little, to take time to think things through, to pray and to write. I've learned the value of meaningful work, work that I can do to help others in a way that many can't or won't. I've learned that everyone needs good friends and that it takes time to cultivate them, that in this age friends aren't a given, we have to actively work on those relationships. I've learned that life is long for a reason. It takes time to figure things out, even for searchers and people like me who think too much. That life is dirty and messy and never perfect, but if we take our time and we pray, if we aren't afraid to go backwards in order to move our lives forward, we can patch together some kind of crazy, mixed-up life that has at its core a deep meaning, and that maybe helps tilt the earth's balance a little towards love."

"That's beautiful, John. I'm almost starting to believe you…"

"Well then, believe me when I tell you that I have loved you since the first time that I saw you, and I want to spend the rest of my life with you. I don't have it all figured out, but I know we can make it work. Simply, intentionally, and together. I've been carrying around something for you for a long time. I bought it in Uganda and have held on to it as a dream and a prayer."

John pulled a simple silver ring out of his pocket. There was a small diamond tightly surrounded by several others. He slipped off the chair, resting his right knee on the floor.

"Jessica, will you marry me?"

She looked at him for a long time. Surprised and joyful, tears began to form in the corners of her eyes. John held his breath, second-guessing everything he had said, the way he had said it, the suddenness of the proposal, all of it.

After what seemed an eternity she said quietly, "What song do you wish was playing right now?"

He laughed and thought a minute… "Okay, wait a minute, I know which one." He scrolled through his phone for a few seconds and found it. As the sweet guitar sound of "I Had to Tell You", Poi Dog Pondering's cover of the Roky Erickson song began, she smiled through her tears.

Taking his cold hands into her warm ones she pulled him back to his chair as they listened to the perfect words and the beautiful melody. When it was quiet again she looked into John's eyes and said, "That is the best gift that anyone has ever given me."

She then took the ring from his palm and slipped it onto her finger. And at that moment, when the separation of the temporal and the eternal was so thin that it was translucent, when both of them could see the past, present and future as one, when time had completely ceased to have meaning and the kingdom of God was as real as the oxygen in their lungs, when all was stripped away and revealed, they knew that everything was going to be alright.

Acknowledgments

The author wishes to acknowledge the generous support, encouragement, and inspiration of:

Holly McKissick and all at Peace Christian Church; Eric Garbison, Jodi Garbison, and all at Cherith Brook Catholic Worker House; Ibrahima Kodio and all of my Medical Missions Foundation and Grace Mission friends; all of the wonderful health care workers that I've been privileged to work with over the years; Jamie Langston, Susan Pomeroy, DeAnn Corbin, Dan Dryer, Doug Pomeroy, Peggy Mallow, Roxanne Nydegger, Alison Janssen; and especially Lucie, Sofia, and Jackson Pomeroy who tolerate a tremendous amount of nonsense.

www.ingramcontent.com/pod-product-compliance
Lightning Source LLC
Chambersburg PA
CBHW031211020726
47499CB00002B/542